"*Fire!*"

Cyclops fired seven broadsides before the two ships drew abeam. The Spaniards fired back with increasing irregularity as the dreadful precision of the British cannon smashed into their vessel's fabric.

Even so they carried away *Cyclops*'s mizen mast above the upper hounds. More rigging parted and the main topsail, shot through in a dozen places, suddenly dissolved into a flapping, cracking mess of torn canvas as the gale finished the work the cannon balls had started.

Suddenly the two frigates were abeam, the sea rushing black between them. The moon appeared from behind the obscurity of a cloud. Details of the enemy stood out and etched themselves into Drinkwater's brain. He could see men in the tops, officers on her quarterdeck and the activity of gun crews on the upper deck. A musket ball smacked into the mast above him, then another and another.

"Fire!" he yelled.

AN EYE OF THE FLEET

RICHARD WOODMAN

PINNACLE BOOKS  NEW YORK

This is a work of fiction. All the characters and events portrayed in this book are fictional, and any resemblance to real people or incidents is purely coincidental.

AN EYE OF THE FLEET

A Pinnacle Book, first published in Great Britain by John Murray Limited in 1981.

First printing, October 1983

ISBN: 0-523-41976-7

Can. ISBN: 0-523-43038-8

Cover illustration by Bruce Minney

Printed in the United States of America

PINNACLE BOOKS, INC.
1430 Broadway
New York, New York 10018

9 8 7 6 5 4 3 2 1

Contents

Author's Note

The major incidents in this novel are matters of historical fact. Some of the peripheral characters, such as Admirals Kempenfelt and Arbuthnot, Captain Calvert, Jonathan Poulter and Wilfred Collingwood are also factual and the personalities are depicted, tally with the images they have left later generations.

The exploits of *Cyclops*, though fictional, are both nautically and politically within the bounds of possibility. The continental currency of Congress was indeed worthless to the extent of almost ruining the Revolution. Fighting in the Carolinas and Georgia was characterised by atrocities, though the Galuda River does not exist.

No nautical claim has been made which was impossible. The details of the Moonlight Battle, for instance, can be verified from other sources, though the actual capture of *Santa Teresa* is *Cyclops*'s own 'part' in the action.

Pains have been taken over the accuracy of facts concerning the life on board men-of-war during the American War of Independence and pedants may like to note that at the time Drinkwater went to sea commissioned officers messed in the gunroom, midshipmen and master's mates in the cockpit. By the beginning of the next century the latter occupied the gunroom with the warrant officer gunner exercising a sort of parental authority and schoolmasters appointed to attempt the education of the 'young gentlemen'. By this time the officers had a grander 'wardroom'.

AN EYE OF THE FLEET

I am taking all Frigates about me I possible can; for if I . . . let the Enemy escape for want of 'the eyes of the Fleet', I should consider myself as most highly reprehensible.

NELSON

Chapter One October–December 1779

The Greenhorn

A baleful sun broke through the overcast to shed a patch of pale light on the frigate. The fresh westerly wind and the opposing flood tide combined to throw up a vicious sea as the ship, under topsails and staysails, drove east down the Prince's Channel clear of the Thames.

Upon her quarterdeck the sailing master ordered the helm eased to prevent her driving too close to the Pansand, the four helmsmen struggling to hold the ship as the wheelspokes flickered through their fingers.

"Mr. Drinkwater!" The old master, his white hair streaming in the wind, addressed a lean youth of medium height with fine, almost feminine features and an unhealthily pallid complexion. The midshipman stepped forward, nervously eager.

"Sir?"

"My compliments to the Captain. Please inform him we are abeam of the Pansand Beacon."

"Yes, sir." He turned to go.

"Mr. Drinkwater!"

"Sir?"

"Please repeat my message and answer correctly."

The youth flushed deeply, his Adam's apple bobbing with embarrassment.

"Y . . . your compliments to the Captain and we're abeam the Pansand Beacon, aye, aye, sir."

"Very good."

Drinkwater darted away beneath the quarterdeck to

where the red-coated marine sentinel indicated the holy presence of the Captain of His Britannic Majesty's 36-gun frigate *Cyclops*.

Captain Hope was shaving when the midshipman knocked on the door. He nodded as the message was delivered.

Drinkwater hovered uncertainly, not knowing whether he was dismissed. After what seemed an age the Captain appeared satisfied with his chin, wiped off the lather and began to tie his stock. He fixed the young midshipman with a pair of watery blue eyes set in a deeply lined and cadaverous face.

"And you are . . . ?" He left the question unfinished.

"M . . . Mister Drinkwater, sir, midshipman . . ."

"Ah yes, it was the Rector of Monken Hadley requested your place, I recollect it well . . ." The Captain reached for his coat. "Do your duty, cully, and you have nothing to fear, but make damned sure you know what you duty is . . ."

"Yes . . . I mean aye, aye, sir."

"Very well. Tell the Master I'll be up shortly when I've finished my breakfast."

Captain Hope smoothed the coat down and turned to look out through the stern windows as the door closed behind the retreating Drinkwater.

He sighed. He judged the boy to be old for a new entrant and yet he could not escape the thought that it might have been himself nearly forty years ago.

The Captain was fifty-six years of age. He had only held his post rank for three years. Devoid of patronage he would have died a half-pay commander had not an unpopular war with the rebellious American Colonies forced the Admiralty to employ him. Many competent naval officers had refused to serve against the colonists, particularly those with Whig sympathies and independent means. As the rebels acquired powerful allies the Royal navy was stretched to the limit, watching the cautiously hostile Dutch, the partisan "neutrals" of the Baltic and the actively hostile French and Spanish. In their plight their Lordships had scraped the barrel and in the lees at the bottom had discovered the able person of Henry Hope.

Hope was more than a competent seaman. He had served as lieutenant at Quiberon Bay and distinguished himself several times during the Seven Years' War. Command of a sloop had come at the end of the war, but by then he was forty with little hope of further advancement. He had a widowed mother, tended by a sister whose husband had fallen before Ticonderoga in Abercrombie's bungled attack, but no family of his own. He was a man used to care and tribulation, a man well suited to command of a ship.

But as he stared out of the stern windows at the yeasty, bubbling wake that cut a smooth through the choppy waters of the outer estuary, he remembered a more youthful Hope. Now his name silently taunted him. He idly wondered about the young man who had just left the cabin. Then he dismissed the thought as his servant brought in breakfast.

Cyclops anchored in the Downs for three days while she gathered a small convoy of merchantmen about her and waited for a favorable wind to proceed west. When she and her covey of charges weighed they thought they would carry a pleasant easterly down Channel. In the event the wind veered and for a week *Cyclops* beat to windward against the last of the equinoctial gales.

Nathaniel Drinkwater was forced to endure a brief, hard schooling. He lay aloft with the topmen, shivering with cold and terror as the recalcitrant topgallants billowed and thundered about his ears. There was no redress when an overzealous bosun's mate accidentally sliced his buttocks with a starter. Cruelty was a fact of life and its evils were only augmented between the stinking decks of an overcrowded British man o'war. Worn out by a week's incessant labour in conditions of unaccustomed cold; forced by necessity to eat indifferent food washed down by small beer of incomparable badness; bullied and shouted at, Drinkwater had broken down one night.

He wept into his hammock with bitter loneliness. His dreams of glory and service to a grateful country melted into the desperate release of tears and in his misery he took refuge in thoughts of home.

He remembered his careworn mother, desperate to see her sons maintain their station in life; her delight when the Rector had called with a letter from the relative of a friend, a Captain Henry Hope, accepting Nathaniel as midshipman aboard *Cyclops*, and how jubilant she had been that her elder son at least had reached the respectability of a King's officer.

He wept too for his brother, the carefree, irrepressible Ned, who was always in trouble and whom the Rector himself had flogged for scrumping apples: Ned with whom he used to practise single stick on Barnet common, of whom his mother used to say despairingly that only a father's firmness would make of him a gentleman. Ned had laughed at that, tossed his head and laughed, while across the room Nathaniel had caught his mother's eyes and been ashamed for his brother's callousness.

Nathaniel had only one recollection of his father, a dim, shadowy being who had tossed him in the air, smelled of wine and tobacco, and laughed wildly before dashing his own brains out in a riding accident. Ned had all his father's reckless passion and love of horses, while Nathaniel inherited the mother's quieter fortitude.

But upon that miserable night when fatigue, hunger, sickness, cold and hopelessness lay siege to his spirit, Nathaniel was exposed to the vicissitudes of fate and in the surrounding darkness his sobbing was overheard by his neighbor, the senior midshipman.

At dinner the following day as eight or nine of *Cyclops*'s dozen midshipmen struggled through their pease pudding, the president of the cockpit, Mr. Midshipman Augustus Morris rose solemnly from his place at the head of the filthy table.

"We have a coward amongst us, gentlemen," he announced, a peculiarly malevolent gleam in his hooded eyes. The midshipmen, whose ages varied between twelve and twenty-four, looked from one to another wondering on whom the wrath of Mr. Morris was about to descend.

Drinkwater was already cringing under the onslaught he instinctively felt was destined for him. As Morris's eyes raked over the upturned faces they fell, one by one, to dumb regard of the pewter plates and tankards sliding about before them. None of them would encourage Morris neither would they interfere with whatever malice he had planned.

"*Mister* Drinkwater," Morris sarcastically emphasized the title, "I shall endeavor to correct your predilection for tears by compelling you arse to weep a little—get over that chest!"

Drinkwater knew it was pointless to resist. At the mention of his name he had risen unsteadily to his feet. He looked dumbly round at the indicated sea chest, his legs shaking but refusing to move. Then a cruel fate made *Cyclops* lurch and the tableau dissolved, Drinkwater was thrown across the chest by the forces of nature. With an unnatural eagerness Morris flung himself on Drinkwater, threw aside the blue cloth coattails and, inserting his fingers in the waistband of Drinkwater's trousers, bared his victim's buttocks to an accompaniment of tearing calico. It was this act more than the six brutal stripes that Morris laid on his posterior that burnt itself into Drinkwater's memory. For his mother had laboured on those trousers, her arthritic fingers carefully passing the needle, the tears filling her eyes at the prospect of parting with her elder son. Somehow, with the resilience of youth, Drinkwater survived that passage to Spithead. Despite the pain in his buttocks he had been forced to learn much about the details of handling a ship under sail for the westerly gale compelled the frigate to wear and wear again in a hard, ruthless fight to windward and it was the second week in October 1779 before she brought to her anchor in St. Helen's Roads under the lee of Bembridge.

Hardly had *Cyclops* gathered sternway, her main topsail aback, and the cable gone rumbling through the hawse than the third lieutenant was calling away the captain's gig. Morris acted as the gig's coxswain. He ordered Drinkwater to the bow where a grinning seaman handed the youth a boat-hook. The gig bobbed alongside the wooden whales of the frigate's side, the hook lodged in the mainchains. Above him, but unseen, Drinkwater could hear the thumping of the marines' boots as they fell in at the entry port. Then came the twittering of the pipes. He looked up. At the entry port, fingers to his hat, stood Captain Hope. It was only the second time Drinkwater had seen him face to face since their brief interview. Their eyes met, the boy's full of awe, the man's blank with indifference. Hope turned around, grasped the manropes and leaned outboard. He descended the side until a foot above the gunwhale of the boat he paused waiting for the boat to rise. As it did so he jumped aboard, landing with little dignity between stroke and second stroke. He clambered over the intervening thwart from which the seamen deferentially drew aside and sat himself down.

"Toss oars!" yelled Morris.

"Bear off forrard!" Drinkwater pushed mightily against his boat-hook. It caught in the iron work of the chains; he tried to disengage it as the boat's head fell off but it refused to move, its shaft drawing through his hand and sticking incongruously outwards from the ship's side. He leaned further outboard and grabbed the end of the handle, the sweat of exertion and humiliation poured off him. He lunged again and nearly fell overboard.

"Sit down forrard!" roared Morris, and Drinkwater subsided in the bows, his cup of agony overflowing.

"Give way together!"

The oars bit the water and groaned in the thole pins. In minutes the men's backs were dark with perspiration. Drinkwater darted a glance aft. Morris was staring ahead, his hand on the tiller. The captain was gazing abstractedly at the green shores of the Isle of Wight away to larboard.

Then a thought struck Drinkwater. He had left the boat-hook protruding from the frigate's side. What in God's name was he going to use when they reached the flagship? His mind was overcome by sudden panic as he cast about the bow sheets for another boat hook. There was none.

For nearly twenty minutes as the gig danced over the sparkling sea and the westerly breeze dashed spray off the wavecaps, Drinkwater cast about him in an agony of indecision. He knew their destination was the flagship, *HMS Sandwich* of 90 guns, where even the seamen would look haughtily on the frigate's unremarkable gig. Any irregularities in the boat-handling would be commented upon to the disservice of *Cyclops*. Then a second thought struck him. Any such display of poor seamanship would reflect equally upon Mr. Midshipman Morris and he was unlikely to let Drinkwater discredit him unscathed. The prospect of another beating further terrified the boy.

Drinkwater stared ahead of the boat. The low shore of Hampshire lay before him, the sun shining on the dun blocks of the forts at Gosport and Southsea, guarding the entrance to Portsmouth Harbour. Between the gig and the shoreline a long row of ships of the line lay at anchor, their hulls massive beneath the masts and crossed yards. Large ensigns snapped briskly at their sterns and the gaudy flutter of the union flags over their fo'c's'les gave the vista a festive air. Here and there the square flag of a rear or vice-admiral flew at a masthead. Sunlight glittered on gilded figureheads and quarter galleries as the battleships swung head to wind at the slackwater. The sea surrounding them was dotted with small craft. Coastal vessels crowded on sail to avoid pulling boats of every conceivable size. Small launches and gigs conveyed officers and commanders; larger long boats and cutters under pint-size midshipmen or grizzled master's mates brought stores, powder or shot off from the dockyard. Water hoys and shallops, their civilian crews abusive under their protection from the press gangs, bucked alongside the battleships. A verbal duel between their masters and anxious naval lieutenants who waved requisition orders at them, seemed endless. The sheer energy and scale of activity was like nothing Drinkwater had ever witnessed before. They passed a small cutter aboard which half a dozen painted doxies sat, pallid with the boat's motion. Two of them waved saucily at the gig's crew amongst whom a ripple of lust passed at the unaccustomed sight of swelling bodices.

"Eyes in the boat!" yelled Morris self-importantly, himself glancing at the lushness exhibited by over-tight stays.

The *Sandwich* was nearer now and a cold sweat broke out again on Drinkwater's forehead. Then, by accident, he solved his problem. Wriggling round to view the prospect before him his hand encountered something sharp. He looked down. Beneath the grating he caught sight of something hook-like. He shifted his weight and lifted the slatted wood. In the bilge lay a small grapnel. It had an eye at the end of the shank. It was this that saved his backside another tanning. Fishing it out he bent on the end of the gig's painter and coiled the bight in his hand. He now possessed a substitute boat-hook and relaxed. Once again he looked about him.

It was a splendid sight. Beyond the line of battleships several frigates lay at anchor. They had already passed one lying as guardship at the Warner and had Drinkwater been less perturbed by the loss of his boat-hook he might have been more attentive. But now he could feast his eyes on a sight that his provincial breeding had previously denied him. Beyond Fort Gilkicker more masts rose from hulls grey blue with distance. Drinkwater's inexperienced eyes did not recognize the lines of transports.

It was a powerful fleet; a great effort by Britain to avert the threat to her West Indian possessions and succor the ailing ships on the North American station. For two years since the surrender of Burgoyne's army Britian had been trying to bring the wily Washington to battle while simultaneously holding off the increasing combination of European enemies from snapping up distant colonies when her attention was occupied elsewhere.

That this effort had been further strained by the corruption, peculation and plain jobbery that infected public life in general and Lord Sandwich's navy in particular was not a matter to concern Drinkwater for grander spectacles were before him. As the gig drew close to the massive side of *Sandwich* Captain Hope drew the attention of Morris to something. The midshipman turned the boat head to sea.

"Oars!" he ordered and the blades rose dripping to the horizontal.

Drinkwater looked round for somereason for this cessation of activity. There was none as far as he could see. Looking again at *Sandwich* he noted a flurry about her decks.

Glittering officers in blue and white, pointed polished telescopes astern, in the direction of Portsmouth. Drinkwater could just see the crowns of the marines' black hats as they fell in. Then a drum rolled and the black specks were topped by a line of silver bayonets as the marines shouldered arms. A pipe shrilled out and all activity aboard *Sandwich* ceased. The great ship seemed to wait expectantly as a small black ball rose to the truck of her mainmast.

Then round her stern and into view from *Cyclops*'s gig swept and admiral's barge. At its bow fluttered the red cross of St. George. The oarsmen bent to their task with unanimous precision, their red and white striped shirts moving in unison, their heads crowned by black beavers. A small dapper midshipman stood upright in the stern, hand on tiller. His uniform was immaculate, his hat set at a rakish angle. Drinkwater stared down at his own crumpled coat and badly cobbled trousers; he felt distinctly uncomfortable.

Also in the stern of the barge sat an old-looking man wrapped in a boat cloak. The lasting impression made on Drinkwater was a thin, hard mouth, then the barge was alongside *Sandwich* and Admiral Sir George Brydges Rodney was ascending the side of the flagship. A squeal of pipes, a roll of drums and a twinkle of light as the bayonets flashed to the present; at the main masthead the black ball broke out and revealed itself as the red cross of St. George. At this sight the guns of the fleet roared out in salute.

Admiral Rodney had arrived to take command of the fleet.

A few minutes later Drinkwater hurled his grapnel at *Sandwich's* mainchains. By good fortune it held first time and, to indifferent ceremonial, Captain Hope reported to his superior.

Chapter Two January 1780

The Danish Brig

On New Year's Day, 1780, Rodney's armada was at sea. In addition to the scouting frigates and twenty-one line of battleships no less than three hundred merchantmen cleared the Channel that chill morning. In accordance with her instructions *Cyclops* was part of the escort attending the transports and so took no part in the action of 8th January.

A Spanish squadron of four frigates, two corvettes and the 64-gun ship *Guipuscoaño* was encountered off Cape Finisterre with a convoy of fifteen merchantmen. The entire force was surrounded and taken. Prize crews were put on board and the captured vessels escorted back to England by the *Guipuscoaño*, renamed *Prince William* in honor of the Duke of Clarence, then a midshipman with the fleet. The captured vessels which contained victuals were retained to augment the supplies destined for Gibraltar.

As the concourse of ships plodded its slow way down the Iberian coast of the afternoon of the 15th, Drinkwater sat in the foretop of the *Cyclops*. It was his action station and he had come to regard it as something of his own domain, guarded as it was by its musket rests and a small swivel gun. Here he was free of the rank taint between decks, the bullying senselessness of Morris and here too, in the dog watches, he was able to learn some of the finer points of the seaman's art from an able seaman named Tregembo.

Young Nathaniel was quick to learn and impressed most of his superiors with his eager enthusiasm to attempt any task. But on this afternoon he was enjoying a rest, soaking up the unaccustomed luxury of January sunshine. It seemed impossible that only a couple of months previously he had known nothing of this life. So packed with events and impressions had the period been that it seemed another lifetime in which he had bid his widowed mother and younger brother farewell. Now, he reflected with the beginnings of pride, he was part of the complex organization that made *Cyclops* a man o'war.

Drinkwater gazed over the ship which creaked below him. He saw Captain Hope as an old, remote figure in stark contrast to his first lieutenant. The Honourable John Devaux was the third son of an earl, an aristocrat to his fingertips, albeit an impoverished one, and a Whig to boot. He and Hope were political opponents and Devaux's haughty youth annoyed the captain. Henry Hope had been too long in the service to let it show too frequently since Devaux, with influence, was not to be antagonized. In truth, the younger man's competence was never in doubt. Unlike many of his class he had taken an interest in the business of naval war which was motivated by more than an instinct for survival. Had his politics been different or the government Whig he might have been in Hope's shoes and Hope in his. It was a fact both had the intelligence to acknowledge and though friction was never far from the surface it was always veiled.

As for *Cyclops* herself she had shaken down as well as any ship manned under the system of the press. Her crew had exercised at the great guns under their divisional officers and her signalling system had been sorely strained trying to maintain order amongst the unruly merchantmen but, by and large both captain and first lieutenant agreed, she would do. Hope had no illusions about glory so fanaticism was absent from his character. If his officers were able and his crew willing, he asked no more of them.

To Nathaniel Drinkwater, dozing in his top *Cyclops* had become his only real world. His doubts had begun to evaporate under the influence of a change in the weather and youthful adaptability. He was slowly learning that the midshipmen's berth was an environment in which it was just possible to exist. Although he loathed Morris and disliked several of the older members of his mess, the majority were pleasant enough boys. They got on well together, bearing Morris's bullying with fortitude and commiserating in their hatred of him.

Drinkwater regarded Lieutenant Devaux with awe and the old sailing master, Blackmore, whose duties included the instruction of the midshipmen in the rudiments of navigation, with the respect he might have felt for his father had the latter been living. The nearest he came to friendship was with the topman Tregembo who handled the foretop swivel gun in action. He proved an endless source of wisdom and information about the frigate and her minutae. A Cornishman of uncertain age, he had been caught with a dubious cargo in the fish-well of his father's lugger off the Lizard by a revenue cutter. His father had offered the officers armed resistance and been hanged for his pains. As an act of clemency his son was given a lighter sentence which, the justices assured the court, would mitigate the grief felt by the wife of the dastardly smuggler: impressment. Tregembo had hardly stepped ashore since.

Drinkwater smiled to himself feeling, up here in his little kingdom, the self-satisfaction of youth seeping through him. Below on deck one bell rang through the ship. He was on watch in fifteen minutes. He rose and looked up.

Above him the topmast met the topgallant and at the upper hounds sat the lookout. A mood of devilment seized him; he would ascend to the hounds and from there slide down the backstay to the deck. The long descent would be an impressive demonstration of his proficiency as a seaman. He began to climb.

Casting his leg over the topgallant yard he joined the man on lookout. Far below him *Cyclops* rolled gently. His view of the deck was broken by the bellying sails and lent perspective by the diminishing rigging, each rope leading down to its respective belaying pin or eyebolt.

The seaman made shift for him and Drinkwater looked around. The blue circle of the sea was broken by some two hundred odd white specks as the armada sailed south. In that direction, below the horizon, the advanced frigates reconnoitred. Behind them in three divisions came the dark hulls of the ships of the line, a few of them wearing the yellow gunstrakes that would soon become uniform. In the center of the middle column *Sandwich* carried Admiral Rodney, the man responsible for all this puissance. Behind the battleships a couple of cutters and a schooner, tenders to the fleet, followed like dogs in the wake of their master. Then in a great mass came the convoy of troopships, storeships, cargo vessels with an escort of four frigates and two sloops of war. *Cyclops*'s station on the inshore bow of the convoy made her the nearest frigate to the rear division of battleships and the most advanced ship of the convoy itself.

From his elevated position Drinkwater looked out to larboard. Eight or nine leagues distant, slightly dun coloured in the westering sun, the coast of Portugal was clearly visible. His eyes raked over the horizon casually and he was about to descend to the deck when his attention was caught by an irregularity. A small speck of white almost abeam of them was set against the backdrop of the coast. He nudged the seaman and pointed.

"Sail, sir," the man responded matter-of-factly.

"Yes—I'll hail," then in as manly a voice as he could muster: "Deck there!"

Faintly the voice of Keene, the third lieutenant came back, "Aye, aye?"

"Sail eight points to larboard!" Drinkwater reached for the backstay and began his spectacular hand over hand descent. In the excitement of the strange sail nobody noticed him.

"Signal from flag, sir," said Lieutenant Keene to Captain Hope as Drinkwater came aft.

"Well?"

"Our number. Chase."

"Acknowledge," said the Captain, "Mr. Keene put the ship before the wind."

Drinkwater assisted making up the answering signal as the lieutenant turned to bellow orders through his speaking trumpet. Bosun's mates chivvied the people and the helm was put up. *Cyclops* swung to the east, the braces rattling through the sheaves as the yards swung round.

"All sail if you please Mr. Keens."

"Aye, aye, sir!" There was enthusiasm in the lieutenant's voice and a ripple of excitement ran through the ship. Free of the constrictions necessary in keeping station the frigate spread her wings. Clew and bunt-lines were cast off the pins as the topmen spread out along the footropes loosening the canvas. As the master's mates stationed at the bunt of each sail waved to the deck the order was given to sheet home. The topgallants billowed, collapsed and billowed again as the waisters tallied onto the halliards and the yards rose from the caps. *Cyclops* leaned to the increase of power, the hempen rigging drew tight and the vessel began to tremble gently as she gathered speed. The frigate surged through the dark Atlantic, the white vee of her wake creaming out from under her transom.

On deck the watch changed and the waist cleared as men, drawn on deck by the excitement, went below again.

Drinkwater found the captain staring at him. "Sir?" he ventured.

"Mr., er . . ."

"Drinkwater, sir."

"Ahh. Mr. Drinkwater take a glass to the foremasthead and see what you make of her. D'you think you can do that?"

"Aye, aye, sir." Drinkwater took from a rack an exceedingly battered telescope which was provided by a generous Navy Board for the exclusive use of the ship's "young gentlemen". He started for the foremast rigging.

It was nearly a quarter of an hour before he returned to the deck. Aware that Hope was testing his ability he had waited until he had something positive to report.

He touched his hat to the captain.

"She's a brig, sir. Not flying colors, sir."

"Very well, Mr. Drinkwater."

"See her from the deck now, sir," drawled Devaux who had come up on deck.

The captain nodded. "Clear away the bow chasers, Mr. Devaux . . ."

Drinkwater too could see the two masted vessel they were bearing down upon. He watched for the bright spot of color that must surely appear soon to denote her nationality. A dozen other telescopes were endeavoring to glean the same information. A red speck rose to her peak, red with a white cross.

"Danish!" A dozen people snapped out simultaneously.

Cyclops tore down on her quarry and on a nod from Hope a gun barked from forward, its smoke rolling slowly ahead of the onrushing frigate.

A white spout rose ahead of the Danish ship. It was a cable short but it had the desired effect as the Dane backed his main topsail and hove to.

"Mr. Devaux, you'll board."

Orders flew. Where previously every idler in the ship had been intently watching the chase, chaos erupted. Out of this apparent disorder the main and forecourses rose in their buntlines and groups of organized men appeared to lower the lee quarter boat as *Cyclops* turned to back her main topsail.

Devaux shouted more orders and Drinkwater heard his own name in the confusion.

"Get in that boat, cully!" roared the first lieutenant and Nathaniel ran to the waist where a net had been flung over the side. The boat's crew were aboard but extra seamen armed with cutlasses were swarming down into her. Drinkwater cocked a foot over the rail, caught the leg of his trousers on a belaying pin and heard the fabric rip. But this time it did not seem to matter.

He scrambled down into the boat. To his surprise Devaux was already there, still shouting.

"Where in God's name is Wheeler?" he roared at nobody in particular. Then as the red-coated marine lieutenant and six of his men clumsily descended the netting, their Tower muskets tangling in the cordage.

"Come on you bloody lobsters!" Devaux yelled to the appreciative grins of the seamen. Lieutenant Wheeler resented the insult to his service, but he was unable to retaliate due to his preoccupation with getting himself and his hanger into the boat without a total loss of dignity.

"Shove off! Out oars! Give way together and put your backs into it!"

The big boat drove forward and Devaux pushed the tiller into Drinkwater's hand.

"Take her alongside his lee side and keep her there." He turned to Wheeler, "She's a neutral so don't board unless you hear me shout." He raised his voice, "Bosun's mate!" The petty officer with the armed seamen stood up in the bow.

"Sir?"

"Make no attempt to board unless I need help—if I shout I want the whole bloody lot of you!"

The seamen grinned and fingered their blades. Minutes later Drinkwater's cracking voice was bellowing "Oars! . . . Toss Oars! . . . Hook on!" Lieutenant Devaux leapt for the Dane's chains. For a second or two his elegant legs dangled incongruously, then he had hoisted himself to the deck of the brig.

The boat bounced up and down the side of the strange ship. Occasionally a towheaded face looked curiously overside at them. All in the boat were nervous. A few cannon balls dropped from the rail would plummet through the boat's planking. It seemed to Drinkwater that the first lieutenant had been gone hours. He watched the rail advance and recede as the Atlantic shoved the boat up the Dane's side then dropped her down again. He looked anxiously at Wheeler. The marine officer just smiled, "Don't worry cully. When the Hon. John is in trouble he'll squeal."

At last, to his infinite relief, Drinkwater saw Devaux's legs swing over the rail. He heard the lieutenant's suave voice, all trace of coarseness gone.

"Y're servant ma'am," and the next instant he had tumbled into the boat. He grabbed the tiller from Drinkwater without ceremony.

"Shove off! . . . Oars! . . . Give way together and pull you buggers!" Devaux crouched in the stern his body bent with urgency.

"Pull! Pull! Pull like you'd pull a Frenchman off y're mother!" The men grinned at the obscenity. Devaux knew his business and the seamen bent their oar looms with effort, the blades sprang form the water and flew forward for the next stroke. Astern of them the Dane made sail. Once Devaux looked back and, following his gaze, Drinkwater made out a flash of color where a woman waved.

"Wheeler," said Devaux, "we've work to do." Quite deliberately Devaux told Wheeler the news. He knew the men within hearing would pass it on to the lower deck. Equally he knew Hope would not bother to do so, only a garbled version might reach the innermost recesses of *Cyclops* unless Devaux disseminated the information himself. These men could shortly be called upon to die and the first lieutenant sought to infect them with blood lust. He had seen what a fighting madness such enthusiasm could induce in British seamen and he knew *Cyclops* might need just such an infection in the coming hours.

"That Dane has just sailed from Cadiz. The Dons are at sea, a fleet of 'em. Bit of luck he was pro-British." He paused reflectively. "Married to an English girl. Dammed handsome woman too . . ." he grinned, the marines grinned too—the message was going home.

It was dark when *Cyclops* rejoined the fleet. A full moon enabled Hope to take her in amongst the concourse of ships to where the three horizontal lanterns in *Sandwich*'s rigging marked the presence of the Admiral.

Shortening sail, the frigate sent a boat across and Devaux had reported to Rodney. The outcome of this momentous news was that *Cyclops* had been ordered to make sail and warn the advance frigates. The fleet had shortened sail at sunset to avoid dispersal and aid station keeping so that *Cyclops* soon drew ahead of the battleships, passing down the regular lines of massive sides which dwarfed the swifter frigate as they lumbered along, creaking in the moonlight.

At dawn *Cyclops* was in sight of the frigates. Astern of her the fleet's topsails were just visible with one ship, the two decked seventy-four-gun *Bedford*, crowding on sail to come up with the cruisers.

Hampered by the poor signalling code in use Hope had difficulty in conveying the meaning of his message to the more distant frigates. By a happy coincidence, however, he chose "Clear for action" and two hours later *Bedford* came up flying the same signal, her two lines of gun muzzles already visible, for Rodney had thrown out the order to his fleet at dawn.

At first beat of the marine drummer's sticks Drinkwater had sensed the tension in *Cyclops*. He raced for his station in the foretop where the swivel was loaded and primed. But there was no occasion for haste. All morning the British stood at action stations without any sign of the enemy. During the forenoon division after division of the fleet had altered course to the south east, rounding the pink cliffs of Cape Saint Vincent and heading for the Straits of Gibraltar. At noon half of *Cyclops*'s company stood down for a meal of beer, flip and biscuit.

After a hasty meal Drinkwater, eager not to miss a moment of what popular comment was saying would be a fleet action, returned to the foretop. He looked around him. The frigates had drawn back on the main body and *Bedford* had come up to occupy the inshore station.

In the foretop his men had loaded their muskets. Tregembo was musingly caressing the toy swivel gun. Astern in the main top Morris's blue coat could clearly be seen. He was bending over a young Devon seaman whose good looks had excited some crude jibes from his messmates. Drinkwater could not quite identify the feeling engendered by the sight of Morris thus engaged beyond the fact that it was vaguely disquieting. He was still a comparative innocent to the perversions of humanity.

Astern of Morris Sergeant Hagan commanded the mizzen top and its marine sharpshooters. Their scarlet coats were a splash of vivd color against the black hemp rigging that almost obscured the view. Looking down, Nathaniel had an unimpeded view of the quarterdeck as, cleared for action, the maincourse and cross-jack were clewed up.

He saw Captain Hope and Lieutenant Devaux there with the old sailing master standing by the quartermaster and helmsmen. A gaggle of midshipmen and master's mates were also in attendance to run messages and transmit signals. But as well as blue there was scarlet aft. Wheeler, resplendent in his brilliant coat, crimson sash and the glittering gorget of a military officer had his hanger drawn. He carried it negligently in the crook of his arm but the flash of its blade was a wicked reminder of death. It was very different from the ash single stick Drinkwater had thrust and parried with at home. He had not much considered death or the possibility of dying. Falling from the rigging had at first terrified him but he had overcome that. But supposing a mast, the foremast perhaps, was shot away? He looked down again to where nets were stretched above the deck to keep falling spars and rigging off the guns' crews toiling below. At the moment those gun crews were lazing around their pieces. Just visible to Nathaniel, below him on the main deck, beneath the gratings the second and third lieutenants conferred with one another on the frigates centreline. Their demeanour was studiously casual as they waited to command their batteries.

Apart from the creaking of the ship's fabric, the passage of the wind and the noise of her bow wave, *Cyclops* was a silent thing. Upwards of two hundred and fifty men waited expectantly, as did the crews of all the fleet.

At one o'clock in the afternoon *Bedford* fired a gun, signalled *Sandwich* and let fly her topsail sheets. For those too distant to see the signal the flutter of her topsails was a time honored indication of the presence of an enemy fleet in sight.

"Wind's getting up," said Tregembo to no one in particular but breaking the silence in the foretop.

Chapter Three January 1780

The Moonlight Battle

The battle that followed was one of the most dramatic ever fought by the Royal Navy. The waters over which the opposing fleets contended were to be immortalized twenty-five years later when Nelson was to conquer and die off Cape Trafalgar, but the night action of the 16th/17th January 1780 was to be known by no geographical name.

In an age when admirals were absolutely bound, upon pain of death, to the tactical concept of the unbroken line ranged against that of the enemy, Rodney's unleashing of his ships was an innovation of the utmost importance, and the manner of its doing in that wild Moonlight Battle was an act of daring unsurpassed by sailing warships in such large numbers.

Tregembo had been right. An hour after *Bedford*'s sighting of eleven Spanish battleships and two frigates the sky had clouded over. The wind backed westerly and began to freshen.

At *Bedford*'s signal Rodney had thrown out the "General Chase" to his warships. Each captain now sought to outdo the rest and the vessels fitted with the new copper bottoms forged ahead. The two-deckers *Defence*, *Resolution* and *Edgar* began taking the lead. Officers anxiously checked their gear as captains, reckless as schoolboys, held on to sail. Still the wind rose. Telescopes trained with equal anxiety on the Spaniards who, faced with such overwhelming odds, turned away to leeward and the shelter of Cadiz.

Seeing the retrograde movement Rodney signaled his ships to engage from leeward, thereby conveying to his captains the tactical concept of overhauling the enemy and interposing themselves between the Spanish and safety.

It had become a race.

As the British ships tore forward dead before the wind, puffs of smoke appeared from their fo'c's'les as gunners tried ranging shots. At first the plumes of water, difficult to see among breaking wave crests, were a long way astern of the Spaniards. But slowly, as the minutes ran into an hour, they got nearer.

Aboard *Cyclops* Devaux stood poised on the fo'c's'le glass to eye as the frigate's long nine-pounders barked at the enemy as she lifted her bow. Almost directly above Drinkwater watched eagerly. His inexperienced eyes missed the fall of shot but the excitement of the scene riveted his attention. *Cyclops* trembled with the thrill of the chase and giving expression to the corporate feeling of the ship, O'Malley, the mad Irish cook, sat cross-legged on the capstan top scraping his fiddle. The insane jig was mixed with the hiss and splash of the sea around them and the moan of the gale as it strummed the hempen rigging.

Captain Hope had taken *Cyclops* across the slower *Bedford's* bows and was heading for the northernmost Spaniard, a frigate of almost equal size. To the south of their quarry the high stern of the Spanish line of battleships stretched in a ragged line, the second frigate hidden behind them to the east.

A sudden column of white rose close to the *Cyclops's* plunging bowsprit. Drinkwater looked up. Held under the galleries of a Spanish two-decker by the following wind a puff of white smoke lingered.

Tregembo swore. "That's good shooting for Dagoes," he said. It was only then that Drinkwater realized he was under fire.

As *Cyclops* crossed the stern of the two decker in

chase of the frigate the battleships had tried a ranging shot. Suddenly there was a rush of air and the sound of two corks being drawn from bottles. Looking up Drinkwater saw a hole in the fore-topsail and another in the main. It was uncomfortably close. As their sterns rose to the following seas the Spaniards were firing at the oncoming British silhouetted against the setting sun.

Drinkwater shivered. The brief winter warmth was gone and the fresh breeze had become a gale. He looked again at the Spanish fleet. They were appreciably nearer. Then he saw two plumes of white rise under the Spaniard's quarter. Their own guns were silent. He looked interrogatively at Tregembo.

"What the . . . ?" Then the seaman pointed.

To starboard, hidden from the huddling midshipman by the mast, *Resolution*, a newly coppered seventy-four, was passing the frigate. Conditions now favored the heavier ships. *Resolution* was overhauling the Spaniards rapidly and beyond her *Edgar* and *Defence* were bearing down on the enemy. Before the sun set behind a bank of cloud its final rays picked out the *Resolution*.

The almost horizontal light accentuated every detail of the scene. The sea, piling up from the west, its shadowed surfaces a deep indigo, constantly moving and flashing golden where it caught the sun, seemed to render the warship on it a thing of stillness. The *Resolution*'s hull was dark with the menace of her larboard batteries as she passed scarcely two cables from *Cyclops*. Her sails drew out, pulling the great vessel along, transmitting their power down through the masts and rigging until the giant oak hull with its weight of artillery and 750 men made ten knots through the water.

Drinkwater could see the heads of her upper-deck gunners and a line of red and silver marines on the poop. At her stern and peak battle ensigns stood out, pointing accusingly at the enemy ahead. Her bow chasers barked again. This time there was no white column . Devaux's glass swung round. "She's hit 'em, by God!" he shouted.

Somebody on the fo'c's'le cheered. He was joined by another as *Cyclop*'s crew roared their approval at the sight of *Resolution* sailing into battle. Drinkwater found himself cheering wildly with the other men in the top. Tears poured down Tregembo's cheeks. "The bastards, the fucking bastards . . ." he sobbed. Drinkwater was not sure who the bastards were, nor, at the time, did it seem to matter. It is doubtful if Tregembo himself knew. What he was expressing was his helplessness. The feeling of magnificent anger that overcame these men: the impressed, the drunkards, the jail birds and the petty thieves. All the dregs of eighteenth-century society forced into a tiny hull and kept in order by a ruthless discipline, sailed into a storm of lead and iron death cheering. Stirred to their souls by emotions they could not understand or control the sight of puissant *Resolution* had torn from their breasts the cheers of desperation. It is with such spontaneous inspiration that the makers of war have always gulled their warriors and transformed them into heroes. Thus did the glamor of action infect these men with the fighting anger that served their political masters supremely well.

Perhaps it was to the latter that the barely articulate Tregembo alluded.

"Silence! Silence there!" Hope was roaring from the quarterdeck and the cheering died as men grinned at one another, suddenly sheepish after the outburst of emotion.

Faintly across the intervening sea a cheer echoed from *Resolution* and Drinkwater realised *Cyclops* must appear similarly magnificent from the seventy-four. A shudder of pride and cold rippled his back.

Before darkness isolated the admiral from his ships Rodney threw out a final command to captains: "Engage the enemy more closely." He thus encouraged them to press the enemy to the utmost degree. Both fleets were tearing down upon a lee shore with off-lying shoals. By five o'clock it was nearly dark. The wind had risen to a gale and gloomy clouds raced across the sky. But the moon was rising, a full yellow moon that shone forth from between the racing scud, shedding a fitful light upon the baleful scene.

At sunset *Resolution*, *Edgar* and *Defence* had drawn level with the rearmost Spanish ships. Exchanging broadsides as they passed they kept on, heading the leeward enemy off from Cadiz.

"Larboard battery make ready!" The order rang out. Drinkwater transferred his attention to port as *Cyclops* was instantly transformed. The waiting was over, tension was released as gunners leapt to their pieces and the British frigate rode down the Spanish.

The enemy was close on *Cyclop*'s larboard bow. Below Drinkwater a chaser rang out and a hole appeared in the Spaniard's main topsail.

Devaux ran aft along the larboard gangboard. He was yelling orders to the lieutenants on the gun deck below. He joined Hope on the quarterdeck where the two men studied their enemy. At last the captain called one of the midshipmen over.

"M'compliments to Lieutenant Keene, when his battery engages he is to cripple the rigging . . ."

The boy scrambled below. Hope wanted the Spaniard immobilized before both ships, distraced by the fury of battle, ran down to leeward where the low Spanish coast lay. Offshore the shoal of San Lucar waited for the oncoming ships of both nations.

"Mr. Blackmore," Hope called over the sailing master.

"Sir?"

"The San Lucar shoal, how far distant?"

"Three or four leagues, sir," answered the old man after a moment's consideration.

"Very well. Post a mate forward on the fore t'gallant yard. I want to know the instant that shoal is sighted."

A master's mate went forward. On his way aloft he passed Drinkwater who stopped him with a question.

"Old man's worried about the shoals to looard," the mate informed him.

"Oh!" said Drinkwater looking ahead of the frigate. But all he could see was a tumbling waste of black and silver water as clouds crossed the moon, the spume smoking off the wave crests as they tumbled down wind.

A squealing of gun trucks told where the men of the

larboard gun battery were hand-spiking their carriages round to bear on the enemy. The Spanish frigate was ahead of *Cyclops* but when the British ship drew abeam they would be about two cables distant.

"Make ready!"

The order was passed along the dark gun-deck. In his foretop Drinkwater checked the swivel. Under the foot of the topsail he could see the high Spanish poop. Tregembo swung the swivel gun round and pointed it at where he judged the Spanish officers would be. The other seamen cocked their muskets and drew beads on the enemy's mizen top where they knew Spanish soldiers would be aiming at their own officers.

The Spanish frigate was only two points forward of *Cyclops*'s beam. In the darkness of the gun-deck Lieutenant Keene, commanding the larboard battery of twelve pounders, looked along the barrel of his aftermost gun. When it bore on the enemy's stern his entire broadside would be aimed at the frigate.

A midshipman dodged up to him touching his hat. "Captain's compliments, sir, and you may open fire when your guns bear." Keene acknowledged and looked along the deck. Accustomed to the gloom he could see the long line of cannon, lit here and there by lanterns. The men were crouched round their pieces tensely awaiting the order to open fire. The gun captains looked his way expectantly, each grasping his linstock. Every gun was shotted canister on ball . . .

A ragged flash of fire flickered along the Spaniard's side. The noise of the broadside was muted by the gale. Several balls thumped home into the hull, tearing off long oak splinters and sending them lancing down the crowded decks. A man screamed, another was lifted bodily from the deck and his bloodily pulped corpse smashed against a cannon breech.

Aloft, holes appeared in the topgallant sails and the master's mate astride the fore topgallant yard had his shoes ripped off by the passage of a ball. With a twang several ropes parted, the main royal yard, its sail furled, came down with a rush.

Orders were shouted at the topmen to secure the loose gear.

Meanwhile Keene still watched from his after gunport. He could see nothing but sea and sky, the night filled with the raging of the gale and the responsive hiss of the sea.

Then the stern of the Spanish frigate plunged into view, dark and menacing; another ragged broadside rippled along her side. He stepped back and waited for the upward roll:

"Fire!"

Chapter Four January 1780

The Spanish Frigate

Frigates varied in size and design but basically they comprised a single gundeck running the full length of the ship. In battle the temporary bulkheads providing the captain and officers' accommodation were removed when the ship cleared for action. Above the gun deck and running forward almost to the main mast was the quarterdeck from where the ship was conned. A few light cannon and anti-personnel weapons were situated here. At the bow a similar raised deck, or fo'c's'le, extended aft round the base of the foremast. The fo'c's'le and quarterdeck were connected along the ship's side by wooden gangways which extended over that part of the gundeck otherwise exposed and known as 'the waist'. However the open space between the gangways was beamed in and supported chocks for the ship's boats so that the ventilation that the opening was supposed to provide the gun deck was, at best, poor.

When the larboard battery opened fire the confined space of the gun deck became a cacophonous hell. The flashes of the guns alternately plunged the scene from brilliance to blackness. Despite the season of the year the seamen were soon running in sweat as they sponged, rammed and fired their brutish artillery. The concussion of the guns and rumbling of the trucks as they recoiled and were hauled forward again was deafening. The tight knots of men labored round each gun, the lieutenants and master's mates controling their aim as they broke from broadsides to firing at will. Dashing about the sanded deck the little powder monkeys, scraps of undernourished urchins, scrambled from the gloomier orlop deck below to where the gunner had retired in his felt slippers to preside over the alchemical mysteries of cartridge preparation.

At the companionways the marine sentries stood, bayonets fixed to their loaded muskets. They had orders to shoot any but approved messengers or stretcher parties on their way to the orlop. Panic and cowardice were thus nicely discouraged. The only ways for a man to pass below was to be carried to Mr. Surgeon Appleby and his mates who, like the gunner, held their own esoteric court in the frigate's cockpit. Here the midshipmen's chests became the ship's operating theatre and covered with canvas provided Appleby with the table upon which he was free to butcher his Majesty's subjects. A few feet above the septic stink of rat-infested bilges, in a fetid atmosphere lit by a few guttering oil lamps, the men of Sandwich's navy came for succor and often breathed their last.

Cyclops fired seven broadsides before the two ships drew abeam. The Spaniards fired back with increasing irregularity as the dreadful precision of the British cannon smashed into their vessel's fabric.

Even so they carried away *Cyclops*'s mizen mast above the upper hounds. More rigging parted and the main topsail, shot through in a dozen places, suddenly dissolved into a flapping, cracking mess of torn canvas as the gale finished the work the cannon balls had started.

Suddenly the two frigates were abeam, the sea rushing black between them. The moon appeared from behind the obscurity of a cloud. Details of the enemy stood out and etched themselves into Drinkwater's brain. He could see men in the tops, officers on her quarterdeck and the activity of gun crews on the upper deck. A musket ball smacked into the mast above him, then another and another.

"Fire!" he yelled unnecessarily loudly at his topmen. Astern of him the main top loosed off, then Tregembo fired the swivel. Drinkwater saw the scatter of the langridge tearing up the Spaniard's decks. He watched fascinated as a man, puppet-like in the bizarre light, fell jerking to the deck with a dark stain spreading round him. Someone lurched against Drinkwater and sat down against the mast. A black hole existed where the man's right eye had been. Drinkwater caught his musket and sighted along it. He focused on a shadowy figure reloading in the enemy's main top. He did it as coolly as shooting at Barnet fair, squeezing the trigger. The flint sparked and the musket jerked against his shoulder. The man fell.

Tregembo had reloaded the swivel and the moon disappeared behind a cloud as it roared.

The concussion wave of a terrific explosion swept the two vessels, momentarily stopping the combatants. Away to the south six hundred men had ceased to exist as the seventy gun *San Domingo* blew up, fire reaching her magazine and causing her disintegration.

The interruption of the explosion reminded them all of the other ships engaged to the southward. Drinkwater reloaded the musket. Enemy balls no longer whizzed round him. He looked up, leveling the barrel. The Spanish frigate's main-mast leaned drunkenly forward. Stays snapped and the great spars collapsed, dragging the mizen topmast with it. *Cyclops* drew ahead.

Hope and Blackmore stared anxiously astern where the crippled Spaniard wallowed. Wreckage hung over her side as she swung to starboard. If the Spanish captain was quick he could rake *Cyclops*, his whole broadside pouring in through the latter's wide stern and the shot travelling the length of the crowded decks.

It was every commander's nightmare to be raked, especially from astern where the comparative fragility of the stern windows offered little resistance to the enemy shot. The wreckage over her side was drawing the Spaniard round. One of her larboard guns fired and splinters shot up from *Cyclops*'s quarter. Certainly someone appreciated the opportunity.

Cyclops's helm was put down in an attempt to bring

Cyclops on a parallel course but the spanker burst as the Spaniard fired, then the mizen topmast went and *Cyclops* lost the necessary leverage to force her stern around.

It was a ragged broadside compared with that of the British but its effects were no less lethal. Although nearly a quarter of a mile distant, the damaged enemy had fought back with devastating success. As Captain Hope surveyed the damage with Devaux a voice hailed them:

"Deck there! Breakers on the lee bow!"

Although the British frigate had started her turn the loss of her after sails deprived her of maneuverability. There were anxious faces on the quarterdeck.

The officers looked aloft. The lower mizen mast still stood, broken off some six feet above the top. The wreckage was hanging over the larboard side, dragging the frigate back that way while the gale in the forward sails still drove the ship inexorably downwind to where the San Lucar shoal awaited them. Axes were already at work clearing the raffle.

Hope saw a chance and ordered the helm hard over to continue the swing to port. Devaux looked forward and then at the captain.

"Set the cro'jack, bend on a new spanker and get the fore top'l clewed up!" The captain snapped at him. The first lieutenant ran forward screaming for topmen, anyone, pulling the upperdeck gun crews from their pieces, thrusting bosun's mates here and there . . .

Men raced for the rigging . . . disappeared below, hurrying and scurrying under the first lieutenant's hysterical direction.

"Wheeler, get your lobsters to brace the cro'jack yard!"

"Aye, aye, sir!"

Wheeler's booted men stomped away with the mizen braces as the topmen shook out the sail. A master's mate unmade the weather sheet, he was joined by another, they both hauled as two or three seamen under a bosun's mate loosed the clew and buntlines. The great sail exploded white in the moonlight, flogging in the gale; then it drew taut and *Cyclops* began to swing.

Still in his top Drinkwater could see the shoal now, a line of grey ahead of them perhaps four or five miles away. He became aware of a voice hailing him.

"Foretop there!"

"Aye sir?" he looked over the edge at the first lieutenant staring up at him.

"Aloft and furl that tops'l!"

Drinkwater started up. The fore topsail was already losing its power as the sheets slackened and the clew and buntlines drew it up to the yard. It was flogging madly, the trembling mast attesting to the fact that many of its stays must have been shot away.

Tregembo was already in the rigging as Drinkwater forsook the familiar top. He was lightheaded with the insane excitement of the night. When they had finished battling with the sail Drinkwater lay over the yard exhausted with hunger and cold. He looked to starboard. The white line on the bank seemed very near now and *Cyclops* was rolling as the swell built up in the shoaling water. But she was reaching now, sailing across the wind and roughly parallel with the shoal. She would still make leeway but she was no longer running directly on to the bank.

To the south and west dark shapes and flashes told of where the two fleets did battle. Nearer, and to larboard now, the Spanish frigate wallowed, beam on to wind and sea and rolling down onto the shoal.

Drawn from the gun-deck a party of powder-blackened and exhausted men toiled to get the spare spanker on deck. The long sausage of hard canvas snaked out of the tiers and onto the deck. Thirteen minutes later the new sail rose on the undamaged spars.

Cyclops was once more under control. The cross-jack was furled and the headsail sheets slackened. Again her bowsprit turned towards the shoal as Hope anxiously wore ship to bring her onto the starboard tack, heading where the Spanish frigate still wallowed helplessly.

The British frigate paid off before the wind. Then her

bowsprit swung away from the shoal. The wind came over the starboard quarter . . . then the beam. The yards were hauled round, the headsail sheets hardened in. The wind howled over the starboard bow, stronger now they were heading into it. *Cyclops* plunged into a sea and a shower of stinging spray swept aft. Half naked gunners scurried away below to tend their cannon.

Hope gave orders to re-engage as *Cyclops* bore down on her adversary, slowly drawing the crippled Spaniard under her lee.

Cyclops's guns rolled again and the Spaniard fired back.

Devaux was shouting at Blackmore above the crash of the guns. "Why don't he anchor Master?"

"And have us reach up and down ahead of him raking him?" scoffed the older man.

"What else can he do? Besides there's a limit to how long we can hang on here. What we want is offing . . ."

Hope heard him. Released from the tension of immediate danger now his command was again under control, the conversation irritated him.

"I'll trouble you to fight the ship, Mr. Devaux, and leave the tactical decisions to me."

Devaux was silent. He looked sullenly at the Spanish ship and was astonished at Hope's next order: "Get a hawser through an after port, quickly man, quickly!" At first Devaux was uncomprehending then the moon broke forth again and the lieutenant followed Hope's pointing arm, "Look man, look!"

The red and gold of Castile was absent from the stern. The Spanish frigate had struck.

"Cease fire! Cease fire!"

Cyclops's guns fell silent as she plunged past the enemy, the exhausted gunners collapsing with their exertions. But Devaux, all thoughts of arguing dispelled by the turn of events, was once more amongst them, rousing them to further efforts. Devaux shouted orders, bosun's mates swung their starters and the realization of the Spanish surrender swept the ship in a flash. Fatigue vanished in a trice for she was a war prize if they could save her from going ashore on the San Lucar shoal.

Even the aristocratic Devaux did not despise his captain's avarice. The chance of augmenting his paltry patrimony would be eagerly seized upon. He found himself hoping *Cyclops* had not done too much damage . . .

On the quarterdeck Captain Hope was enduring the master's objections. The only person on board who could legitimately contest the captain's decisions, from the navigational point of view, Blackmore vigorously protested the inadvisability of taking *Cyclops* to leeward again to tow off a frigate no more than half a league from a dangerous shoal.

But the exertions of the night affected men differently. As Blackmore turned away in defeat Hope saw his last opportunity. Shedding years at the prospect of such a prize his caution fell a prey to temptation. After a life spent in a Service which had inconsistently robbed him of a reputation for dash or glamor, fate was holding out a fiscal prize of enormous magnitude. All he had to do was apply some of the expertise that his years of seagoing had given him.

"Wear ship, Mr. Blackmore."

The captain turned and bumped into a slim figure hurrying aft.

"B . . . Beg pardon sir."

Drinkwater had descended from the foretop. He touched his hat to the captain.

"Well?"

"Shoal's a mile to leeward, sir." For a minute Hope studied the young face: he showed promise.

"Thank you, Mr., er . . ."

"Drinkwater, sir."

"Quite so. Remain with me; my messenger's gone . . ." The captain indicated the remains of his twelve-year-old midshipman messenger. The sight of the small, broken body made Drinkwater feel very light headed. He was cold and very hungry. He was aware that the frigate was maneuvering close to the crippled Spaniard, paying off downwind . . .

"First lieutenant's on the gun deck see how long he'll be." Uncomprehending the midshipman hurried off. Below the shadowy scene in the gundeck was ordered. A hundred gunners lugged a huge rope aft. Drinkwater discovered the first lieutenant right aft and passed the message. Devaux grunted and then, over his shoulder ordered, 'Follow me.' They both ran back to the quarterdeck.

"Nearly ready, sir," said Devaux striding past the captain to the taffrail. He lugged out his hanger and cut the log ship from its line and called Drinkwater.

"Coil that for heaving, young shaver." He indicated the long log line coiled in its basket. For an instant the boy stood uncertainly then, recollecting the way Tregembo had taught him he began to coil the line.

Devaux was bustling round a party of sailors bringing a coil of four inch rope aft. He hung over the taffrail, dangling one end and shouting at someone below. Eventually the end was caught, drawn inboard and secured to the heavy cable. Devaux stood upright and one of the seamen took the log line and secured it to the four inch rope.

Devaux seemed satisfied. "Banyard," he said to the seaman. "Heave that at the Spaniard when I give the word."

Cyclops was closing the crippled frigate. She seemed impossibly large as the two ships closed, the rise and fall between them fifteen to twenty feet.

The two ships were very close now. The Spaniard's bowsprit rose and fell, raking aft along *Cyclops*'s side. Figures were visible on her fo'c's'le as the bowsprit jutted menacingly over the knot of figures at the after end of *Cyclops*.If it ripped the spanker *Cyclops* was doomed since she would again become unmanageable, falling off before the gale. The spar rose again then fell as the frigate wallowed in a trough. It hit *Cyclops*'s taffrail, caught for an instant then tore free with a splintering of wood. At a signal from Devaux Banyard's line snaked dextrously out to tangle at the gammoning of the bowsprit dipping towards the British stern.

"Come on, boy!" shouted Devaux. In an instant he

had leapt up and caught the spar, heaving himself over it, legs kicking out behind him. Without thinking, impelled by the force of the first lieutenant's determination Drinkwater had followed. Below them *Cyclops* dropped away and was past.

The wind tore at Drinkwater's coat tails as he cautiously followed Devaux aft along the spar. The dangling raffle of gear afforded plenty of handholds and it was not long before he stood with his superior on the Spanish forecastle.

A resplendently attired officer was footing a bow at Devaux and proferring his sword. Devaux, impatient at the inactivity of the Spaniards, ignored him. He made signs at the officer who had first secured the heaving line and a party of seamen were soon heaving in the four inch rope. The moon emerged again and Devaux turned to Drinkwater. He nodded at the insistently bobbing Spaniard.

"For God's sake take it. Then return it—we need their help."

Nathaniel Drinkwater thus received the surrender of the thirty-eight gun frigate *Santa Teresa*. He managed a clumsy bow on the plunging deck and as graciously as he knew how, aware of his own gawkiness, he handed the weapon back. The moonlight shone keenly on the straight Toledo blade.

Devaux was shouting again: "Men! Men! Hombres! Hombres!" The four inch had arrived on board and the weight of the big hawser was already on it. Gesticulating wildly and miming with his body Devaux urged the defeated Spaniards to strenuous activity. He pointed to leeward. "Muerto! Muerto!"

They understood.

To windward Hope was tacking *Cyclops*.It was vital that Devaux secured the tow in seconds. The four inch snaked in. Then it snagged. The big ten-inch rope coming out of the water had caught on something under *Santa Teresa*'s bow.

"Heave!" screamed Devaux, beside himself with excitement. *Cyclops* would feel the drag of that rope. She might fail to pay off on the starboard tack . . .

Suddenly it came aboard with a rush. The floating hemp rose on a wave and swept aboard as *Santa Teresa*'s bow fell into a steep trough.

Drinkwater was astonished. Where she had been rolling wildly the seas had been breaking harmlessly alongside. He sensed something was wrong. That sea had broken over them. He looked around. The sea was white in the moonlight and breaking as on a beach. They were in the breakers of the San Lucar shoal. Above the howl of the wind and the screaming of the Spanish officers the thunder of the Atlantic flinging itself onto the bank was a deep and terrifying rumble.

Devaux sweated over the end of the ten inch rope. "Get a gun fired quick!"

Drinkwater pointed to a cannon and mimed a ramming motion. "Bang!" he shouted.

The sailors understood and a charge was quickly rammed home. Drinkwater grabbed the linstock and jerked it. It fired. He looked anxiously at *Cyclops*.Several Spaniards were staring fearfully to leeward. "*Dios*!" said one, crossing himself. Others did the same.

Slowly Devaux breathed out. *Cyclops* had tacked successfully. The hemp rose from the water and took the strain. It creaked and Drinkwater looked to where Devaux had passed a turn round *Santa Teresa*'s fore mast and wracked lashings on it. More were being passed by the sailors. The *Santa Teresa* trembled. Men looked fearfully at each other. Was it the effect of the tow or had she struck the bottom?

Cyclops's stern rose then plunged downwards. The rope was invisible in the darkness which had again engulfed them but it was secured and *Santa Teresa* began to turn into the wind. Very slowly *Cyclops* hauled her late adversary to the south west, clawing a foot to windward for every yard she made to the south.

Devaux turned to the midshipman and clapped him on the back. His face broke into a boyish grin.

"We've done it, cully, by God, we've done it!"

Drinkwater slid slowly to the deck, the complete oblivion of fatigue enveloping him.

Chapter Five February–April 1780

The Evil that Men do . . .

Rodney's fleet lay at anchor in Gibraltar Bay licking its wounds with a sense of satisfaction. The evidence of their victory was all about them, the Spanish warships wearing British colors over their own.

The battle had annihilated Don Juan de Langara's squadron. Four battleships had struck by midnight. The Admiral in *Fenix* surrendered to Rodney but *Sandwich* had pressed on. At about 2 a.m. on the 17th she overhauled the smaller *Monarcha* and compelled her to strike her colours with one terrible broadside. By this time, as *Cyclops* struggled to secure *Santa Teresa* in tow, both fleets were in shoaling water. Two seventy gun ships, the *San Julian* and *San Eugenio*, ran helplessly aground with terrible loss of life. The remainder, Spanish and British, managed to claw off to windward.

In the confusion of securing the prizes one Spanish battleship escaped as did the other frigate. With the exception of the *San Domingo* and the escapees, De Langara's squadron had fallen into Rodney's hands. It was a bitter blow to Spanish naval pride, pride that had already suffered humiliation when late the previous year the treasure flota from the Indies had fallen to marauding British cruisers.

Now the great ships lay at anchor. *Fenix* was to become *Gibraltar* and others were to be bought into the British service. Their presence boosted the morale of General Elliott's hard pressed garrison and forced the besiegers to stop and think. Behind the fleet the convoy had arrived safely and the military dined their naval colleagues. Midshipmen, however, at least those of *Cyclops*, dined aboard, on hardtack, pease pudding and salt pork.

During her stay at Gibraltar *Cyclops* became a happy ship. She had come through a fleet action with distinction and the experience had united her crew into a true ship's company. Her casualties had been light, four dead and twenty-one wounded, mostly by splinters or falling wreckage. Every morning as the hands turned up there was not a man among them who did not cast his eyes in the direction of the *Santa Teresa*. The Spanish frigate was their own, special badge of honor.

The men worked enthusiastically, repairing the damage to *Cyclops*. It was a task that fascinated Drinkwater. The elements of seamanship he already knew were augmented by the higher technicalities of masting and rigging and when Lieutenant Devaux turned his attention to the *Santa Teresa* his knowledge was further increased. The first lieutenant had taken a liking to Drinkwater after their sojourn together on the captured frigate. Revived from his faint, Devaux had found him an eager and intelligent pupil once his stomach had been filled.

Cyclops's crew spared no effort to efface as much of the damage their own cannon had done to the *Santa Teresa* so that the frigate presented as good an appearance as possible to the prize court. Presided over by Adam Duncan, Rodney's Vice-Admiral, this august body was holding preliminary hearings into the condition of the fleet's prizes before despatching those suitable back to England. Once this intelligence had been passed to the hands they worked with a ferocious energy.

The intensive employment of *Cyclops*'s crew meant that the midshipmen were often absent and rarely all on board at the same time. For the first time Drinkwater felt comparatively free of the influence of Morris. Occupied as they all were there was little opportunity for the senior midshipman to bully his hapless juniors. The anticipation of vast sums of prize money induced a euphoria in all minds and even the twisted Morris felt something of this corporate elevation.

Then, for Drinkwater, all this contentment ended.

Cyclops had lain in Gibraltar Bay for eleven days. The repairs were completed and work was almost finished aboard the *Santa Teresa*. Her spars were all prepared and it was time to send up her new topmasts. Devaux had taken almost the entire crew of *Cyclops* over to the Spaniard to make light of the hauling and heaving. Topmen and waisters, marines, gunners, fo'c's'le men were all set to man the carefully arranged tackles and set up the rigging.

Captain Hope was ashore with Lieutenant Keene and only a handful of men under the Master kept the deck. The remainder, off-duty men, slept or idled below. A drowsy atmosphere had settled over the frigate exemplified by Mr. Blackmore and the surgeon, Appleby, who lounged on the quarterdeck, their energies spent by recent exertions.

Drinkwater had been sent with the launch to pass the convoy orders to a dozen transports in the outer bay. These ships were bound for Port Mahon and *Cyclops* would be escorting them.

As he returned to *Cyclops* he passed *Santa Teresa*. The sound of O'Malley's fiddle floated over the calm water. Signs of activity were visible, the creak of tackles lifting heavy weights clearly audible as two spars rose up the newly erected masts. Drinkwater waved to Midshipman Beale as the launch swept round the frigate's stern. The yellow and red of her superimposed ensign almost brushed the oarsmen as it drooped disconsolately under the British colour. Drinkwater brought the launch alongside the mainchains of *Cyclops*.

Mr. Blackmore languidly acknowledged his report. Drinkwater went below. He had half expected to find Morris on deck, not wishing to encounter him in the cockpit. So intense was Drinkwater's loathing of Morris that he would return to the deck rather than remain in his company below. There was something, something indefinable, about him that Nathaniel found distasteful without knowing what it was.

Between decks *Cyclops* was dim and almost silent. The creaking of her fabric went unnoticed by Drinkwater. A few men sat at the mess tables slung between the guns, lounging and talking. Some swung in hammocks and several watched Drinkwater with idle curiosity. Then one, a fox-faced man named Humphries, nudged his neighbour. A large topman turned round. Drinkwater scarcely noticed the malice that appeared in Threddle's eyes.

He descended to the orlop and turned aft to where, screened off with canvas, the frigate's "young gentlemen" lived. Drinkwater was happily oblivious of the menace in the air. The fetid atmosphere of the orlop was dark; a darkness punctured by swinging lanterns suspended at intervals from the low deckhead which glowed dimly in the poor air. Drinkwater approached the canvas flap which answered the midshipmen for a door.

He was stopped in his tracks.

At first he was completely uncomprehending. Then the memory of similar, half-glimpsed, actions, and a pang of instinctive recognition in his own loins brought the realization slamming home to him.

He felt sick.

Morris was naked from the waist down. The handsome young seaman from the main top was bent over a midshipman's chest. There was little doubt what was happening.

For a few seconds Drinkwater was rooted to the spot, helplessly watching Morris's breathless exertions. Then Drinkwater noticed the initials on the chest: "N.D." He turned and ran, stumbling along the orlop, desperate for the cool freshness of the upper deck.

He ran full-tilt into Threddle who hurled him back. Drinkwater staggered and, before he could recover, Threddle and Humphries were lugging him aft. Drinkwater struggled in pure terror at re-entering his dismal quarters.

Threddle threw him forward and he fell on his back.

For a minute he closed his eyes then a kick in the kidneys forced them open. A fully dressed Morris stood looking down at him. Threddle and Humphries were behind the midshipman. The handsome seaman had shrunk into a corner. He was crying.

"What are we goin' to do wiv 'im, Mr. Morris?" asked Humphries, his eyes glittering with possibilities. Morris looked at Drinkwater, his own eyes veiled. He licked his lips considering the physical possibilities himself. Perhaps he read something in Drinkwater's expression, perhaps his lusts were temporarily slaked or perhaps he feared the consequences of discovery. At last he came to his decision and bent over Nathaniel.

"If," Morris labored the word, "if you mention a word of this to anyone we will kill you. It will be easy—an accident. Do you understand that? Or perhaps you'd like friend Threddle here . . ." the seaman shuffled forward eagerly, a hand passing to his belt, ". . . to show you what a buggering is?"

Drinkwater's mouth was quite dry. He swallowed with difficulty.

"I . . . I understand."

"Then get on deck where you belong, lickspittle."

Drinkwater fled. The normality of the scene on deck shocked him profoundly. As he arrived in the waist Tregembo came up and gave him an odd look, but the midshipman was too terrified to notice.

"Mr. Blackmore wants you, sir," called Tregembo as he rushed past. Drinkwater went aft his heart thumping, doing his best to master his shaking limbs.

A week later Gibraltar was once more closely invested by the besieging Spanish. Rodney had sent the transports on to Minorca and the units of the Channel fleet back to home waters under Rear Admiral Digby. The empty transports had gone with them. His task fulfilled the Admiral sailed for the West Indies with reinforcements for that station.

It is 500 miles from Gibraltar to Port Mahon. The brief respite in the weather was over. A Lleventades blew in their teeth as *Cyclops* and her consort *Meteor* struggled to keep the transports and storeships in order. The convoy beat to windward, tack upon weary tack. At first they kept well south, avoiding the unfavorable current along the Spanish coast and the flyspeck island of Alboran but, having made sufficient easting, they held to a more northerly course until they raised the high, snow-capped peaks of the Sierra Nevadas and could weather Cape da Gata. With more sea room the convoy spread out and the escorts and even more trouble shepherding their charges.

The weather worsened. *Cyclops* was a misery. Damp permeated every corner of the ship. Fungi grew in wet places. The companionways were battened down and the closed gunports leaked water so that the bilges required constant pumping. The lack of ventilation between decks filled the living spaces with a foul miasma that made men gasp as they came below. Watch relieved watch, four hours on, four off. The galley fire went out and only the daily grog ration kept the men going, that and fear of the lash. Even so tempers flared, fights occurred and men's names were listed in the punishment book.

Things did not improve when *Meteor* signalled that she would keep the convoy company in Port Mahon while *Cyclops* cruised offshore and waited for the ships to discharge. *Meteor*'s captain, though half the age of Hope, was the senior. He was known to have a weakness for good wine, dark-haired women and the tables. It was *Meteor* therefore that secured to a buoy in the Lazaretto Reach and *Cyclops* that stood on and off the coast, hard-reefed and half-hearted in her lookout for Spanish cruisers.

The fourth day after they had seen the convoy safe into Mahon Humphries went overboard. No one saw it happen, he just failed to answer the muster and a search of the ship revealed nothing. When he heard the news Drinkwater was suddenly afraid. Morris shot him a malignant glance.

On the seventh day the weather began to moderate,

but the ocean with typical perversity, sent one misery to succeed the last. Towards evening the wind fell away altogether and left *Cyclops* rolling viciously in a cross sea, a swell rolling up from the south east.

So chaos remained to plague the frigate and filled Midshipman Drinkwater's cup of misery to overflowing. Somehow the happiness he had felt in Gibraltar seemed unreal, a false emotion with no substance. He felt his own ingenuous naivety had betrayed him. The ugliness of Morris and his perverted circle of lower deck cronies seemed to infect the ship like the dampness and the rank stink. Indeed it so associated itself in his mind with the smell of malodorous bodies in cramped, unventilated spaces that he could never afterwards sense the taint in his nostrils without the image of Morris swimming into his mind. It had a name this thing; Morris had used it with pride. The very recollection made Drinkwater sweat. He began to see signs of it everywhere though in truth there were about a dozen men in *Cyclops*'s crew of over two hundred and sixty who were homosexual. But to Drinkwater, himself in the fever of adolescence, they posed a threat that was lent substance by the continuing tyranny of Morris and the knowledge that Morris possessed henchmen in the form of the physically heavyweight Threddle and his cronies.

Drinkwater began to live in a cocoon of fear. He wrestled unresolvedly with the possession of knowledge he longed to share.

Free of the disturbances of bad weather at last *Cyclops* cruised a week in pleasant circumstances. Light to fresh breezes and warmer winds took March into April. The frigate smelled sweeter between decks as fresh air blew through the living spaces. Vinegar wash was applied liberally and Devaux had the waisters and landsmen painting and varnishing until the waterways gleamed crimson, the quarterdeck panelling glistened and the brasswork sparkled in the spring sunshine.

On the last Sunday in March, instead of the Anglican service, Captain Hope had read the Articles of War.

Drinkwater stood with the other midshipmen as Hope intoned the grim catechism of Admiralty. He felt himself flush, ashamed at his own weakness as Hope read the 29th Article: "If any person in the Fleet shall commit the unnatural and detestable crime of buggery or sodomy with man or beast he shall be punished with death . . ."

He bit his lip and with an effort mastered the visceral fear he felt, but he still avoided the eyes of those he knew were staring at him.

After the solemnly oppressive reminder of the Captain's power the hands had been made to witness punishment. In the recent bad weather two men had been persistent offenders. Hope was not a vicious commander and Devaux, with a simple aristocratic faith in being obeyed, never pressed for strict action, infinitely preferring the indolence of inaction. He was content that the bosun's mates kept *Cyclops*'s people at their duty. But these two men had developed a vendetta and neither captain nor first lieutenant could afford to stand for that.

A drum rolled and the marines stamped to attention as a grating was triced up in the main rigging. A man was called out. Before passing sentence Hope had endeavored to discover the source of the trouble but to no avail. The lower deck kept its own counsel and guarded its own secrets. The man came forward to where two bosun's mates grabbed him and lashed his wrists to the grating. A piece of leather was jammed into his mouth to prevent him from biting through his own tongue. It was Tregembo.

The drum rolled and a third bosun's mate wielded the supple cat o'nine tails and laid on the first dozen. He was relieved for the second and his relief for the third. After a bucket of water had been thrown over the wretched prisoner's body he was cut down.

With difficulty Tregembo staggered back to his place among the sullen hands. The second man was led out. Threddle's powerful back testified to previous punishment but he bore his three dozen as bravely as

Tregembo. When he too was cut down he stood unsupported, his eyes glittering with tears and fierce hatred. He looked directly at Drinkwater.

The midshipman had become inured to the brutality of these public floggings; in some curious way the spectacle affected him far less than the sonorous intonation of that 29th Article of War.

Like many of the officers and men he managed to think of something else, to concentrate on the way the row of fire buckets, each with its elaborately painted royal cipher, swung to the motion of the ship. He found the device reassuring, helping him to master himself after the disquiet of that uncompromising sentence. It was thus disarmed that Threddle caught his eye.

Drinkwater felt the occult force of loathing hit him with near physical impact. The midshipman was certain that he was in some strange way connected with the animosity that existed between these two men that had broken out in persistent and disruptive fighting. It was only with difficulty that Drinkwater prevented himself from fainting. One seaman did. It was the handsome young topman who had been Morris's pathic.

Later in the day Drinkwater passed close to Tregembo as the man worked painfully at a splice.

"I am sorry you were flogged, Tregembo," he said quietly.

The man looked up. Beads of sweat stood out on his brow, evidence of the agony of working with a back lashed to a bloody ruin.

"You don' have to worry, zur," he replied. Then he added as an afterthought, "It shouldn't have to come to that . . ." Drinkwater passed on, musing on the man's last, incomprehensible remark.

Later that night the wind freshened. At 4 a.m. Drinkwater was called to go on watch. Stumbling forward to the companionway he was aware that once more *Cyclops* was pitching and tossing. "They'll shorten sail soon," he muttered to himself struggling into his tarpaulin as he emerged on deck. The night was black and chilly. A patter of spray came aboard, stinging his face. He relieved Beale who gave him a friendly grin.

At a quarter after four the order came to double reef the topsails. Drinkwater went aloft. He thought little of it now, nimbly working his way out to the place of honor at the yardarm. After ten minutes the huge sail was reduced and the men were making their way to the backstays, disappearing into the darkness as they returned to the deck. As he came in from the yardarm and transferred his weight to a backstay a hand gripped his wrist.

"What the hell . . . ?" He nearly fell. Then a face appeared out of the windtorn blackness. It was the good-looking topman from the main top and there was a wild appeal in his eyes.

"Sir! For Christ's sake help me!" Drinkwater, swaying a hundred feet above *Cyclops*'s heaving deck, yet felt revulsion at the man's touch. But even in the gloom he saw the tears in the other's eyes. He tried to withdraw his hand but his precarious situation prevented it.

"I'm not one of them, sir, honest. They make me do it . . . they force me into it, sir. If I don't they . . . kick me, sir . . ."

Drinkwater felt the nausea subside. "Kick you? What d'ye mean?" He could hardly hear the man now as the wind whipped the shouted confidences away to leeward.

"The bollocks, sir . . ." he sobbed, "For Christ's sake help me . . ."

The grip relaxed. Drinkwater tore himself away and descended to the deck. For the remainder of the watch as dawn lit the east and daylight spread over the sea he pondered the problem. He could see no solution. If he told an officer about Morris would he be believed? And it was a serious allegation. Had he not heard Captain Hope read the 29th Article of War? For the crime of sodomy the punishment was death . . . it was a serious, a terrible allegation to make against a man and Drinkwater quailed from the possibility of being instrumental in having a man hanged . . . and Morris was evil, of that he was certain, evil beyond his own perversion, for

Morris was allied to the huge physical bulk of Able-Seaman Threddle and what would Threddle not stop at?

Drinkwater remained in an agony of fear for himself and helplessness at his inabiliy to aid the topman. He felt he was failing his first test as an officer . . . Who could he turn to?

Then he remembered Tregembo's remark. What was it he had said? He dredged the sentence out of the recesses of his memory: "It shouldn't have to come to that." To what? What had Tregembo said before his final remark . . .

"You don't have to worry." That was it.

Meaning that he, Drinkwater, did not have to worry. But another doubt seized him. He had only expressed regret that the seaman had been flogged for fighting. Then he realized the truth. Tregembo had been flogged for fighting Threddle and had said the midshipman did not have to worry. Tregembo must, therefore know something of what had gone on. "It" should not have to come to Drinkwater himself worrying? Would the lower deck carry out its own rough justice? Had it already passed sentence on and executed Humphries?

Then Drinkwater realised that he had known all along. Threddle's eyes had blamed his flogging of Nathaniel and subconsciously Drinkwater had acknowledged his responsibility for Tregembo's pain.

He resolved that he would consult Tregembo . . .

It was the second dog watch before he got Tregembo to one side on the pretext of overhauling the log for Mr. Blackmore.

"Tregembo," he began cautiously, "why did you fight Threddle?" Tregembo was silent for a while. Then he sighed and said, "Now why would you'm be axing that, zur?"

Drinkwater took a deep breath. "Because if it was over what I believe it to have been then it touches the midshipmen as well as the lower deck . . ." He watched Tregembo's puzzled frown smooth out in comprehension.

"I know, zur," he said quietly and, looking directly at

Drinkwater, added "I saw what they'm did to you in Gib, zur . . ." It was Tregembo's turn to be embarrassed.

"I kind of took to 'ee, zur," he flushed, then resumed with a candid simplicity, "that's why I did fur 'Umphries."

Drinkwater was shocked: "You murdered Humphries?"

" 'E slipped and I 'elped 'im a bit." Tregembo shrugged. "Off'n the jibboom, zur. 'E ent the fust," he said to alleviate Drinkwater's obvious horror. The midshipman absorbed the knowledge slowly. The burden he had borne was doubled, not halved as he had hoped. The respect for the law engendered by his upbringing was suffering a further assault. Tregembo's lawless, smuggling, devil-may-care attitude was a phenomenon new to him. His face betrayed his concern.

"Doan ye worry yerself, Mr. Drinkwater. We're used to buggers and their ways. Most ships 'ave 'em but we doan like it when they doan keep it to 'emselves . . ." He indicated the handsome seaman coiling a rope amidships. He looked up at them. There was appeal and desperation in his eyes, as though he knew the substance of a conversation taking place sixty feet away.

"Yon Sharples is a good topm'n but 'e's scared of 'em, see. I doan wonder if ye'd seen what they done to 'im . . ." Tregembo reached into a pocket and slipped a quid of tobacco into his mouth.

" 'E won't 'ave owerlong to wait," he concluded ruminatively.

Drinkwater stared sharply at Tregembo. "The lower deck'll look after it's own, zur, but Mr. Morris is a cockpit problem. Cockpits usually 'ave their own justice, zur." Tregembo paused sensing Drinkwater's sense of physical inadequacy.

"You'd easy outnumber 'im, zur, wouldn't 'e?"

The log line was nearly coiled in its basket and Tregembo rose. He walked forward knuckling his forehead to the first lieutenant as he passed. Drinkwater remained aft at the taffrail staring astern unseeing. He felt no shame at the suggestion that he was alone unable to thrash Morris . . . yet it saddened him to think that Morris could terrorize not just him and his fellow midshipmen but the less fortunate Sharples . . . There was so much in the world that he did not comprehend, that was at variance with the picture books and learning had given to his mind's eye . . . perhaps . . . but no it was not possible . . .

He turned to walk forward. The whole of *Cyclops* lay before him. Devaux and Blackmore were at the foot of the mizen mast. The boom and spanker overhead. She was a thing of great beauty, this ship, this product of man's ingenuity and resolve to conquer. For mankind went onwards, following and undirected destiny at no matter what cost to himself. And in the echo of that resolve, exemplified by the frigate, he cast about for the will to do what he thought was right.

Chapter Six May 1780

Prize Money

His Britannic Majesty's frigates *Meteor* and *Cyclops* saw their charges into Spithead in the last week of May 1780. News had just come in from the West Indies that Admiral Rodney had fought a fleet action with De Guichen off Martinique on April 17th. But the battle had not been decisive and there were disturbing rumors that Rodney was courtmartialling his captains for disobedience.

The news, though vital to the progress of the war, was of secondary importance to the ship's company of *Cyclops*. All the weary voyage from the Mediterranean the ship had buzzed as every mess speculated on the likely value of the prize.

There was not a man in the entire crew who did not imagine himself in some state of luxury or gross debauch as a result of the purchase of *Santa Teresa* into the Royal Navy. For Henry Hope it meant security in old age; for Devaux the means of re-entering society and, hopefully, contracting an advantageous marriage. To men like Morris, Tregembo and O'Malley fantasies of splendid proportions rose in their imaginations as they prepared to make obeisance at the temples of Bacchus and Aphrodite.

But as the two frigates and their empty convoy sailed northward the initial excitment passed. Arguments broke out as to how much hard money was involved and, more important, how much each man would receive.

Rumor, speculation and conjecture rippled through the ship like wind through standing corn. A chance remark made by an officer, overheard by a quartermaster and passed along the lower deck, sparked off fresh waves of debate on no single thread of fact but by mountains of wishful thinking. Only the previous year frigates like *Cyclops* had taken the annual treasure fleet from the Spanish Indies. It had made their captains fabulously wealthy; even able seamen had received the sum of £182. But it was not always visions of untold wealth that occupied the imaginations of her people. As the frigate drew north other rumors gained currency. Perhaps *Santa Teresa* had been retaken by the Spaniards who were once again besieging Gibraltar. Or sunk by shell-fire, or burned by fireships . . .

If the Spanish could not take her would they not have made an attempt to redress their honor by destroying at least some of the prizes in Gibraltar Bay?

Gloom spread throughout *Cyclops* and as the days passed the talk of prize money occurred less and less frequently. By the time *Cyclops* sighted the Lizard all discussions on the subject had become taboo. A strange superstition had seized the hands, including the officers. A feeling that if the subject were mentioned their greed would raise the ire of the fate that ruled their lives with such arbitrary harshness. No seaman, irrespective of his class or station, could admit the philosophical contention that Atropos, Lachesis or Clotho and their elemental agents acted with impartiality. His own experience continually proved the contrary.

Gales, battles, leaks, dismastings, disease and death; Acts of God, Acts of My Lords Commissioners of the Admiralty and all the other factors which combined to cause maritime discomfort, seemed to direct the whole weight of their malice at Jack Tar. Hardship was a necessary function of existence and the brief appearance of a golden ladder to a haven of wealth and ease became regarded with the deepest suspicion.

When *Cyclops's* cable rumbled through the hawse and she brought up to her bower at Spithead no man dared mention *Santa Teresa*. But when the first lieutenant called away the captain's gig there was not a soul on board whose heartbeat did not quicken.

Hope was absent from the ship for three hours.

Even when he returned to the boat lying at King's Stairs the gig's crew were unable to read anything from his facial expression. Drinkwater was coxswain of the gig and set himself the task of conning her through the maze of small craft that thronged Portsmouth Harbour. In fact Drinkwater had thought less than most about the prize money. Money was something he had no experience of. There had been enough, barely enough, in his home and in his interest in his new profession had both prevented him from dwelling on the subject of poverty or from realising how little he had. As yet the disturbance of lust had been a confused experience in which the romantic concepts imparted by a rudimentary education were at sharp variance with the world he found around him. He had not yet realized the power of money to purchase pleasure and his adolescent view of the opposite sex was one of total ambivalence. Besides, whilst there were no other distractions, he found the business of a sea-officer vastly more interesting and he had changed significantly since his first boat trip on the waters of Spithead. Although he had added little to his girth and height his body had hardened. His muscles were lean and strong, his formerly delicate hands sinewy with hard labor. His features remained fine drawn but there was now a touch of firmness, of authority about the mouth that had banished the feminine cast to his face. A dark shadow was forcing him to shave occasionally and his former pallor was replaced by a weathered complexion.

There remained, however, the bright eagerness that had attracted Devaux's notice so that he used Drinkwater when he wanted a difficult task undertaken by one of the "young gentlemen." The first lieutenant had placed Drinkwater in a post of honour as coxswain of the captain's gig. If he could afford no fancy ribbons about his boat's crew at least Hope could have a keen young middy to swagger, dirk at his side, in the stern sheets.

Blackmore too considered the youth the aptest of his pupils and, had it not been for the specter of Nemesis in the form of Morris, the approbation of his seniors would have brought the keenest pleasure to Nathaniel.

The gig danced over the water. Next to Drinkwater Hope sat in stony silence, digesting the facts that the admiral's secretary had told him. *Santa Teresa* had been purchased as a prize. The court had been assembled under the authority of Rear-Admiral Kempenfelt whose purpose it was to examine the findings of Duncan's preliminary hearing at Gibraltar. Kempenfelt and his prize court had decided that she was a very fine frigate indeed and had purchased her into the Service for the sum of £15,750. Captain Hope's share would amount to £3,937.10 shillings. After years of grinding service with little glory and no material rewards beyond a meager and delayed salary, fate had smiled upon him. He could hardly believe his luck and regarded it with a seaman's cynicism which accounted for his stony visage.

Drinkwater brought the gig alongside. Hope reached the deck and the pipes twittered in salute. Every man upon the upper deck ceased work to look at the captain for some sign of news of the *Santa Teresa*. All they perceived was a stony face.

So, they concluded, their worst fears were realized. Hope walked directly aft and disappeared. The eyes of the ship's company followed the captain's retreating back. One hundred and seventy six men, just then occupied upon the upper deck of *Cyclops* were united in a moment of immobile, silent, bitter disappointment.

Some half-hour later Drinkwater was dispatched again in the gig. Instead of the captain the midshipman had orders to convey Mr. Copping, the purser, ashore. Mr. Copping imparted the intelligence that he was entrusted to buy some special provisions for the captain's table that evening and that the captain was holding a dinner for his officers. He also handed Drinkwater a letter written in the old captain's crabbed hand. The superscription was to "His Excellency Richard Kempenfelt, Rear Admiral"

Drinkwater was to deliver it while the purser attended to his purchases.

Hope had invited all his officers, the master, gunner and the midshipmen. Appleby, the surgeon, was also present. They gathered noisily aft at three bells in the second dog watch with only the first lieutenant and Wheeler absent forming an honor guard to greet the Admiral.

When Hope had impulsively dashed off his invitation to Kempenfelt he was in boyish high spirits. He had suppressed his mirth as he snapped orders at Copping so that that individual had left his commander with the positive belief that the worst fears of the ship's company were realized and had lost no time in sending word forward that further optimism was futile.

Hope saw the Admiral as the true author of his good fortune and in some way wished to acknowledge his gratitude. For Kempenfelt was a popular sea officer whose brilliance shone in an age when brains were not the qualification for flag rank. His innovations were admired throughout the fleet where thinking men discussed the handling of fleets under sail more than jobbery or place seeking. Kempenfelt was, perhaps, more than that to Hope. To the captain, whose post rank he owed to the political faction he despised, the Rear-Admiral was a respected figure, and in an age when lip service of the greatest extravagance disguised base motives, Hope wished to demonstrate honest, simple admiration.

But as his officers collected on the deck above, the captain had his private doubts. Midshipman Drinkwater had brought back the Admiral's acceptance and he was beset by second thoughts. The prank he was playing on his own ship's company was childish—but captains could indulge themselves to some extent with their own people; admirals were rather different. He was not sure now what Kempenfelt would think . . .

Above his head the buzz of speculative conversation came down the skylight. The officers might have got wind of the prize court's decision; it was unlikely that they had not heard by now and were doubtless writing him off as an old fool. Hope flushed but recollected himself when he heard the note of resignation in the babble above. He listened more attentively. He heard the second lieutenant, Mr. Price, his lilting Welsh voice vaguely angry, say "I told you so, eh Blackmore?" Hope could imagine the old sailing master, called in as an ally in disappointment, a man so like himself that the captain could imagine the years of experience formulating a reply to Price.

"That's right, Mr. Price, you'll never see Jolly Jack make a brass farthing out of his business," the remark was made dully, authoritatively, an oft-uttered and oft-heard contention. Hope suddenly grinned—to hell with admirals! He had a surprise for Blackmore, a good surprise too, and of all his ship's company he would be most pleased to see the white-haired master receive his share.

A knock came at the door. "Enter," Devaux stepped inside.

"All ready sir, and the Admiral's barge is in sight." The first lieutenant hesitated, wanting to say more. "Sir . . . ?"

Hope enjoyed Devaux's discomfort. So often the easy mannered savoir faire of the man had irritated him. Assuredly this was Henry Hope's day.

"Yes, Mr. Devaux?"

"The . . . the prize, sir?"

Hope looked up sharply—perhaps his little drama made him overreact but it had its effect on Devaux. The first lieutenant jumped for the captain's threshold like a chastened midshipman.

"The prize, Mr. Devaux, the prize . . ." Hope managed a tone of outraged propriety, "don't talk to me of prizes when there's an Admiral to meet."

Rear Admiral Richard Kempenfelt greeted Captain Hope with a smile. He doffed his tricorne to Wheeler and his guard and nodded to Devaux. His eye rove over *Cyclops* and her company as Hope conducted him aft to where the now silent group of officers waited. Those who noticed such details watched their captain earnestly addressing the admiral. They might also have noticed the admiral's smile broaden and crack open in a brief laugh. At the laugh Hope relaxed. It *was* going to be his day after all.

Hope introduced his officers, the warrant officers and midshipmen. Then Kempenfelt asked to be conducted round the ship.

"I merely want to see something of *Cyclops* and the brave fellows who took that Spaniard."

Someone in the waist raised a formal cheer for the Admiral. To Devaux's ears its very half-heartedness was shameful. He did not notice Kempenfelt's eyes twinkle with amusement.

After his brief tour of the frigate the admiral turned to Hope.

"You've a damned taut ship, Captain Hope. We shall find work for you to do. In the mean time . . ." he lowered his voice. Hope nodded and turned to Devaux. "Call all hands aft, Mr. Devaux."

There was a vast shuffling and scurrying to a twitter of pipes and a bellowing of orders. Red-coated marines stamped aft and gradually a sort of order fell on the ship. Kempenfelt stepped forward and addressed them.

"D'you hear now my lads, Captain Hope has asked that I give ye all the news of your prize, the frigate *Santa Teresa*." He paused to watch the shuffle throughout the assembly. Expectancy, kindled in their faces by the presence of the admiral, now became a restless eagerness. The ragged line wavered.

"You'll be pleased to know she's been purchased for . . ." He tailed off as a buzz that swiftly became a hum broke out.

"Silence there!" yelled Devaux.

". . . she's been purchased for 15,000 guineas sterling and you'll all receive your due according to usage and custom." The admiral stepped back.

Devaux looked at Hope; he was smiling cherubically. Then, sensing the moment was right he called out:

"Three cheers for the Admiral . . ."

It was no longer half-hearted. They heard the noise on *Cerberus* a mile away. As the cheering died down Hope announced to Devaux, "Mr. Devaux, you may allow wives and sweethearts tomorrow, apparently the admiral's office announced us a few days ago . . ."

Captain Hope was having his day. As he ushered the Admiral and his flag lieutenant into the cabin there were more cheers for the captain himself.

The dinner in Captain Hope's cabin that evening was, as naval dinners went, unremarkable. But the setting sun laid a path of glittering gold from the horizon to the very stern windows of *Cyclops* and invested the scene with some of its magic. The excited babble of talk amongst the juniors present and the natural elation due to the unaccustomed wine and natural headiness of the occasion nevertheless lent to the proceedings a degree of memorability.

Copping had provided a banquet within the limits of his materials. If Kempenfelt was unimpressed by the cookery he did not show it and to the short-rationed midshipmen any meal of more than one course automatically assumed the dignity of *haute cuisine*.

Fortunately the *Santa Teresa*'s loot had yielded a sufficiency of both Oporto and Jerez wines which made up for the indifference of Hope's claret. Some Havana cigars were also salved which, after the duff and capons had been consumed, filled the air with the aromatic luxury of their blue smoke.

A bare hour after they had sat down Drinkwater's body was enjoying the pleasant sensations of a mild drugging. His stomach was distended to unusual proportions and his head just beginning to assume that lucid detachment from his limbs that is the pleasantest but also the briefest stage of drunkenness. As for his forgotten legs, they reclined as he had negligently left them before the increase in his cerebral concentration had drawn all the energy from them. He heard without fully comprehending the senior officers discussing Kempenfelt's new code of signals. The admiral's explanation of Rodney's action off Martinique passed through his aural organs and left his brain to seize on and amplify certain graphic phrases that his overwrought imagination dwelt on.

Hope, Price, Keene, Devaux and Blackmore listened to the read-admiral with professional deference, but to Drinkwater the splendid figure of Kempenfelt poured forth the very stuff of dreams.

After the loyal toast Kempenfelt proposed one to the *Cyclops*'s gallantry in the night action off Cadiz. In turn Hope toasted an admiral "without whose ratification their fortunes would have remained uncertain". The admiral prodded his flag lieutenant and that worthy rose unsteadily and read a prepared statement toasting Lieutenant John Devaux and Midshipman Nathaniel Drinkwater for their bold action in boarding the prize and earning a special place in Hope's report. Deveaux rose and bowed to the flag lieutenant and the admiral. Recalling that the midshipman had the post of honor in receiving the Spaniard's surrender he called upon the young gentleman to reply.

Drinkwater was barely aware of what was required of him, but he was suddenly aware of Morris staring at him from the far side of the table with an evil grin upon his face. The face seemed to grow larger, terrifying in its size, oppressive with malice. Conversation died as all turned to stare at him. He was confused. He remembered a succession of his seniors standing in turn and he rose unsteadily to his feet. For a moment or two he stood there swaying slightly. The bored expression of the flag lieutenant changed to one of sudden interest at the prospect of a neat gaffe with which to entertain his fashionable friends.

Drinkwater stared out through the stern windows to where the last shreds of daylight flared above the horizon. Morris's face faded and that of his mother swam before him. He remembered her preparing his sea-kit, sewing a table cloth for her son to use at sea. It lay hidden and unused at the bottom of his chest. It bore a motto. That motto sprang into his midshipman's mind now and he uttered it in a loud, commanding voice:

"Confusion to the king's enemies!" He said it all in one

breath and without a slur. He sat down abruptly as a roar of assent went round the table. The flag lieutenant resumed his bored expression.

He vaguely heard Kempenfelt's approbatory comment: "Damme Captain, a real fire eater!"

Chapter Seven June–July 1780

The Duel

On awakening next morning Drinkwater had only the haziest notions of turning in the previous night. He was not sure at what hour the Admiral had left, for after his toast the evening had become a blur. The blue and white uniforms, the gold braid and pink faces seemed shrouded in more than tobacco smoke. Wheeler's scarlet coat and glittering gorget had glowed like a surrogate sun in the candlelight as they joked and laughed and became serious again. The conversation had turned on a variety of topics; had been general, then particular; bawdy then technical as the portions of the table concentrated, divided then joined again in a verbal tide.

The event had been a triumph for Henry Hope. As a crowning to the evening Blackmore had suggested a little music and word was passed for O'Malley. The diminutive Irish cook entered, stealing sidelong glances at the ruins of the meal and the empty bottles. He produced some sweet and melancholic airs, after the fashion of the time, which brought an appreciative silence to the table. He concluded to loud applause with a frantic jig from his native land which, drawn from the wild turbulence of his people, seemed to Drinkwater to summarize the exhilaration of that Moonlight Battle in which these genial fellows had taken such a part.

Little O'Malley had gone forward two guineas better off with a farewell whose obsequiousness was not that of sobriety but suggested that, in the course of roasting the very capons whose ruins he had so enviously regarded, he had partaken of "pusser's dips".

Despite the vague recollections of a successful evening Drinkwater woke to the disturbing sensation that all was not well. He had a headache due to the quite unaccustomed quantity of wine he had consumed but it was more than that. He groped in his mind for some memory that would give him a clue to his disquiet. At first he thought he had committed some impropriety. His stomach contracted at the thought of an indiscretion in front of the admiral. But the approach of a figure traversing the darkened orlop brought the memory back.

It was Morris coming to call him at one bell to stand the morning anchor watch. Morris's face was lit demoniacally by the lantern. The rest of his body was invisible in the blackness of the cockpit. This apparition finding Drinkwater awake was a very mask of malice which spat out a torrent of invective in a sibilant whisper. Nathaniel was transfixed with horror, a feeling made worse by his prone position. Jealousy and hate burned within Morris, contesting with the fear of Drinkwater's knowledge of himself. The resulting conflict of powerful emotion burned within him in a terrible, bullying anger.

"Come on admiral's lickspittle, get out of your hammock and convey your greasy arse on deck, damn you for a crawling get!"

Drinkwater made no reply, vulnerably shrinking within his blanket. For a second Morris's face hung over him, the male-volence in his eyes an almost physical force. In a sudden, swift movement Morris had a knife out, the lantern catching the dull glint of its blade. It was a microsecond of suspense wherein Drinkwater suddenly, inexplicably, found himself drained of all fear. He simply tensed and awaited the inevitable . . .

Morris slashed with the knife. The hammock lashing parted and with a jarring crash Drinkwater landed on the deck. Fighting out of his blanket he found himself alone in the creaking darkness.

On deck a squall of rain skittered across Spithead and

the wind behind it was cutting. Drinkwater shivered and drew his cloak closer around him. Dawn was not yet visible and Morris's figure was barely discernible, huddled in the paltry shelter of the mizzen rigging.

The figure detached itself and approached Drinkwater. Morris's face, dark now, came close. The older midshipman gripped the arm of the younger. Spittle flecked offensively on to Drinkwater's cheek.

"Now listen," hissed Morris, "just because you are a crawling little bastard don't get any God-dammed ideas about anything. Threddle hasn't forgotten his flogging and neither of us have forgotten Humphries. So don't forget what I'm saying. I mean it." Morris's vehemence was irresistible. Drinkwater shrunk from the voice, from the spittle and the vicious grip upon his arm. Morris's knee came up into his groin. He gasped with pain.

"D'ye understand, God-damn you?" queried Morris, an undetected doubt in his voice.

"Y . . . yes," whispered Drinkwater doubling with agony and nausea, his head swimming. Another figure loomed out of the rain-swept darkness. For a terrifying moment Drinkwater thought it was Threddle but the voice of Tregembo asked, "Everything all right, Mr. Drinkwater?" He felt Morris freeze then relax as he straightened up. Tears flowed down his cheeks but he managed to steady his nerve enough to mutter, "Yes thank you."

In a clipped tone Morris handed over the watch. "The lieutenants are excused watches tonight. Call all hands at three bells." A quartermaster approached, the half-hour glass in his hand. The lower half was almost full.

"Eight bells, Mr. Morris."

"Make it so then."

"Aye, aye, sir."

Four o'clock in the morning.

When Morris had gone below Drinkwater went to the weather side. The rain stung and wet his face. He felt it with relief. The pain in his groin eased and his head felt less thick. Then a wave of nausea swept over him. The pain, the wine and the self-disgust caused him to vomit into the inky, hissing waters of Spithead. After that he felt better. He still stared to windward, his hands gripping the rail. His self-disgust rankled. Why had he not hit Morris back? Just once. He had to face the fact that he was scared, forgetful of the bold resolutions he had formulated and continually put off, pending a more propitious opportunity. He had one now. Morris had assaulted him. Hitherto he had lain low in the hope that by effacing himself Morris would leave him alone. But Morris could not do that . . .

The thing that he knew about Morris he devoutly wished he did not know. It was so disgusting that the very image of it, so vivid in his impressionable mind, was abominable to him.

Drinkwater was terrified of what he had seen almost more than of those who had been doing it. In that terror was submerged the realization of the power he had over Morris. In Morris's aggression all Drinkwater saw was brutality. He failed to perceive the brutality masked fear. He saw nothing of the source, only the source's manifestation.

He was suddenly aware of someone alongside of him.

"H-h'm." A voice coughed apologetically.

Drinkwater nervously began to move away.

"Beg pardon, zur . . ."

"Yes?"

"I saw what 'appened, zur. I saw 'im 'it 'ee . . . if you'm be wantin' a witness, zur."

"No, Tregembo, thank you," Drinkwater paused. He remembered that conversation with Tregembo in the Mediterranean. A brief memory of Humphries flashed in his brain, of Sharples and Threddle, and of the flogging Tregembo had received. Drinkwater looked hard at Tregembo . . . the seaman expected Drinkwater to thrash Morris, Tregembo would otherwise see Drinkwater as a coward . . .

Drinkwater suddenly recalled the moment when fear had left him not an hour earlier. A bold feeling swept over him. He could no longer suffer Morris's tyranny and determined to challenge his senior. It was a desperate throw but in such circumstances resolves are easily made, though less easily carried out. He forced a grim note into his voice. "No Tregembo, this is a cockpit matter, as you said. I'll thank you to hold your tongue . . ."

The man backed away disappointed. He had mistimed his assistance to the young gentleman. Having conceived a respect for the midshipman, Tregembo had assumed that he sought a legitimate means to encompass the destruction of Morris. Tregembo remembered the twenty-ninth Article of War, if ever one man held the other in the palm of his hand Drinkwater held sway over Morris. Tregembo was puzzled. He had "taken" to the youth and could not understand why some attack had not been made on Morris as he had seen many of the youngsters carry out from time to time on various ships. Tregembo was too blunt to be aware of Drinkwater's sensibilities just as Drinkwater was unaware that Morris's bullying concealed a pusillanimous soul, a fact that was very plain to Tregembo.

In the first glimmer of dawn Drinkwater saw the topman's crestfallen retreat.

"Tregembo!"

"Zur?" The man hesitated.

"Quietly have a word with one of the carpenter's mates to get two ash single sticks made up. Each thirty inches long, d'you understand?"

"Aye zur. And thank'ee."

Drinkwater had not the slightest idea why Tregembo had thanked him but suddenly the rain fell sweet upon his upturned face.

The news of *Cyclops's* prize and the promise of allowing visitors on board made her the happiest vessel in the anchorage. Before the morning watch was over the hands, uncommonly cheerful, had swabbed her decks and flaked and coiled all the ropes. When Devaux appeared the brasswork already gleamed in a watery sunshine that promised a fair day after the dawn's wet beginning.

The men were already staring across the leaden water to Fort Gilkicker and Portsmouth Harbour. For days past hired punts and galleys had brought out women and children. Many were full of whores but there had been some with wives of both the churched and commonlaw variety. They had made a forlorn sight, lying just clear of the ship's sides, exchanging unhappy waves or little snatches of conversation with the sailors until the bosun's mates or the officers had driven the men back to their work. The boats too were driven off either by the abuse of the ship's officers and marine sentries, or by the efforts of the guard-boats provided by the units of fleet themselves. This was an especial joy to the seamen who manned them for, if you are denied the pursuit of pleasure yourself there is a certain gratification in denying it to others.

Although *Cyclops* had commissioned at Chatham some of her company, volunteers mainly, had wives in the Portsmouth area. Occasionally a young wife would travel, at God knows what cost and on the chance that leave would be given her to meet her man. But it was the other variety of female that most interested *Cyclops*'s hands that pale morning. Today no guard boat could interrupt them as they took their pleasure, a fact that was doubly appreciated by the messes as they broke their fast to the news that *Meteor* was rowing guard. It was a sweet revenge for their consort's debauch at Port Mahon.

In the gunroom Lieutenant Devaux presided over fresh coffee and toast in evident good humour. "Well Appleby," he said addressing the chubby surgeon, "Why are you looking so damned glum?"

"The reason for my glumness is occasioned by my contemplation of the follies of mankind, Mr. Devaux. Ah, yes, a cup of coffee would be most welcome, I thank you for your courtesy." He sat in the chair indicated by the first lieutenant.

Devaux poured. "The women, Mr. Appleby?" enquired Devaux with a smile.

"The women, Mr. Devaux," replied the surgeon resignedly. "And, of course—the men."

Devaux laughed outright. "Poor Appleby, we win or lose in action but you can never win, poor devil."

"But you've plenty of mercury, I don't doubt, to cope with the inevitable problems?" interjected Lieutenant Price with a sense of nicety in which his sensibility fought a losing action with his curiosity.

Appleby drew a deep breath and Devaux knew he was about to deliver a lengthy peroration, for which he was notorious.

"Mr. Price, the provision of mercury by My Lords Commissioners for the execution of the office of Lord High Admiral, I say the provision of mercury to ships of war is insufficient to combat the outbreak of a chronic dose of syphilis in all but the smallest vessels, since their Lordships have failed to take cognizance of the fact that vessels of the various rates have an increasing number in their complement in inverse proportion to the number of their rating.

"Now—by syphilis I mean that corrupting infection of the blood known colloquially as 'pox' (which euphemism scarcely moderates its effect upon the human body, but only serves to render its acquisition a little easier to the witless sailor who foolishly considers it no worse than the common cold, having been misapprehended by the employment of the common vernacular.) Unfortunately he continues in this mind until, with unsteady tread and wandering mind, disfigured beyond his fellow's toleration, he is led raving to an asylum, to the inevitable shame of his family and the everlasting damnation of his immortal soul." Devaux had heard it before.

"Furthermore," Appleby continued as Devaux groaned, "furthermore, the administration of mercury, in my opinion, only serves to suppress the symptoms rendering the individual's life more agreeable, but enabling him to pass the contagion on to other partners undetected. In time, however, the bacillae attack essential organs and precipitate death by a stroke or other cessations of essential bodily functions."

"Don't you consider the expression of lust an "essential bodily function'?" asked Devaux, winking at Price. The latter was exhibiting a distinct pallor.

"The Honourable John Devaux asks me a question to which a man of his erudition surely knows the answer."

"The expression of lust is a natural manifestation of procreational urges which holy ordinances proclaim sanctified under the matrimonial coverlet. Nature did not intend its indiscriminate proliferation . . ."

"But it *is*, Bones," interrupted Price again, rallying now the discussion was of a less medical nature.

"Aye, Mr. Price, and so is the proliferation of the disease so lately under discussion. Surely a punishment from God."

"Pah! exploded Devaux at last exasperated by the doctor.

"Not 'Pah!', sirrah," droned on Appleby, undeterred. "Consider the evidence. The appearance of Christ on this earth was followed by an expansion of the church under the divine felicity and a thousand years in which the Christion religion gained ground against paganism. Only when the Church of Rome reached a state of corruption offensive to God did the devil descend to tempt men's hearts with temporal arts, and produce what educated people are pleased to call the 'renaissance'. Oft men went in search of 'knowledge'. And what did Columbus bring back from his fabulous Americas? Syphilis!"

"*Bravo medico*!" laughed Devaux sardonically. "Such a simple deduction scarcely becomes a man of science whose profession descends from such self-same intellectual quest; who would be an indigent fellow without it and whose mind has such a high regard for its own opinions."

"I cannot escape my time," replied the good surgeon whose tragic tones were not ennobled by his pudgy frame.

"You sound like a God-damned Wesleyan, Appleby."

"Maybe I have some sympathy with the man."

"Hah! Then I'm damned if ye'll get any more coffee at

my table. Yes Drinkwater?" This last was addressed to the midshipman who had appeared at the gunroom door.

"Beg pardon, sir, but boats approaching." The gleam in Devaux's eye was an eloquent endorsement of the accuracy of Appleby's forebodings.

"Thank you Drinkwater." The midshipman turned away. "Oh, Drinkwater!"

"Sir?"

"Sit down, cully, and listen to some good advice," said the first lieutenant indicating a vacant chair. Drinkwater sat and looked at the two lieutenants with a bewildered expression on his face. "Mr. Appleby has something to say to you, haven't you Appleby?"

Appleby nodded, marshalled his facts and began cannonading the midshipman.

"Now young man, the first lieutenant is alluding to a contagion which is best and successfully avoided by total abstinence . . ."

For a second Devaux watched the look of horror cross Drinkwater's face, then, clapping the tricorne on his head and waving Price out behind him, the two lieutenants quit the gunroom.

". . . total abstinence to which end I do earnestly implore you to bend and address your best endeavours . . ."

The arrival of the women brought all hands on deck. Men craned over the hammock nettings, leaned from gunports and ascended the lower rigging to leer at the wherries bobbing alongside.

The hands gave no thought to the fact that what was to follow was no substitute for proper shore leave, something they could not have for fear they might desert. The immediate preoccupation was a debauch.

Women and gin were aboard.

Whilst Wheeler and his marines made a token effort to maintain order the usage of the service permitted all classes of women to board and all offenses of drunkenness and fornication to be ignored. It was inevitable therefore that the greater part of the women were whores and that the messdeck deteriorated instantly into an inferno of desperate debauchery. The women were of various ages: tired, painted and blowsy doxies in worn and soiled dresses whose vernacular was as explicit as "Jolly Jacks", and younger molls, their youth blown on the winds of experience, their eyes dull with the desperate business of survival.

Some few were bona fide wives. The older among them used to their sisters in trade, the two or three younger astonished and shocked at the dim squalor of the gun deck. Where, perhaps, a poor counting house clerk had been pressed into the service his wife, possessing some slender claim to gentility, found her husband living in the vilest conditions. Such women instantly became a butt for the others to vent their coarse wit upon, which was a double tragedy since their husbands had probably just managed to live down their genteel origins. Legitimate wives were quickly recognized by their demeanor at the entry port, for they waved chits and passes at the marine sentries.

These genuine spouses looked earnestly for their husbands and avoided the leering and grasping propositions of others. For several such wives their journey ended in battle royal. Not expecting their spouses, men were engaged in coupling with whores. One enormous creature, the churched wife of a yeoman of sheets, found her man thus occupied between two twelve pounders. She belaboured his heaving buttocks with the tattered remnants of a parasol. A stream of filthy invective poured from her and she was quickly surrounded by a mass of cheering seamen and harlots who egged the trio on. The wife ceased her beating and took a long pull at a gin bottle someone held out to her. In the interval her husband finished his business and, to a cheer, the girl wriggled out from beneath him, hastily covering herself. She held out her hand for money but changed her mind when she saw the expression in the wife's eyes. She dodged under the barrel of the adjacent cannon as the offended lady screeched at her, "Try and take the money that's mine ye painted trollop, why, ye don't know y're business well enough to axe fur it fust!"

At this remark the yeoman caught his wife's arm and slapped her across the mouth with "And how in hell's name ud youm be knowin' that, my Polly?"

The crowd melted away for this was now a domestic matter and not the common property of the gun deck.

All day the ebb and flow of liaisons took place. What little money the men had soon found its way into the pockets of the women. Mr. Copping, the purser, in the manner of his race, set up a desk at which the eager men could sign a docket relinquishing a portion of their pay or prize money for an advance of cash. Many thus exceeded the dictates of prudence, the favors of a woman being a most urgent requirement. Thus were pursers a hated breed, though rarely a poor one.

Meteor rowed a dismal guard around *Cyclops*.Occasionally a bottle or a woman's drawers would be thrown out of an open gunport to an accompaniment of cheers and shrieks. The cutter's crew visibly smoldered and at one point she ran in and hailed the quarterdeck. The master's mate in charge of the boat was livid.

"Sir," he yelled at Lieutenant Keene, "Y're men show no respect. There are three of them baring their arses at me from y're gun ports . . ."

Appleby joined the chuckling lieutenant who disdained to reply.

"Sure you did not bare yours at Mahon, mister?" enquired the surgeon.

There was no reply. "That found its mark, eh lieutenant?" said Appleby as the man looked sulkily away.

"If the ship offends ye, sirrah, row guard round the rest of the fleet. Ye'll get little pickings from this lot!"

The master's mate spat overside and snarled at his boat's crew "Give way you damned lubbers."

During the forenoon the wife of the man Sharples made her appearance at the entry port. She was very young and, though few knew it, had made the journey from Chatham purely on the chance of seeing her husband. The journey had taken a week and her expectant condition had made it a nightmare.

But Sharples had seen her board and embraced her at the entry port amid the sentimental cheers of his messmates. No one had seen the sour look on the face of Mr. Midshipman Morris, who happened to be passing at the time. No one, that is, except Tregembo who, by another coincidence, was in search of Morris.

As Sharples and his wife, clasped together, stepped over the prostrate, active bodies oblivious of the parodies of love enacted all about them, Tregembo stepped up to Morris and touched his forelock.

"Beg pardon, Mr. Morris," said Tregembo with exaggerated politeness, "Lieutenant Keene's orders and will ye take the launch over to flag for orders."

Morris snarled at Tregembo then a gleam of viciousness showed in his eyes. Calling a bosun's mate known for "starting" he strode forward. As he went he called men's names. They were the least desirable of *Cyclops*'s company. A few, otherwise engaged, told him to go to the devil, one or two he let off, the rest he left to the bosun's mate.

At the forward end of the gun deck Morris ran his quarry to earth. Sharples and his wife lay on the deck. Her head was pillowed on his hammock and her face wore a look of unbelieving horror. Her man, father of her unborn child whose image she had cherished, lay sobbing in her arms. The whole foul story of Morris had poured out of him for there was no way he could be a man to her until he had unburdened himself. Sharples was unaware of the presence of Morris until the author of his misfortune had been standing over the pair for a whole minute.

"Sharples!" called Morris in a voice which cut through the unhappy man's monologue. "You are required for duty."

The girl knew instinctively the identity of the intruder and struggled to her knees, "No! No!" she protested.

Morris grinned. "Are you questioning my orders?"

The girl faced Morris, biting her lip.

"I can report you for obstructing an officer of the execution of his duty. The punishment is a flogging . . . your husband is already guilty of disobeying orders in having a hammock out of the nettings . . ." He spat the words in her face. This threat to his wife revived Sharples who pulled his wife gently aside.

"W-what orders, Mr. Morris?"

"Man the launch."

The topman hesitated. He was not in the boat's crew. "Aye, aye;" then turning to his wife he whispered "I'll be back."

The girl collapsed sobbing on the deck and one of the older women, to whom midshipmen were small fry, put an arm around her. A stream of filth followed Morris down the deck.

The launch was absent three hours. After a while the girl, disgusted with the scenes on the gun deck, sought fresh air and light on deck. Finding her way to the forward conpanionway, she groped her way to the starboard side where she made a little bright patch against the coils of black hemp belayed and hung upon the pinrail.

Staring out over the bright waters of Spithead she touched the life quickening within her. Her heart was full to bursting with her misery. The horrors of her week-long journey rose again before her at a time when she had thought to be burying them in happiness. Shame for her man and for herself, shame for the unborn child and for the depths of degradation to which one human could subject another welled up within her. Tears rolled down her cheeks.

Her eyes stared out unseeing at the ships lying to the tide. She was a small, broken piece of the price Britain paid for its naval puissance.

It was some time before old Blackmore noticed the lonely figure forward. He had relieved Keene of the deck and soon sent Drinkwater to turn the woman below again. Blackmore, trained in the merchant service, retained his civilian prejudice for refusing women leave to come on board. He sighed. In the merchant service a master gave his crew shore leave. If they wished to visit a brothel that was their affair, but they could be relied upon to return to their ship. The navy's fear of desertion prevented any liberty and resulted in the drunken orgy at present in progress between decks. If the old sailing master could do nothing to alter the crazy logic of Admiralty he was damned if he would have the upper deck marred by the presence of a whore.

Drinkwater approached the girl. In her preoccupation she did not hear him. He coughed and she turned, only to blench at his uniform. She drew back against the coils of hemp imagining Morris's threat of a flogging about to be carried out.

"Excuse me ma'am," began Drinkwater, unsure of himself. The woman was obviously distressed. "The Master's compliments and would you please to go below . . ."

She looked at him uncomprehending.

"PLease ma'am," the midshipman pleaded, "None of you, er, ladies are permitted above decks." She began to perceive his meaning and his embarrassment. Her courage rallied. Here was one she could answer back.

"D'you think I'm one of them 'arlots?" she asked indignantly. Drinkwater stepped back and the girl gained more spirit from his discomfiture.

"I'm a proper wife, *Mrs*. Sharples to the likes o'you, and I journeyed a week to see my 'usband Tom . . ." she hesitated and Drinkwater tried to placate her.

"Then, please ma'am, will ye go to Sharples and bide with him."

She rose in scorn. "Aye willingly, Mister Officer, if ye'll return him to me but he's out there. . . ," she waved over the side, "Off in a boat, an' me with child and a week on the road only to find 'im beat and, and . . ." here she could not bring herself to say more and her courage failed her. She stepped forward and fainted into the arms of a confused Drinkwater. Then in an intuitive flash he realized she knew of her husband's humiliation.

He called aft for Appleby and the surgeon puffed up along the gangway. A glance took in the lady's condition and her nervous state. Appleby chafed her wrists and sent Drinkwater off for sal volatile from his chest. A few minutes later the girl recovered consciousness. Blackmore had come up and demanded an explanation. Having made an enquiry on passing through the gun deck en route to the surgeon's chest, Drinkwater was able to tell the master that Sharples had gone off in the launch with Morris. 'But the man's not in the launch crew.'

"I know, Mr. Blackmore," replied Drinkwater.

"Did Morris single him out?"

"It appears so, sir." Drinkwater shrugged and bit his lip.

"D'ye have any idea why?" asked Blackmore, shrewdly noticing the midshipman's face shadowed by doubtful knowledge. Drinkwater hesitated. It was more eloquent than words.

"Come on now, young shaver, if ye know, let's have it out."

The midshipman swallowed hard. He looked at the distressed girl, golden curls fell about a comely face and she looked like a damsel in distress. Drinkwater burnt his boats.

"Morris has been buggering her husband," he said in a low voice.

"And Sharples?" enquired Blackmore.

"He was forced, sir . . ."

Blackmore gave Drinkwater another hard look. He did not have to ask more. Long experience had taught him what had occurred. Morris would have bullied Drinkwater, may even have offered him physical violence or worse. The old man was filled with a loathing for this navy that ran on brutality.

"Let the lady get some air," said Blackmore abruptly and turned aft for the quarterdeck.

When the launch returned Sharples was reunited with his wife. He had endured three hours of abuse and ridicule from Morris and his boat's crew.

Having delivered the Admiral's orders, Morris made his way to the cockpit.

Drinkwater had also been relieved and going below he met Tregembo. The Cornishman was grinning. He held in his hand two ash sticks, each three feet long, with a guard of rattan work obviously untwisted from one of the blacksmith's withy chisels. "Here, zur," said Tregembo. Drinkwater took the sticks.

Drinkwater looked at Tregembo. He had better let the man know what had happened on the upper deck before it became known below.

"The Master knows Morris has been buggering Sharples, Tregembo. You'd better watch Threddle . . ."

A cloud crossed the Cornishman's face and then he brightened again. The midshipman was not such a disappointment after all.

"Ye'll thrash him easy, zur. Good luck . . . ." Drinkwater continued below. He had uttered words that could hang a man, words that he would never have dared to utter at home. And now he felt ice cold, apprehensive but determined . . .

In the cockpit Morris and the other midshipmen were eating, mugs of ale at their places. The messman produced a plate for Drinkwater. He waved it aside, went to his place and, standing, cleared his throat.

"H'hmm." Nobody took any notice. The blood pounded in his throat and adrenalin poured into his blood stream. But still he was cool. "Mr. Morris!" he shouted. He had their attention now.

"Mr. Morris. This morning you threatened me and struck me . . ." A master's mate put his head in through the canvas door. The tableau was lit by two lanterns even at two p.m. here in the orlop. The air crackled with tension. Two master's mates were now looking on.

Morris rose slowly to his feet. Drinkwater did not see the apprehension turning to fear in his eyes. He was too busy remaining cool.

"You struck me, sir," he repeated. He threw a single stick on the table, it knocked over a mug of ale and in the ensuing pause the air was filled with the gurgle of beer running on to the deck.

"Perhaps, gentlemen, you would be kind enough after

dinner to give me room to thrash Mr. Morris at single stick. Now, steward, my dinner if you please . . ."

He sat down grateful that his own mug remained full. The meal was completed in total silence. The two master's mates disappeared.

It was afterwards agreed that Drinkwater had been extremely *sporting* in allowing notice of the forthcoming match to be circulated. It was quite a crowd that eagerly cleared a space for the protagonists while Drinkwater removed his coat and stock. Both combatants were in their shirt-sleeves and Drinkwater took up his stick and tested it for balance. He had chosen the weapon for its familiarity. In Barnet it had been a favorite with the lads. Imitating the gentleman's short sword, it combined the finesse of that weapon with some of the blunt brutality of the quarterstaff. The carpenter's mate had done well.

Drinkwater watched Beale push the last sea-chest back against the ship's side.

"Mr. Beale will 'ee stand second to me?"

"With pleasure, Mr. Blackwater," said the other youngster shooting a sidelong glance at Morris.

The latter looked desperately around him. At last one of the master's mates stood second to Morris rather than spoil the match.

As dueling was illegal on board ship Drinkwater's choice of weapons was fortuitously apt. Although he had been guided by his own proficiency with the weapon and chose the single stick in ignorance, any action by the lieutenants could be circumvented by an explanation that it was a sporting occasion. To this end the seconds conferred and decided to send the messman in search of Wheeler who, despite his commissioned status, could be relied upon for his vanity in presiding over such a match.

It was a tiny space in which they had to fight, about five feet four inches high and some fifteen feet by ten in area. The spectators backed up against the ship's side further restricted it. Someone offered odds and the babble of excited voices attracted more attention. Into this babel, calling for order, strode the resplendent figure of Lieutenant Wheeler. His arrival was accompanied by a rending of canvas as the forward screen was demolished, thus augmenting the spectators by some two score. Wheeler looked about him,

"Damn my eyes, what an evil coven have we here. For the love of God bring more lanterns, a fencing master has to *see*, d'ye hear . . .

The protagonists faced each other and Wheeler issued his instructions.

"Now gentlemen, the rules of foil, hits with the point, on the trunk only. You are unmasked, which I do not like, but as this is only a sporting match," this with a heavy emphasis, "I should not have to caution you." He paused.

"*En garde*!"

"*Est vous pré*?"

"Aye,' Aye," Wheeler grimaced at the common response.

"*Allez*".

Drinkwater's legs were bent ready for the lunge and his left hand was on his hip as there was no room for it in equipoise. Morris had adopted a similar position. Beads of sweat stood out on his forehead.

Drinkwater beat Morris's stick; it gave. He beat again and lunged. The point hit Morris on the breastbone but he side swiped and would have hit Drinkwater's head but the latter parried on the lunge and recovered.

"*Halte*!" yelled Wheeler, then, "*En Garde*!"

This time Drinkwater extended, drew Morris's stick and disengaged, pressing the lunge. His point, blunt though it was, scraped and bruised Morris's upper arm, ripping his shirt away.

"*Halte*!" cried Wheeler but as Drinkwater returned to guard Morris, with a yell of rage, cut at his opponent's flank. The blow stung Drinkwater's sword arm and bruised his ribs so that tears started in his eyes and his arm dropped. But it was only for a second. He lost his temper and jabbed forward. Wheeler was yelling for them to stop but Drinkwater's stick drove savagely into Morris's stomach muscles. Morris stumbled and bent forward. Drinkwater recovered and raised his smarting arm. He beat the length of his stick down upon Morris's back.

"*Halte*! *Halte*!" screamed Wheeler jumping up and down with the excitement.

"Leave 'em! Leave 'em!" yelled the cheering onlookers.

Drinkwater hit Morris again as he went down. His arm was filled now with the pent-up venom in his soul. He struck Morris for himself, for Sharples and for Kate Sharples until someone pinioned him from behind. Morris lay prone. Someone passed a bucket along. A woman shouted it was full of "lady's pee" and the crowd roared its approval as it was emptied over Morris's back.

Lieutenant Devaux, disturbed from the quiet consumption of a third bottle of looted Madeira by the yelling and stamping, elbowed his way through the crowd. He was blear-eyed and disheveled. He regarded the scene with a jaundiced eye.

"Our bloody little fire-eater, eh?"

Silence fell. Punters melted away into the darkness. "Send this rabble forward. Wheeler! What in God's name are you doing here? Who's in charge? Wheeler, what's the meaning of all this tomfoolery?"

But as Wheeler began to explain an astonished Lieutenant Price came in. Looking at the tableau in ill-disguised regret that he had missed the rout, he addressed the first lieutenant.

"Captain's compliments, Mr. Devaux, and will you attend him in the cabin immediately."

For answer Devaux swore horribly and left the company. A few moments later, hair clubbed, hatted and coated he made his way aft.

"Orders to sail, I believe," Price said quietly to Wheeler by way of explanation.

Drinkwater overheard. He drew a deep, deep breath and turned his back on the shakily standing Morris. They could sail to hell and back now, thought Nathaniel, for he no longer felt oppressed by his boyhood.

Chapter Eight July–August 1780

The Capture of the Algonquin

Cyclops was under easy canvas standing southward. At noon the ship was hove to and soundings tried for the Labadie Bank. As the yards swung round there was a sudden cry from the masthead: "Sail Ho!"

Devaux ordered Drinkwater up with a glass. When he returned Hope was on deck.

"Schooner, sir," the midshipman reported.

"Raked masts?"

"Aye, sir."

"Yankee," snapped Hope. "Belay that nonsense, Mr. Blackmore. Mr. Devaux all sail, steer south."

Blackmore looked crestfallen, holding the lead and examining the arming, but around him the ship burst into activity. The topgallant sails were cast loose in their slack buntlines and the yards hoisted. Within minutes, braced round to catch the wind, the canvas tautened. *Cyclops* drove forward.

"Royals, sir?" queried Devaux as he and Hope gauged the wind strength.

"Royals, sir," assented the captain. "Royal halyards . . . hoist away!"

The light yards were set flying, sent aloft at the run to the bare poles above the straining topgallants. As the frigate spread her kites, Hope walked forward and carefully ascended the foremast. Behind him Devaux, already querying the wisdom of setting royals in the prevailing breeze, expressed his opinion of captains who could not trust their officers to make reports. Ten minutes later the captain descended. Approaching the knot of officers on the quarterdeck he said, "She's Yankee all right. Small, light and stuffed full of men. Luckily for us she's to loo'ard and the wind's inclined to freshen."

"Should catch him then," said Devaux, looking pointedly aloft.

"Aye," ruminated Blackmore, still peeved at the captain's disregard for his navigational technicalities, "but if he once gets to windward he'll stand closer than us . . ."

"Quite!" snapped Hope, "and now Mr. Devaux we will clear for action."

Since sailing from Spithead on a cruise against enemy privateers and commerce raiders, the mood in *Cyclops*'s cockpit changed. The affair of Morris and Drinkwater had been the ship's own *cause célèbre* since many, particularly on the lower deck, knew the background to the quarrel. The immediate consequences for the protagonists had been a mast-heading each after which Morris lost all credibility in the mess and, aware of the thinness of the ice upon which he now skated, assumed an attitude of almost total self-effacement. The change in his attitude was quite incredible and while he nursed a venomous hatred for Drinkwater he was himself now haunted by the noose.

Drinkwater, on the other hand, had become overnight a popular hero. His own stature increased with the hands and his self confidence grew daily. Wheeler had made of him a sort of friend and had undertaken to school him in the smallsword. Drinkwater rapidly became adept at fencing and was once or twice invited to dine in the gunroom. Tregembo and Sharples attached themselves to the midshipman and formed a sort of bodyguard.

After the scrap Blackwater had taken Drinkwater aside and quizzed him further about Morris. Drinkwater had not wanted to press charges and Blackmore saw to it that Morris knew this. The old man was confident that

Morris would give no more trouble on the present cruise.

The sighting of the Yankee schooner was the first opportunity *Cyclops* had had of intercepting all but merchant ships, and the crew were in high spirits as she bore down on her quarry.

The chase had seen *Cyclops* but failed to recognize the danger until too late. Approaching end-on, the Americans had taken the frigate for a merchantman and a potential prize. The appearance of *Cyclops's* gun muzzles, however, urged the rebels to flee. The schooner's helm was put up and she made off before the wind.

She was a small, low vessel, a fast soft-wood craft built in the shipyards of Rhode Island. But *Cyclops*, now carrying her studding sails in the freshening breeze, was tearing down on her. The Americans held his canvas but his smaller vessel labored with its huge gaff sails, threatening to bury her bow and broach her. The British frigate came on with a great white bone in her teeth. On her fo'c's'le Devaux waited for her bow to rise. The bow chaser barked.

"Short by God!" The gun's crew loaded again. Smoke belched a second time from the muzzle as the frigate scended.

A dozen glasses were pointed at the schooner fine to larboard. The knot of officers on the quarterdeck muttered their opinions to each other. Drinkwater lingered, retained as messenger to the captain.

"We're closing all right."

"He still hasn't hoisted colors."

"There they are." The American ensign rose to the peak and snapped out in the wind. The schooner was driving forward under too great a press of canvas. White water surged beneath her bow and along her side. A brief puff of smoke appeared, instantly dissipated by the wind. A hole opened in the frigate's forecourse.

"Good shooting by heaven!"

"Aye, and Hon. Johnny will be bloody cross . . ."

Devaux's long nine-pounder barked again. A hole was visible in the schooner's mainsail.

"*Quid pro quo*," said Keene.

"What'd you do now?" asked Wheeler of no one in particular.

"I'd stand to windward as fast as I could, once up wind of us he'll get away," said Lieutenant Price. Everyone knew the schooner, with her fore and aft rig, could haul a bowline faster than a square-rigged frigate, but Price's opinion was contested by Drinkwater who could no longer hold himself silent.

"Beg pardon, Mr. Price, but he's his booms to larboard with the wind aft. To stand to wind'ard he has to gybe on to the larboard tack. To do so on the starboard he must needs cross our bow . . ."

"He'll have to do something," said Price irritably . . ."

"Look!" said several voices at once.

The American commander knew his business. Aware that his desperate gamble of overcarrying canvas had failed, he decided to stand to windward on the larboard tack. But the risk of a gybe that would carry away gear was unacceptable if he was to escape, and he had to think of something to reduce this risk. Hope had been intently studying the Yankee, had reasoned along the lines that Drinkwater had followed and was anticipating some move by the rebel ship.

What the officers had seen was the scandalizing of the two big gaff sails. The wooden gaffs began to hang down on their peak halyards, taking the power out of the canvas. But Hope had already noticed the topping lifts tighten to take the weight of the booms even before the peak halyards were started. He began roaring orders.

"Hands to braces! Move damn you!"

"Foretack! Maintack!"

The officers and men were galvanized to action. Hope looked again at the schooner, her speed had slackened. As Devaux's gun barked again the shot went over. The schooner began to turn. Now her stern was towards *Cyclops*.Through the glass Drinkwater read her name: *Algonquin, Newport*. He reported it to Hope. The schooner rolled to starboard as she came round, then her booms whipped over as she gybed. But the Americans were skilful. The main and foresheets were overhauled and the wind spilled from the scandalized sails.

"Down helm!"

"Lee braces!"

"Mainsail Haul!"

"Let go an' haul!"

Even as *Algonquin*'s gaffs rose again and her sails were hauled flat, *Cyclops* was turning. Hope's task was to traverse the base of a triangle the hypotenuse of which formed *Algonquin*'s track. The schooner pointed to windward better than the frigate and if she reached the angle of the triangle before *Cyclops*, without damage, her escape was almost certain.

On the fo'c's'le Devaux was transferring his attention to the starboard bow chaser as *Cyclops* steadied on her new course, heeling over under her press of canvas.

A crack came from aloft. The main royal had dissolved into tattered strips.

"Aloft and secure that raffle!"

The *Algonquin* was pointing well up but still carrying too much canvas. Nevertheless she was head-reaching on the British frigate. For a few minutes the two ships raced on, the wind in the rigging and the hiss of water along their hulls the only significant sounds accompanying their grim contest. Then Devaux fired the starboard bow chaser. The shot passed through *Algonquin*'s mainsail close to the first hole. A seam opened up and the sail flogged in two . . . three pieces.

Cyclops came up with her victim and hove-to just to windward. The Yankee ensign remained at the gaff.

Hope turned to Drinkwater. "My compliments to Mr. Devaux and he may fire the first division at that fellow." Drinkwater hurried forward and delivered his message. The first lieutenant descended to the gun deck and the six leading twelve pounders in the starboard battery roared their command. The American struck.

"Mr. Price, take a midshipman, two quartermasters, two bosun's mates and twenty men. Plymouth or Falmouth, Mr. Price. Mr. Wheeler a file of your marines!"

"Aye, aye, sir!"

The long boat was swayed up from the waist and over the side, the yardarms blocks clicking with the efforts of the seamen. Once in the water men tumbled down into it. Drinkwater heard his own name called out by Price.

"Mr. Drinkwater, see the Master for our position and a chart."

"Aye, aye, sir!" The midshipman went in search of Blackmore. The old master was still grumbling about interruptions to his soundings on the Labadie Bank, but he wrote out the estimated latitude and longitude quickly enough. As Drinkwater turned away the old man grabbed his arm.

"Be careful, lad," he said, full of concern, "Yon's not like the Don."

Drinkwater swallowed. In the excitement he had not realized the implications of boarding the prize. He went off to join the longboat. In minutes it was pulling across the water between the two ships.

Once clear of the ship's lee the force of the wind tore off the wave caps, dashing the spray into the boat. Sergeant Hagan reminded his men to cover their primings and the marines moved as one man to place their hands over the pans. Halfway between *Cyclops* and *Algonquin* the longboat swooped into the wave troughs so that only the mastheads of the two ships were visible. Then those of *Cyclops* receded as those of the rebel ship loomed over them.

Drinkwater had a peculiarly empty feeling in the pit of his stomach. He was aware of the collective tension of the prize crew as they sat, stony-faced, each man wrapped in his own apprehension. Drinkwater felt vulnerably small, sitting alongside Price, as they took the frail boat over this turbulent circle of the vast ocean. Astern of them *Cyclops*, the mighty home of thirteen score of men, dwindled into insignificance.

Hope was deliberately detailed a large body of men for taking the privateer. He knew she would have a numerous and aggressive crew capable of manning her own prizes. As the long boat neared the privateer Drinkwater realized Blackmore's predictions would be right. This was no comparison with the boarding of the *Santa Teresa*. There, wrapped in the powerful protection of a victorious fleet, he had felt no qualms. The dramatic circumstances of the Moonlight Battle and the rapid succession of events that had resulted in him accepting a surrendered sword, had combined into an experience of almost sublime exhilaration. The remnants of chivalric war were absent now. The bayonets of the marines glittered cruelly. With a dreadful pang of nauseous fear Drinkwater imagined what it would be like to be pierced by so ghastly a weapon. He shrank from the thought.

The next moment they were alongside the schooner.

The twenty seamen followed Price up the side, Hagan and his marines brought up the rear. Lieutenant Price addressed a blue-coated man who appeared to be the commander.

"I must ask you for your vessel's papers, sir." The blue-coated one turned away.

Sergeant Hagan swept his men through the ship. She had a crew of forty seven seamen. Having ascertained the large fo'c's'le was secured by one hatch, he herded them below. Under the guns of *Cyclops* three cables distant they went resentfully but without resistance.

Price, having possessed himself of the ship, had a man run up British colors and set his men to securing and repairing the mainsail. The privateer's officers were confined in the cabin aft and a marine sentry put on guard. Next the lieutenant turned two of the quarter guns inboard to sweep the deck and had them loaded with grapeshot. The keys of the magazine were secured and the vessel's details passed down into the waiting longboat for return to *Cyclops*.

With a damaged mainsail Price was limited to the gaff foresail and a staysail but he set course and trimmed the sheets. In twenty three minutes the privateer *Algonquin* of Newport, Rhode Island, operating under letters of marque from the Continental Congress, was seized by his Britannic Majesty's navy.

The blue-coated man remained on deck. He was

staring at the frigate that had taken his ship from him. The distance between the two vessels was increasing. He banged his fist on the rail then turned to find the British Lieutenant at his elbow.

"I am sorry, sir, to be the agent of your distress, but you are operating illegally under the authority of a rebel organization which does not possess that authority. Will you give me your parole not to attempt to retake this ship or must I confine you like a felon?" Price's courteously modulated Welsh voice could not disguise his mistrust of the silent American.

At last the man spoke in the colonial drawl.

"You, sir, are the practitioners of piracy. You and all your country's perfidious acts and tyrannous oppressions be damned! I shall give you no parole and I shall take back my ship. You are outnumbered and may rest assured that my men will not take kindly to you confining them forward. You will get little sleep lootenant, so you think on that and be damned to 'ee!"

Blue coat turned away. Price nodded to Hagan who, with two marines, roughly urged the commander below.

Price looked about him. The sail repair was progressing. Midshipman Drinkwater and the two quartermasters had organized the deck, the tiller was manned and the course set for the Channel. Lieutenant Price looked astern. *Cyclops* was already only a speck on the horizon, resuming her cruise. He felt lonely. During his eight years at sea he had been prizemaster on several occasions but the prizes had invariably been docile, undermanned merchantmen. True their masters and crews had resented capture but they had given little trouble in the face of armed might.

In the dreary years of the war with the Americans the British had learned their opponents possessed an almost unfair capacity for seizing opportunities. True their generalissimo, Washington, continually faced mutiny in his own army, but when the British might be caught at a disadvantage the damned Yankees would appear like magic. Burgoyne had found that out. So had St. Leger. Even when the greatest American tactician, Benedict

Arnold, changed sides, the laconic British High Command learned too late the value of such talents.

The fate of Lieutenant Price was sealed in that same restless energy. He was surprised, even in death, that men of his own race could treat his humanity with such contempt.

For two days *Algonquin* steered southwest to pass south of the Scillies before hauling up Channel. The big mainsail had been repaired and hoisted. Drinkwater took a keen interest in the sailing of the schooner. Unfamiliar with the qualities of fore and aft rig, he was fascinated by her performance. He had no idea a vessel could move so fast with a beam wind and listened with interest when the two quartermasters fell to arguing as to whether it was possible to sail faster than the wind itself. Indeed the fears planted by Blackmore were withering as Nathaniel experienced the joys of independence.

The weather remained sunny and pleasant, the wind light but favorable. The Americans appeared in small groups on deck forward for daily exercise and Sergeant Hagan and his marines saw to the policing of the schooner.

The American mates gave little trouble, remaining confined in one cabin whilst the privateer's commander was locked in the other. They were allowed on deck at different times so that one or other of them was usually to be seen standing close to the mainmast shrouds during daylight.

The principal stern cabin had been seized by Price and the Midshipmen whilst the seamen and marines used the hold tween decks for accomodation. This space had been intended to house the crew of prizes taken by the *Algonquin*.

By the evening of the second day Price had relaxed a little. An hour earlier one of the American sailors had asked to see him. Price had gone forward. A man had stepped out and asked if they could provide a cook since the food they were receiving was making them ill. If the "lootenant" would agree to this they would promise to behave.

Price considered the matter and agreed they could supply a cook but that no further relaxation of their regimen could be allowed. He estimated his position to be some ten leagues south of the Lizard and hoped to stand north the following day and make Falmouth.

But that night the wind fell light and then died away altogether. As dawn filtered through it revealed a misty morning. The schooner lay rolling in the water as a lazy swell caused her blocks to rattle and her gear to chafe.

When Price was called he was in a passion at the change of weather. By noon there was still no sign of wind and he had the big gaff sails lowered to reduce chafe. The hands were engaged with this work as the American cook went forward, a pot of stew in his hands.

Drinkwater was standing right aft. As the big mainsail was lowered he hove in the slack of the sheet and coiled it down.

There was a sudden scream from forward.

The marine sentry, bending down to open the companionway for the prisoners' cook had had the boiling contents of the pot dashed into his face.

In a trice the American had picked up the marine's musket and threatened the four seaman lowering the foresail. For a split-second every man on *Algonquin*'s deck was motionless then, with a whoop, the Americans were pouring aft. They hurled themselves at the unarmed seamen as the latter let go the halyards, they pulled belaying pins from the rail and rolled aft, a screaming human tide. The foresail came down in a rush, adding to the confusion.

The seamen forward were quickly overpowered but further aft Hagan had got several marines to present. The muskets cracked and three Americans went down. Lieutenant Price lugged out his hanger and leapt for the lanyard of the starboard quarter gun. He tugged it. A flash and roar emanated through the fog as the grape cut a swathe through friend and foe. Momentarily the human tide was stemmed. Then it rolled aft again.

Drinkwater remained rooted to the spot. This was all a dream. In a moment the fog would clear and *Algonquin* become her ordered self again. A pistol ball smacked into the rail beside him. He saw Price, mouth drawn back into a snarl, whirling the slender hanger. One, two rebels received its needle point in their bodies then, with a sickening thud, a handspike whirled by a giant half-caste Indian split the lieutenant's skull.

Drinkwater suddenly felt inexplicably angry. Nothing could withstand the furious onslaught of the Americans. He was dimly aware of struggling British seamen and marines being held by three or four of the privateersmen. He knew he was about to die and felt furious at the knowledge. He choked on his rage, tears leaping into his eyes. Suddenly his dirk was in his hand and he was lunging forward. The big half-caste saw him coming too late. The man had picked up Price's hanger out of curiosity. Suddenly aware of the midshipman rushing towards him he bent and held it outwards like a hunting knife.

Drinkwater remembered his fencing. As the Indian jabbed the sword upwards Drinkwater's dirk took the hanger's foible in a semi-circular parry. Taking the blade he exerted a *prise-de-fer*, raised his point and his own momentum forced his toy weapon into the stomach of the Indian.

The man howled with pain and surprise as they collided. Then he collapsed on top of him. For a moment Drinkwater's anger evaporated into sudden, chilling fear, a fear mingled with an overwhelming sense of relief. Then he received a blow on the head and was plunged into a whirlpool of oblivion.

When Drinkwater recovered consciousness it was several minutes before he realized what had happened. He was confused by total darkness and a regular creaking sound that terminated in a number of almost simultaneous dull knocks before starting again.

"Wh . . . where the hell am I?" he asked out loud.

A groan came from alongside him. Then a hand grasped his knee.

"Mister Drinkwater?" A strained voice enquired, pain and anxiety in the tone of it.

"Yes."

"Grattan, sir, marine."

"Eh . . . Oh, yes."

"We're in the fo'c's'le . . . just the wounded, sir . . ."

"Wounded?"

"Aye, sir, you were unconscious. My arm's broken . . ."

"Oh, I'm sorry . . ."

"Thank you, sir." Drinkwater's brain was beginning to grasp the situation and an enormous and painful bump on the crown of his head testified to the accuracy of the marine's report. Recollection came back to him. He sat up and took stock.

"What's that noise then?"

"Sweepin', sir . . . that's what the others are doin'."

Before he could ask more the hatch flew open. A few cold drops of moisture dripped into Drinkwater's upturned face, then the shape of a man lowering himself down blotted out the foggy daylight.

The man bent over each of the prisoners in turn. When he got to Drinkwater he grunted: "You're fit. Get on deck!" He grabbed Drinkwater's arm and dragged him to his feet.

A few moments later Drinkwater stood unsteadily on the deck of *Algonquin* and looked aft. The source of the strange noise revealed itself. Still shrouded in fog, *Algonquin* was making slow but steady headway over the calm, grey sea. Between the gun ports oak thole pins had been driven into the caprail. At each set of pins a long oar, or sweep, was shipped. Two men were stationed at each sweep, heaving it back and forth so that the schooner made way to the southward. The men at the sweeps were nearly all British. One of the American mates walked up and down the deck with a rope's end. Every now and again he brought it down on the bare back of a seaman or the sweat-darkened red coat of a marine.

Drinkwater was pushed along the deck, given a pannikin of green water from the scuttle butt and shoved alongside a marine pulling the aftermost larboard sweep. The man was Hagan. He was running with sweat as the rigging dripped with foggy dew.

Hagan grunted a welcome and Drinkwater grasped the loom of the sweep. It was slippery with blood and plasma of the man he had relieved. Within a quarter of an hour Drinkwater knew why the privateer was under sweeps. The progress through the fog was an advantage to the American commander but it was also the most efficient way of exhausting the British. An exhausted prize crew would not attempt further resistance.

After an hour Drinkwater had reached a state of physical numbness that utterly overpowered him. He had ceased to feel the mate's starter. His head throbbed but his brain had ceased to function. It was Hagan who roused him from his torpor. The marine sergeant hissed between clenched teeth, 'Breeze comin'.'

Drinkwater raised his head and wiped the sweat out of his eyes. A catspaw rippled the greasy surface of the sea. The sun was brighter now, warmer. He had no idea of the time nor of how long he had been semi-conscious. The fog began to disperse. Imperceptibly at first, wind and sunshine broke through the murk.

An hour later there was a breeze. Light and fitful, it steadied to become a north westerly air. From a zephyr it graduated to a breeze and the American commander ordered the sweeps inboard and the sails hoisted. Before they were herded below into the fo'c's'le Drinkwater was aware that *Algonquin* was headed south east for he had heard the helm order. As the hatch closed over the British the schooner heeled and the water of the Channel hissed past her washboards with increasing speed.

Chapter Nine August 1780

A Turning of Tables

The British prize crew aboard the *Algonquin* were in a pathetic state. It had been evening when the Americans had retaken their ship. All that night the British had swept the craft south, away from the Cornish coast. It was the following dawn when the midshipman, recovering consciousness, had been forced on deck. By the time the breeze sprang up the day was far advanced.

In the stinking fo'c's'le the British sprawled in all attitudes of exhausted abandon. After a while the eyes adjusted to the darkness and Drinkwater could see the men asleep. He looked for Grattan. The man tossed restlessly, his eyes staring. He was the only other man awake. Another, whose name Drinkwater did not know, was dead. His head had been injured and dried blood blackened his face. He lay stiff, his mouth open, emitting a silent cry that would echo forever. Drinkwater shivered.

Grattan was muttering incoherently, for the pain of his arm had brought on a fever.

At noon the hatch was shoved open. A pan of thin soup, some biscuit and water were lowered down. The hatch was being closed again when Drinkwater roused himself and called, "We've a dead man down here."

The hatch stopped and the silhouette of a man's head and shoulders were visible against the sky.

"So?" he drawled.

"Will you permit him to be taken on deck?" There was a pause.

"He's one of yours. You brought him: you keep him." A gobbet of spittle flew down and the hatch slammed shut.

The exchange had woken the men. They made for the food, improvising means of eating it, dunking the biscuit and sucking it greedily.

After a while Sergeant Hagan crawled over to the midshipman.

"Beg pardon, Mr. Drinkwater, but 'ave you any orders?"

"Eh? What's that?" Drinkwater was uncomprehending.

"Mr. Price is dead. You're in charge, sir."

Drinkwater looked at the quartermasters and the marines. They were all older than him. They had all been at sea longer than he had. Surely they were not expecting him to . . . ? He looked at Hagan. Hagan with twenty-odd years of sea-soldiering to his credit, Hagan with his bragging stories of service under Hawke and Boscawen, Hagan with his resource and courage . . .

But Hagan was looking at *him*. Drinkwater's mouth opened to protest his unsuitability. He had not the slightest idea what to do. He closed it again.

Hagan came to his rescue.

"Right lads, Mr. Drinkwater wants a roll-call," he said, "so let's see how many of us there are . . . Right . . . ," Hagan coughed, "Marines speak up!" Apart from the sergeant there were five marines left.

"Quartermasters?" The two quartermasters were both still alive and unwounded.

"Bosun's mates?" There was silence.

"Seamen?" Eleven voices were eventually identified, one of whom complained of a sprained ankle.

Hagan turned to Drinkwater. "That's . . . er, counting yerself, sir, that's exactly a score, though one is unfit, sir . . ." Hagan seemed to think that this round figure represented some triumph for the British.

"Thank you, Sergeant," Drinkwater managed, unconsciously aping Devaux in his diction. He wondered what was next expected of him. Hagan asked:

"Where d'ye think they mean to take us, sir?"

Drinkwater was about to snap that he had not the faintest idea when he remembered the helm orders as he left the deck.

"Southeast," he said. Recalling the chart he repeated their course and added their destination. "Southeast, to France . . ."

"Aye," said one of the quartermasters, "The bloody rebels have found some fine friends with the frog-eating Johnny Crapo's. They'll be takin' us to Morlaix or St. Malo . . ."

Hagan spoke again. His simple words came like a cold douche to Drinkwater. Hagan was the fighter, Hagan the expediter of plans. Hagan would not shrink from a physical task once that task had been assigned to him. But he looked to the quality to provide the ideas. To him Drinkwater, in his half-fledged manhood, represented the quality. In the general scheme of things it was assumed a person of Drinkwater's rank automatically had the answer. He was what was known on a King's ship as a "young gentleman".

"What do we do, sir?"

Drinkwater's mouth flapped open again. Then he collected himself and spoke, realising their plight was hourly more desperate.

"We retake the ship!"

A pathetically feeble, yet strangely gratifying, cheer went round the men.

Drinkwater went on, gaining confidence as he strung his thoughts together.

"Every mile this ship covers takes her nearer to France and you all know what that means . . ." There was a morose grumble that indicated they knew only too well. ". . . There are nineteen fit men here against what? . . . about three dozen Americans? Does anyone know approximately how many were killed on deck?"

A speculative buzz arose, indicative of rising morale.

"Lots went down when the lieutenant fired the gun, sir . . ." Drinkwater recognized Sharples's voice. In the bustle of events he had forgotten all about Sharples and his being in the prize crew. He was oddly comforted by the man's presence. ". . . and we fixed a few, you did for one, sir . . ." admiration was clear in the man's voice.

Hagan interrupted. It was a sergeant's business to estimate casualties. "I'd say we did for a dozen, Mr. Drinkwater . . . say three dozen left." Grunts of agreement came from the men.

"Right, three dozen it is," Drinkwater continued. An idea had germinated in his brain. "They're armed, we're not. We're in the fo'c's'le which is sealed from the rest of the ship. It was the one place *we* chose to put *them*." He paused.

"They got out because they made a plan long before we took them. As a . . . er . . . contingency . . . I heard the American captain tell Lieutenant Price he would retake his ship. It was almost like a boast. I've heard Americans have a reputation for boasting . . ." A desperate cackle that passed for a laugh emanated from the gloomy darkness.

Hagan interrupted again. "But I don't see how this helps us, sir. They got out."

"Yes, Mr. Hagan. They got out by using their plan. They were model prisoners until they had made their arrangements. They lulled us until the last possible moment then they took back their ship. If we hadn't run into fog we might have been under the lee of the Lizard by now . . ." he paused again, collecting his thoughts, his heart thumping at the possibility . . .

"Someone told me these Yankee ships were mostly made of softwood and liable to rot." A murmur of agreement came from one or two of the older hands.

"Perhaps we could break through the bulkhead or deck into the hold, and work our way aft. Then we could turn the tables on them . . ."

There was an immediate buzz of interest. Hagan, however, was unconvinced and adopted an avuncular attitude. "But, Nat lad, if we can do that why didn't the Yankees?"

"Aye, aye" said several voices.

But Drinkwater was convinced it was their only hope. "Well I'm not sure," he replied, "but I think they didn't want to raise our suspicions by any noise. It is going to be difficult for us . . . Anyway, if I am right they already had a plan worked out which relied on us behaving in a predictable manner. Now we've got to better them. Let's start searching for somewhere to begin."

In the darkness it took them an hour to find a weak, spongy plank in the deck of the fo'c's'le. Hagan produced the answer to their lack of tools by employing his boots. The joke this produced raised morale still further, for the booted marines, the unpopular policemen of a man o' war, were the butt of many a barefoot sailor's wit.

Hagan smashed in enough to get a hand through, timing his kicks to coincide with the plunging of the *Algonquin*'s bow into the short Channel seas. For the wind veered and the schooner was laid well over, going to windward like a thoroughbred. Regularly and rhythmically she thumped into each wave and as she did so she disguised the noise of demolition.

The deck lifted easily once an aperture had been made. Access was swiftly gained to the cable tier below. Drinkwater descended himself.

The schooner's cable lay on a platform of wooden slats. Beneath these the swirl and rush of bilge water revealed a passage aft. It was totally dark below but, doing his best to ignore the stench, he pressed on driven by desperation. He wriggled over the coils of rope and in one corner, unencumbered by cable he found the athwartships bulkhead that divided the forepart of the ship from the hold. Here he found the slatting broken and ill-fitting.

He had to get aft of the bulkhead. He struggled down in the corner, worming his way beneath the cable tier platform where they failed to meet the ship's side properly. Something ran over his foot. He shuddered in cold terror, never having mastered a fear of rats. Fighting back his nausea he lowered himself into the bilgewater. Its cold stink rose up on his legs and lapped at his genitals. For a long moment he hung poised, the malodorously filthy water clammily disgusting him. Then a strange, detached feeling came over him: as if he watched himself. In that moment he gained strength to go on. Continuing his immersion, Nathaniel Drinkwater finally forsook adolescence.

Algonquin was on the larboard tack, leaning to starboard. By sheer good fortune Drinkwater's descent was on the larboard side. There was therefore a greater amount of water to starboard and a "dry" space for him to cling to. Even so it was slippery with stinking slime. He could see nothing, and yet his eyes stared apprehensively into darkness. All his senses were alert, that of smell almost overpowered by the stench of the bilge. But although he gagged several times he was possessed now by an access of power that drove him relentlessly on, ignoring his bodily weaknesses, impelled by his will.

He moved aft over each of *Algonquin*'s timbers. Eventually he found what he hardly dared hope he would discover. The schooner's builders had not constructed the pine planking of the bulkhead down to the timbers. It extended to cross "floors" which supported the "ceiling" that formed the bottom of the hold. Between that and the ship's skin a small bilge space ran the length of the vessel.

Drinkwater continued aft. Having eventually completed his reconnaissance he began to return to his fellow prisoners. He was excited so that that twice he slipped, once going into the foul water up to his chest, but at last he wriggled back into the fo'c's'le. The men were expectantly awaiting his return. They offered him a pull at the water pannikin which he accepted gratefully. Then he looked round the barely discernible circle of faces.

"Now my lads," he said with new-found authority, "this is what we'll do . . ."

* * *

Captain Josiah King, commander of the privateer *Algonquin*, sat in the neat stern cabin of his schooner drinking a looted bottle of Malmsey. He would be in Morlaix by morning if the wind did not veer again. There he could disencumber himself of these British prisoners. He shuddered at the recollection of losing his ship, but as quickly consoled himself with his own forethought. The contingency plan had worked well—the British lieutenant had been a fool. The British always were. King had been with Whipple when the Rhode Islanders burnt the Government schooner *Gaspée*, back in '72. He remembered her captain, Lieutenant Duddingstone, acting the hero waving a sword about. A thrust in the groin soon incapacitated him. They had cast the unfortunate lieutenant adrift in a small boat. King smiled at the memory. When the magistrates eventually examined the cause of the burning, the entire population of the town protested ignorance. King knew every spirited man in Newport had answered Whipple's summons. The American smiled again.

Burgoyne had been a fool too with his clap-trap about honourable terms of surrender. Never mind that Gates had promised his army a safe-conduct to the coast. The British had surrendered and then locked up for their pains. That was what war was about: winning. Simply that and nothing else.

Warmed by recollection and wine he did not hear the slight scuffle of feet in the alleyway outside . . .

Drinkwater's plan worked perfectly. They had waited until well after dark. By this time such food as the Americans allowed them had been consumed. Each fit man was detailed off to follow in order and keep in contact with the man ahead.

The midshipman led the way. The wind had eased and *Algonquin* heeled less. The passage of the bilge was foul. Rats scrabbled out of their way, squealing a protest into the darkness, but no one complained. The filthy fo'c's'le was stinking with the corpse's corruption and their own excrement. Activity, even in a malodourous bilge, was preferable to the miasma of death prevailing in their cramped quarters.

When he reached the after end of the hold Drinkwater moved out to the side. Here there were gratings that ran round the schooner's lazarette. The wooden powder magazine was set in the center of the ship with the catwalk all around. This was decked with the gratings that now barred their passage. Upon these the gunner's mates walked round tending the lanterns that, shining through glass, safely illuminated the gunner within and enabled him to make up his cartridges.

Sergeant Hagan followed Drinkwater. Between them they lifted a grating and got through. Men followed silently. They were still in darkness but a faint current of air told where a small hatch led on deck at the top of a panelled trunking. it was locked. Drinkwater and Hagan felt round the space. Behind the ladder they found a door that led into the after quarters. It too was locked.

Hagan swore. They knew that once they were through that door they had a fair chance of success. In there were the officers' quarters. On either side of the alleyway beyond there were a couple of cabins and at the end, athwart the ship, the stern cabin. If they failed to capture the deck possession of the after quarters would probably result in the capture of an officer who might be useful as a hostage. But the door was secured against them.

Drinkwater dared not rattle the lock. In the darkness he could hear his men breathing. They all relied on him; what could he do now? He felt the hot tears of frustrated anger begin to collect and he was for the first time thankful for the darkness.

"Beg pardon, sir . . . ?" A voice whispered.

"Yes?"

"Locked door, sir?"

"Yes." He replied without hope.

"Let me have a look, sir."

There was a pushing and a shoving. A man came past. There was a silence as eighteen men held their breath, the creaking of the schooner and hiss of the sea seemed inaudible. Then a faint click was heard.

A man shoved back into the queue.

"Try it now, sir."

Drinkwater found the handle and turned it very slowly. The door gave. He pulled it to again. "What's your name?"

"Best you don't know it sir."

There was a muffled snigger. The man was doubtless one of *Cyclops*'s many thieves. With the scum of London pressed in her crew it was not surprising. Nevertheless the man's nefarious skill had saved the situation.

"Are you ready?" Drinkwater enquired generally in a loud whisper.

"Aye! Aye! . . ." The replies were muffled but nothing could disguise their eagerness.

Drinkwater opened the door. He made directly for the companionway. Hagan and the marine behind him made for the arms chest outside the stern cabin. Alternately a marine and a seamen emerged blinking into the dimly lit alleyway. The marines armed themselves with the cutlasses Hagan thrust at them; then in pairs they burst into the cabins. They took Josiah King before the Rhode Islander's feet hit the deck. His flimsy cabin door was dashed to matchwood and Hagan, his face contorted into a furious grimace presented the point of a cutlass to King's chest.

Drinkwater dashed on deck. His heart was pounding and fear lent a ferocity to him. The companionway emerged on deck abaft a skylight that let on to the passageway. Fortunately for the British a canvas cover was pulled over this to prevent the light disturbing the helmsman. But the helmsman stood immediately aft of the hatch, behind the binnacle. He leant against the huge tiller, straining with the effort of maintaining weather helm.

The mate on deck was a little further forward but he turned at the helmsman's exclamation. Drinkwater ran full tilt at the mate, knocking him over. The two men behind him secured the helmsman. He was tossed howling over the stern while the next man grabbed the tiller so that *Algonquin* scarcely faltered on her course.

The American officer rolled breathless on the deck. He attempted to rise and summon the assistance of the watch but Drinkwater, recovering from his butting charge, had whipped a belaying pin from the rail. The hardwood cracked on the man's head and laid him unconscious on his own deck.

Drinkwater stood panting with effort. The noise of blood and energy roared in his ears. It was impossible that the *Algonquin*'s crew had not been awakened by the din. Around him the British, several armed by Hagan's marines, gathered like black shadows. As one man they rolled forward. Too late the Americans on deck realized something was amiss. They went down howling and fighting. One attempted to wake those below. But resistance was useless. Men threatened with imprisonment in a French hulk or the benches of a galley are desperate. Five Americans perished through drowning, hurled over *Algonquin*'s side. Several were concussed into insanity. Eight were killed by their own edged weapons, weapons intended to intimidate unarmed merchantmen. The remainder were penned into the hold so lately reserved for their victims.

In ten minutes the ship was retaken.

Half an hour later she was put about, the sheets eased and, on a broad reach, steadied on course for England.

Chapter Ten August 1780

Elizabeth

Drinkwater leaned over the chart. Beside him a quartermaster named Stewart was pointing out the navigational dangers. Stewart had served as mate of a merchant ship and Drinkwater was thankful for his advice.

"I think Falmouth, Mr. Drinkwater," the man said. "You'll find the distance less and you'll not need to fear the Eddystone. The lighthouse is fine but the light feeble. Nay I'd say the twin cressets of the Lizard will be a better mark."

Drinkwater heeded Stewart. The former mate was a tough and experienced mariner which the incongruous paradoxes of human social order placed under his orders.

"Very well. Falmouth it is. But I fear them retaking the ship. We have at least twenty leagues to run before sighting the Lizard . . ."

"I do not think they will attempt it. Hagan's guard won't let them trick us again. The boys'll spit them with their baynits before asking any questions. Just you refuse them all requests and favours, Mr. Drinkwater."

Rolling the charts up they went on deck.

Algonquin raced along, her canvas straining under the force of the wind. On either side of her the white water hissed urgently as her keel tramped down the waters of the Channel underfoot.

The breeze was fresh but steady, allowing them to keep sail on the schooner and reel off a steady seven knots. At eight bells the next morning the sun caught the twin white towers of the Lizard and at noon *Algonquin* ran into Falmouth Harbour, under the guns of St. Mawes and Pandennis castles. At her peak she flew British over American colors. Drinkwater brought her to an anchor under the guns of a frigate lying in Carrick Roads.

Drinkwater was reluctant to leave *Algonquin* and report to the frigate, but the warship sent her own boat. Amidst a crowd of unfamiliar faces he was rowed across to her. She proved to be the *Galatea*.

Reporting to the third lieutenant he was informed the Captain was in lodgings ashore but that the first lieutenant would receive his report.

Drinkwater was conducted aft to where a tall, thin officer was bent almost double under the deck beams. He was coughing violently.

"Beg pardon, sir, this is Midshipman Drinkwater of the *Cyclops*. Prizemaster of the schooner yonder . . ." Drinkwater was suddenly a boy again, the responsibility of command lifted from him in the presence of this intimidating stranger. He felt very tired, tired and dirty.

The tall man looked at him and smiled. Then in an unmistakably Northumbrian accent he said, "Watched you anchor, mister. Well done. You'll have prisoners, no doubt?"

"Aye, sir, about twenty."

The lieutenant frowned. "About?" He fell to coughing again.

"I haven't allowed them on deck, sir. I'm not sure how many were killed last night."

The officer's frown deepened. "You say you're from *Cyclops*, lad?"

"Aye, sir, that's correct."

"She's off Ireland or thereaboots, so how were you fighting last night?"

Drinkwater explained how the Americans had retaken the ship, how Lieutenant Price had been killed and briefly related the prizecrew's desperate attempt to retrieve the situation. The first lieutenant's frown was replaced by a wry grin.

"You'll be wantin' to be rid of such troublesome fellars then."

"Yes, sir."

"I'll send some men and our long boat over. You'll have to take them to Pendennis. After that report to Captain Edgecumbe at the Crown." The tall man indicated first the squat tower of Pendennis on its headland above the harbor and then the huddle of houses and cottages that constituted the market town of Falmouth. He broke into another fit of coughing.

"Thank you, sir."

"My pleasure, lad," said the tall man moving away.

"Beg pardon, sir?" The man turned, a bloody handkerchief to his mouth.

"May I ask your name?"

"Collingwood," coughed the tall lieutenant.

Lieutenant Wilfred Collingwood was as good as his word. Half an hour later *Galatea's* longboat was alongside and a file of marines came aboard. Hagan had done his best to smarten the crew up but they did not compare with *Galatea's* men.

The Americans were herded into the boat. Drinkwater ordered *Algonquin's* boat into the water and was rowed ashore with Stewart. On the stone pier of Falmouth's inner harbour the marines were lining the American prisoners up. Josiah King was paraded scowling at the head of his men and the scarlet coats were lined along either side of the downcast little column. Drinkwater, his trousers still damp and smelling of bilge, swaggered at their head while Stewart and six seamen followed with cutlasses.

Hagan, also stinking of bilge, marched beside Drinkwater. The column moved off. It was market day and Falmouth was crowded. The people cheered the little procession as it tramped through the narrow streets. Drinkwater was conscious of the eyes of girls and women, and found the sensation thus produced arousing. But such is the vanity of humanity that Sergeant Hagan threw out his chest and received the same glances with the same assurance that they were for him.

Whereas in truth they were intended for the handsome, sulking American commander who, in the romantic hour of his defeat appealed to the perverse preference of the women.

Josiah King burned with a furious rage that seemed to roar in his skull like a fire. He burned with shame at losing his ship a second time. He burned with impotent anger that fate had wrested the laurels of victory from him, Josiah King of Newport, Rhode Island, and conferred them on the skinny young midshipman whose wet and smelly ducks stuck to his legs with every swaggering stride he took. He burned too with the knowledge that he had been outwitted at the very moment he had been congratulating himself on his forethought. That was, perhaps the bitterest, most private, part of the affair. Behind him his men trooped disconsolately as the column moved out of the town and began to climb the headland.

The road passed the end of the hornworks ascending through low undergrowth. It was hot and the sun beat down upon them. Suddenly the ramparts rose on their left and they swung over the fosse, under the Italianate guardhouse inside which the huge expanse of the castle enclosure revealed itself.

The guard had called the sergeant and the sergeant called his captain. The captain despatched an ensign to attend to the matter and continued his post-prandial doze. The ensign was insufferably pompous, having discovered that the escort was commanded by a none too clean midshipman. His condescending manner annoyed the exhausted Drinkwater who was compelled to endure the tedium of the unfamiliar and bewildering paperwork without which even the business of war could not be expedited. Each individual American had to be identified and signed for both by the ensign and the midshipman. All the while the sun beat down and Drinkwater felt the fatigue of a sleepless night merge with the euphoric relief from responsibility. At last the disdainful officer was satisfied.

The marines had fallen in again and the little party began to descend to the town.

With Stewart, Drinkwater repaired to the Crown Inn.

Captain Edgecumbe of His Britannic Majesty's frigate *Galatea* was an officer of the old school. When a ragamuffin midshipman appeared before him in filthy ducks the Captain was rightly wrathful. When that same scruffy midshipman attempted to report the arrival of the captured privateer *Algonquin* the captain refused to be side-tracked by incidentals. He also disliked interruptions.

The diatribe to which he subjected Drinkwater was as lengthy as it was unnecessary. In the end the midshipman stood silent, discovering, after some minutes had elapsed, that he was not even listening. Outside the hot sun shone and he had an odd longing to be doing nothing but lounging in that sunshine and perhaps have his arm about the waist of one of those pretty girls he had seen earlier. The sweet scent of Cornwall wafted in through the open window, distracting his senses from the path of duty. Only when the Captain ceased his tirade did the sudden silence break into his reverie and drag his conscious mind back to the inn room. He looked at the Captain.

Sitting in his shirt-sleeves Edgecumbe looked what he was, a dissipated and incompetent officer, living out of his ship and indulging his sexual appetites with local ladies. Drinkwater felt a sudden surge of contempt for him.

He touched his forehead. "Aye, aye, sir. Thank you, sir." He turned and marched smartly from the room.

Downstairs he found Stewart in the taproom. He was chaffing with a red-cheeked girl. Drinkwater noticed with a flutter in his stomach the girl had bright eyes and apple breasts.

Stewart, slightly abashed, bought the midshipman a pot of beer.

"Be *'e* y're Cap'n?" the girl asked Stewart, giggling

incredulously and setting the tankard down in front of Drinkwater.

The quartermaster nodded, flushing a little.

Drinkwater was confused by the unaccustomed proximity of the girl, but he felt Stewart's deference to his apparent importance as a spur to his manhood. She leaned over him boldly.

"Does y're honor need anything?" she inquired solicitously.

The heaving bosom no longer embarrassed him in his newfound confidence. He sucked greedily at the tankard, staring at the girl over its rim and enjoying her discomfiture as the beer warmed his belly. He was, after all, prize-master of the *Algonquin*, who had strutted through Falmouth under the admiring glances of scores of women . . .

He finished the beer. "To tell the truth ma'am, I have not the means to purchase more than a pot or two of beer . . ."

The girl plumped herself on the bench next to Stewart. She knew the quartermaster had a guinea or half sovereign about him, for she had seen the glint of gold in his hand. Stewart's experience insured he never ventured ashore without the price of a little dalliance or a good bottle about his person. The girl smiled at Drinkwater. It was a pity, she thought, he looked a nice young man, handsome in a pale sort of way. She felt Stewart's arm encircle her. Ah, well a girl had to live . . .

"Y're honor'll have matters of great importance to deal with," she said pointedly. She began to nestle up to Stewart who was staring at him. Drinkwater was aware of the pressure of Stewart's arm on a large breast. The white flesh swelled up, threatening to eject itself from the ineffectively grubby confines of the girl's bodice.

Drinkwater smiled lightheadedly. Rising, he tossed a few coppers onto the table.

"Be on board by sunset, Mr. Stewart."

On his return to *Algonquin* Drinkwater found the schooner being washed down. Upon deck lay a bundle.

It was a dead man. The other wounded were up and about, Grattan had had his arm splinted by the surgeon of *Galatea*. In the absence of the midshipman Collingwood had been aboard the schooner and arranged for *Cyclops*'s injured to attend *Galatea* for medical attention. He had also ordered the remaining into cleaning their prize.

Collingwood took an interest in the *Algonquin* for he was shortly to be posted to the West Indies where such vessels abounded. Besides he had liked the look of the young midshipman, who had done well by all accounts. A little discreet questioning among *Algonquin*'s prize crew told how well. The lieutenant left a message that Drinkwater should report to him on his return aboard.

The quarterdeck of *Galatea* reminded Drinkwater of *Cyclops* and he experienced a pang of nostalgia for his own frigate. Collingwood took him to one side and questioned him.

"Did you see Captain Edgecumbe?"

"Yes, sir." The lieutenant broke into a fit of coughing.

"What orders did he give you?" he asked at last.

"None, sir."

"None?" queried the lieutenant, a mock frown creasing his forehead.

"Well, sir . . ." Drinkwater faltered. What did one say to a first lieutenant whose captain had filled you with contempt?

"He told me to change my uniform, sir, and to . . . and to . . ."

"To report to the Flag Officer, Plymouth, I don't doubt. Ain't that so, lad?"

Drinkwater looked at Collingwod and through his fatigue the light slowly dawned on him.

"Oh! Yes . . . yes, sir, that's correct." He paused.

"Very well. I'd get under way tomorrow if I were you."

"Aye, Aye, sir." The midshipman knuckled his forehead and turned away.

"Oh, and Mr. Drinkwater!"

"Sir?"

"You cannot bury that man in the harbor. My carpenter is making a coffin. I have taken the liberty of arranging a burial service later this afternoon. You will attend the church of St. Charles the Martyr at four o'clock. Do you give thanks to the Lord for your deliverance . . ." The tall lieutenant turned away in another paroxysm of coughing.

Drinkwater slept briefly and at five bells was called to find his ducks cleaned and pressed. Hagan had spruced up his marines and the little party that solemnly marched to the parish church with their dismal burden carried with them a kind of rough dignity. The organization of a church burial for one of their number was a touch that Drinkwater did not really appreciate at the time.

Called upon to squander their life's blood in the service of an ungrateful country, the British seaman was inured to being treated worse than a beast. When gestures such as that made by Wilfred Collingwood touched their hearts they became an emotional breed. While Edgecumbe pursued the libertine path of the insensitive autocrat, Collingwood and others were learning the true trade of leadership. No one was to play upon the sailor's heartstrings as well as Horatio Nelson, but he was not the only one to learn.

The church was marvelously cool after the heat of the afternoon. The little congregation shuffled awkwardly, sensing the incongruity of the occasion. Afterwards, under the yew trees, the heat wrapped itself around the party again. Three men wept as the plain coffin was laid to rest, worn out with exertion and over-strung nerves.

The brief burial over, the seamen and marines prepared to march into town. The priest, a thin shrivelled man who wore his hair to the shoulder in the old fashioned manner, came over to the midshipman.

"I would be honored, sir, if you would take a dish of tea with me at the vicarage yonder."

"Thank you, sir," Drinkwater bowed.

The two men entered the house which contained something of the cool of the church. It reminded Drinkwater abruptly and painfully of his own home. A table was set for three. It seemed that the priest had some knowledge of the prize crew's exploits for he addressed Drinkwater in enthusiastic tones.

"I am but the interregnum here, but I am sure that the incumbent would wish me to welcome the opportunity of entertaining a naval hero in his home . . ."

He motioned Drinkwater to a chair.

"You are most kind, sir," Drinkwater replied, "but I do not think my actions were those of an hero . . ."

"Come, come . . ."

"No, sir. I fear the threat of a French prison revived our spirits . . ." He rose as a woman came in bearing a tea kettle.

"Ahh, my dear, the tea . . ." The old man bobbed up and down wringing his hands.

"Mr. Drinkwater, I'd like to present my daughter Elizabeth. Elizabeth, my dear, this is Mr. Drinkwater . . . I fear I do not know the gentleman's Christian name though it would be an honor to do so . . ." He made little introductory gestures with his hands, opening and closing them like an inexpertly-managed glove puppet.

"Nathaniel, sir." volunteered Drinkwater. The woman turned and Drinkwater looked into the eyes of a striking girl of about his own age. He took her hand and managed a clumsy little bow as he flushed with surprise and discomfiture. Her fingers were cool like the church. He mumbled:

"Y're servant ma'am."

"Honored, sir." Her voice was low and clear.

The trio sat. Drinkwater felt immediately oppressed by the quality of the crockery. The delicacy of the china after months of shipboard life made him feel clumsy.

The appearance of a plate of bread and cucumber, however, soon dispelled his misgivings.

"Nathaniel, eh," muttered the old man. "Well, well . . . 'a gift of God'", he chuckled softly to himself, ". . . most appropriate . . . really most appropriate . . ."

Drinkwater felt a sudden surge of pure joy. The little

parlor, bright with chintzes and painted porcelain reminded him poignantly of home. There was even the air of threadbare gentility, of a pride that sometimes served as a substitute for more tangible sustenance.

As she poured the tea Drinkwater looked at the girl. He could see now that she was indeed his own age, though her old fashioned dress had conveyed an initial impression of greater maturity. She bit her lower lip as she concentrated on pouring the tea, revealing a row of even and near perfect teeth. Her dark hair was drawn back behind her head in an unpretentious tress and it combined with her eyes, eyes of a deep and understanding brown, to give her face the inescapable impression of sadness.

So struck was he with this melancholy that when she looked up to pass him his cup he held her gaze. She smiled and then he was surprised at the sudden vivacity in her face, a liveliness free of any reproach that his directness deserved. He felt contentment change into happiness absent from his life for many months. He felt a keen desire to please this girl, not out of mere gratuitous bravado, but because she had about her the soothing aura of calm and tranquility. In the turmoil of his recent life he felt a powerful longing for spiritual peace.

Occupied with such thoughts he was unaware that he had consumed the greater part of the sandwiches single handed.

Isaac Bower and his daughter showed some surprise.

"Pardon me for the liberty, sir, but you have not eaten for some time?"

"I have not eaten like this for near a twelvemonth, sir . . ." smiled Drinkwater unabashed.

"But on board ship you eat like gentlemen and keep a good table?"

Drinkwater gave a short laugh. He told them of what his diet consisted. When the parson showed a shocked surprise he learned himself how ignorant the people of Britain were as to the condition of their seamen. The old man was genuinely upset and questioned the midshipman closely on the food, daily routines and duties of the respective persons aboard a man o' war, punctuating Drinkwater's replies with "'Pon my soul" and "Well, well, well" and copious sighs and shakings of his venerable head. As for Drinkwater he discoursed with the enthusiastic and encyclopedic knowledge of the professional proselyte who had done nothing but imbibe the details of his employment. His picture of life on a frigate, though slightly lurid and excusably self-important, was, once sifted by the old man's shrewdness, not far from the truth.

While the men talked Elizabeth refilled their cups and studied her guest. Ignoring the soiled state of the linen about his neck and wrists she found him presentable enough. His mop of dark hair was drawn carelessly back into a queue and framed a face that had weathered to a pale tan, a tan that accentuated the premature creases around his eyes. These were of a cloudy grey, like the sky over the Lizard in a sou' westerly gale, and they were shadowed by the blue bruises of fatigue and worry.

As he talked his face blazed with infectious enthusiasm and a growing self-confidence that, if it was not apparent to its owner, was clear to Elizabeth.

For she was more than the sheltered daughter of a country parson. She had experienced near poverty since her father had lost his living some two years previously. He had unwisely attacked the profligacy of his patron's heir and suffered the heir's revenge when that worthy succeeded suddenly to the estate. The death of his wife shortly afterwards had left Bower with the child of their declining years to bring up unaided.

In the event the girl had matured quickly and assumed the burden of housekeeping without demur. Although brought up in the shadow of her father's profession, the hardships and rigors of life had not left her untouched. In his younger days Bower had been an active man, committed to his flock. Within the circumscribed world of a country parish events had served to temper Elizabeth's growing character. Much of her adolescence had been spent nursing her consumptive mother and during the last weeks of her life Elizabeth had come face to face with the concomitants of sickness and death.

As she contemplated the ruins of a fruitcake that would have lasted the parson and herself a week, she found herself smiling. She too felt grateful for the tea-party. Drinkwater had blown in with some of the freshness of youth absent from her life until that moment. It was a refreshing change from the overbearing bombast of the red-faced squireens, or the languid indolence of the garrison infantry officers who had been until then almost the only eligible members of the male sex that she had met. She detected a sympathy about the young man sitting opposite, a sensitivity in him; something contained in his expression and given emphasis by the early lines appearing on his face, the umbra of nervous strain about his eyes.

At last the discussion ceased. Both men were, by now, firm friends. Drinkwater apologized for monopolizing the conversation and ignoring his hostess.

"It is quite unnecessary to apologize, Mr. Drinkwater, since my father has too little of such stimulating talk." She smiled again. "Indeed I am glad that you have come, albeit in such circumstances." With a little pang of conscience Drinkwater remembered he had that afternoon attended a funeral.

"Thank you, Miss Bower."

"But tell me, Mr. Drinkwater, in all these comings and goings did you not feel afraid?"

Drinkwater answered without hesitation. "Aye greatly . . . as I told your father earlier . . . but I think fear may be the mainspring of courage . . ." he paused. It was suddenly imperative that he convey exactly what he meant. He did not wish the young woman opposite to misunderstand, to misjudge him.

"Not that I wish to boast of courage, but I found the more I feared the consequences of inactivity, the more I found the . . . the resolve to do my utmost to alter our circumstances. In this I was most ably supported by the other members of the prize crew."

She smiled without coquetry.

Nathaniel basked in the radiance of that smile. It seemed to illuminate the whole room.

The cake consumed, the tea drunk, and the conversation lapsing into the silences of companionable surfeit, Drinkwater rose. The sun was westering and the room already full of shadows. He took his leave of the parson. The old man pressed his hand.

"Goodbye my boy. Please feel free to call upon us any time you are in Falmouth, though I do not yet know how much longer we shall be here." His face clouded briefly with uncertainty then brightened again as he took the young man's hand. "May God bless you, Nathaniel . . ."

Drinkwater turned away strangely moved. He bowed towards Elizabeth.

"Y'r servant, Miss Bower . . ."

She did not answer but turned to her father. "I shall see Mr. Drinkwater to the gate, father, do you sit and rest for you look tired after your long talk." The old man nodded and wearily resumed his seat.

Elated at thus receiving a moment or two alone with the girl Drinkwater followed Elizabeth as she moved ahead of him, flinging a shawl about her shoulders as she left the house.

She opened the gate and stepped down into the lane. He stood beside her, looking down into her face and fumbling with his hat, suddenly miserable with the knowledge that he had enjoyed his simple tea with all its reminders of home and English domesticity. But it was more than that. It had been the presence of this girl that had made the afternoon and evening so memorable. He swallowed hard.

"Thank you for your hospitality, Miss Bower . . ."

The air was heavy with the scent of foliage. In the gathering gloom of the Cornish lane fern fronds curled like fingers of pale green fire in the crevices of rocks that marked the boundary of the glebe. Overhead swifts screamed and swooped.

"Thank you for your very kind hospitality, Miss Bower . . ." She smiled and held out her hand. He grasped it eagerly, holding her eyes with an exhilarating boldness.

"Elizabeth . . . ," she said defying the bounds of propriety yet leaving her hand intensely passive in his firm grip, "please call me Elizabeth . . ."

"Then call me Nathaniel . . ." They paused, uncertainly. For a second the specter of awkwardness hovered between them. Then they smiled and laughed simultaneously.

"I thought . . ." she began.

"Yes . . .?"

"I thought . . . I hoped you would not disappear completely . . . it would be pleasant to see you again . . ."

In answer Nathaniel raised her hand to his lips. He felt again the coolness of her flesh, not the coolness of rejection but the balm of serenity.

"I am," he said with absolute conviction, "your very devoted servant, Elizabeth . . ." He held her hand a moment longer and turned away.

He looked back once before the lane bent away in descent. He could see her face pale in the twilight, and the flutter of her hand raised in farewell.

That night *Algonquin* seemed to him a prison . . .

Chapter Eleven August–October 1780

Interlude

It was autumn before Drinkwater rejoined *Cyclops*. News had arrived in England of the defection of Benedict Arnold to the King's cause and the consequent shameful hanging of Major John André. To Drinkwater, however, languishing at Plymouth, it scarcely seemed possible that a ferocious war was taking place at all.

Arriving in that port with *Algonquin* he had been swiftly dispossessed of the schooner which passed to the port admiral's hands. He found himself with Stewart, Sharples and the rest, kicking his heels on the guardship. This vessel, an obsolete 64-gun battleship, was overcrowded and stinking, filled with newly-pressed seamen awaiting ships and young officers like himself daily expecting the return of their own vessels or the arrival of new posting. The prevailing conditions on board necessitated the vessel being run like a prison and the consequent corruption found in those institutions therefore prevailed. Gambling, rat-baiting and cockfighting were clandestinely practiced. Drunken and sexual orgies took place almost nightly and the enforced idleness of twelve hundred and seventy men gave the devil's agents excessive scope for improvisation.

From command of his own ship Drinkwater became less than nothing, one of many midshipmen and master's mates with sufficient time to reflect on the paradoxes of a sea officer's career.

It was a dismal time for him. The thought of Elizabeth

Bower plagued him. Falmouth was not too far away. He panicked at the thought of her father's interregnum ending and the pair being sent God knew where. He had never been in love before and submitted to the self-centred lassitude of the besotted in an atmosphere utterly conducive to the nurturing of such unsociable emotions.

Week succeeded week and the period was one of utter misery. Yet in its way the amorous depression that accompanied the congested privation served to keep him away from other more immediate amusements. His romantic preoccupations encouraged him to read, or at least to daydream over, such books as the guardship possessed.

As time passed the memory of Elizabeth faded a little and he read more diligently. He spent some of his small stock of gold on books purchased from messmates needing ready cash for betting. In this way he acquired a copy of Robertson's "Elements of Navigation" and one of Falconer, reflecting that the money, some loose Spanish coin he had found on *Algonquin* and rightly the property of the crown, was being correctly spent on the training of a King's officer and not lining the pockets of an Admiralty lackey.

After ten weeks of ennui Drinkwater had a stroke of luck. One morning an elaborately decorated cutter anchored in Jennycliff Bay. A boat pulled over to the guardship with a request to the commanding officer for the loan of one master's mate or midshipman. It so happened that the second mate of the cutter had been taken ill and her master required a replacement for a few days.

By chance Drinkwater happened to be on deck and the first person the lieutenant dispatched to find a "volunteer" clapped eyes on. Within minutes he was in the cutter's gig and being rowed across the steely waters of the Sound. A sprinkling rain began to patter on the water.

The boat rounded the cutter's stern and Drinkwater looked up to see the state cabin windows richly ornamented with gilt work and a coat of arms consisting of four ships quartered by St. George's Cross. The ensign at the vessel's stern was red and bore a similar device in the fly. The officer in charge of the boat, who happened to be the mate of the cutter, explained that she was the Trinity House Yacht, bound to the Scillies to attend St. Agnes lighthouse.

Drinkwater had heard of the Elder Brethren of the Trinity House who maintained buoys in the Thames estuary and some lighthouses around the coast. However, his main source of information had been Blackmore. As a sailing master in the Royal Navy Blackmore had had to suffer examination by the Brethren, who passed the navy's navigators, before he could obtain his warrant. Blackmore, the former master of a Baltic trader had resented the fact and commented somewhat acidly on the practice.

However Drinkwater was immediately impressed by the immaculate appearance of the Trinity Yacht. The crew, all volunteers exempt from the press-gang, were smart and well fed when compared with the Royal Navy's raggamuffins. The master, one John Poulter, seemed a pleasant man and welcomed Drinkwater cordially. On explaining his lack of clothing (since his chest remained on *Cyclops*) the master offered him fresh ducks, a tarpaulin and a pea jacket.

A great sensation of relief flooded over Drinkwater as he settled into his tiny cabin. He luxuriated in the privacy which, although he had partaken of it aboard *Algonquin*, had not been without the worrying responsibility of command. Until that moment he had not realised the extent of the guardship's oppression upon his spirit.

Later he went on deck. It was now raining steadily. The Cawsand shore was blurred into grey mist but the rain fell with the hiss of freedom. Pulling the tarpaulin round him, he examined the vessel. She was sturdily built and mounted a few swivel guns on either side. Her mainsail was clearly larger than *Algonquin*'s and she had a soldier, more permanent feel about her. This was due to her oak construction and opulent appointments, for she fairly dripped with gilt gingerbread-work. Her spars gleamed even in the dreary weather and Drinkwater examined the details of her rigging with great interest.

Captain Poulter had come on deck and walked over to him.

"Well, cully, had much experience with this kind of vessel?" His accent was unmistakably that of the capital.

"Not a cutter, sir, but I was lately prizemaster of a schooner."

"Good. I hope I shall not detain you long from the King's business but I am bound for the Scilly Islands with Captain Calvert to examine the lighthouse there. Perhaps a King's officer may find that interesting." Drinkwater detected the flicker of insinuation in Poulter's voice. He recognized it as a device used by old Blackmore and other merchant masters who resented the navy's social superiority. To his credit he coloured.

"To tell the truth, sir, I am greatly obliged to you for removing me from yonder guardship. Methought I might die of boredom before I saw action again."

"That's well," said Poulter turning to windward and sniffing the air. "Plague on this damn coast. It's always raining."

The Trinity Yacht left Plymouth two days later. August had passed into September. The rain had given way to windy, mist-laden days. But the weather had no power to depress the young midshipman's spirits. After the claustrophobic atmosphere of the guardship, service on the Trinity Yacht was stimulating in the extreme. Here was a fine little ship run as efficiently as a first-rate without the lash and human degradation prevalent in His Majesty's Service.

Captain Poulter and his mate proved generous instructors and Drinkwater quickly learned more of the subtleties of handling the fore and aft rig of the big cutter than he had mastered aboard *Algonquin*.

He found Captain Anthony Calvert willing to discourse with him, even interested to hear how Drinkwater would undertake certain navigational problems. He joined the Elder Brother and Poulter at dinner one evening. Calvert was treated with as much deference as Drinkwater had seen accorded to Admiral Kempenfelt. Indeed the captain flew his own flag at the cutter's masthead, although his privileges and responsibilities were considered to be exterior to the management of the yacht. Nevertheless he proved to be an interesting and and interested man. As the cutter bucked her way to the west, Drinkwater found himself recounting the story of the recapture of the *Algonquin*. At midnight Drinkwater left Poulter and Calvert to relieve the mate. It was still blowing hard, the night black, wet and inhospitable.

The mate had to bellow in Drinkwater's ear as he passed over the position and course.

"Keep her off on the starboard tack another hour. You're well off the Wolf Rock now but keep a sharp lookout when you stand north. We should be well west of it by now but the flood's away and will be fierce as the devil's eyebrows with this wind behind it. Ye'll be well advised to use caution."

"Aye, aye," replied Drinkwater, shouting back to the black figure whose tarpaulin ran with rain and spray. He was left to the night ruminating on the dangers of the unmarked Wolf. This totally isolated pinnacle of rock was, with Eddystone, the most feared danger to mariners on the south coast of England. Continually swept by swells on even the calmest days, it was to be 1795 before an abortive attempt was made to erect a beacon on it. This structure collapsed at the first gale and it was to be a generation before a permanent seamark was finally grouted into that formidable outcrop.

It was claimed by some that in certain sea conditions a subterraneous cavern produced a howling noise and this had given the rock its name, but, howling noise or not, nothing could have been heard that night above the roar of the gale and the creak and crash of the Trinity Yacht as she drove to the south-southwest.

Poulter had put four reefs into the enormous mainsail before dark. He was in no hurry since he wished to heave to off the Scillies to observe the light at St. Agnes.

It was for this purpose Calvert had journeyed from London.

At two bells, Drinkwater prepared to put about on to the port tack. Before doing so he went forward to inspect the headsails. The staysail was reefed down but out on the long bowsprit a small spitfire jib stood against the gale. Drinkwater had learned that to balance the huge mainsail a jib had to be kept as near the end of the bowsprit as conditions permitted. He watched the big spar stab at a wave-crest even as the bow he stood on pitched down off its predecessor. Beneath him the figurehead of a lion guardant disappeared in a welter of white water that rolled hissing away from the cutter's steadily advancing stern.

He returned aft, calling the watch to their stations, glanced at the compass then up at Calvert's flag standing out from the masthead like a board. Two men leaned against the big tiller. He shouted at them:

"Down Helm!" They grunted with exertion.

The yacht's heel reduced, she came upright, her canvas slatting madly, cracking like thunder. The hull swooped and ducked as she met the seas head on.

Drinkwater bit his lip. She took her time passing through the eye of the wind but her crew clearly knew their business. His orders were as much for his own satisfaction as the vessel's management. As she paid slowly off to starboard the little spitfire jib was held aback. The wind caught it and suddenly it exerted its tremendous leverage at the extremity of the bowsprit. The cutter spun on her heel, the mainsail filled, then the staysail was hauled over. Finally the weather jib sheet was started and the canvas cracked like a gun before it was tamed by the lee sheet. The yacht sped away to the northwest and Drinkwater breathed a sigh of relief.

There was no opportunity to study the chart in the prevailing conditions. The deck was continually sluiced by seas coming aboard so that the two boats on chocks amidships appeared to be afloat of their own accord.

After a further hour of this the sails suddenly slatted. At once several men perceived the veering of the wind.

"Keep her full and bye," roared Drinkwater to the helmsmen, to which a slightly reproachful voice answered, "Aye, aye, but that's north, sir."

Drinkwater checked himself reflecting that this was no king's ship and the helmsman's reply was not insubordinate but informative.

North.

He shook his head to clear away fatigue and too much of Calvert's port. With leeway and a roaring flood tide to set them east he might be setting on to the Wolf Rock! A knot of panic gripped his stomach until he mastered it with the thought that the total area of the rock was less than that of the cutter's deck. Surely the odds were impossibly against them striking that isolated spot?

A figure loomed up beside him. It was Poulter.

"Heard her luff, cully. You'll be concerned about the Wolf." It was not a question but a statement simply made. Drinkwater felt the load lifted from his shoulders. His brain cleared and he was able to think.

"D'ye wish me to put about again Captain Poulter, with the shift of wind she'll hold a more westerly course, sir . . . ?"

Poulter was glancing at the dimly lit compass. Drinkwater thought he caught a glimpse of a smile in the wet darkness.

"That will do very well, Mr. Drinkwater. See to it if ye please."

"Aye, aye, sir . . ."

The Trinity Yacht arrived off Hugh Town later that day and remained there for several days. Calvert and Poulter had themselves pulled across to St. Agnes and the crew discharged several chauldrons of coal into their boats to feed the light's chauffer-fires.

Ten days after leaving Plymouth Calvert pronounced himself satisfied with the lighthouse and on coming aboard from a final visit Drinkwater overheard him talking to Poulter.

"Well Jonathan, we'll make passage tomorrow at first light observing the cresset again tonight. I'll post to London from Falmouth and you may then proceed to the east'ard." Calvert's words fell dully on Drinkwater's ears until he mentioned Falmouth.

Falmouth meant Elizabeth.

On arrival at Falmouth it was discovered that the yacht's second mate had recovered sufficiently to rejoin the ship. Drinkwater was therefore discharged by Poulter with a letter explaining his absence and a certificate as to his proficiency. Greatly delighted with his luck he was even more astonished when Calvert sent for him and presented him with four guineas for his services and another certificate testifying that as an Elder Brother of the Trinity House he had examined Mr. Drinkwater and found him to be competent in navigation and seamanship. The document he presented to Drinkwater certified that he had passed the examination for master's mate.

"There, Mr. Drinkwater. Under the latest regulations you are now permitted to board prizes as prize-master in your own right. Good luck to ye."

Stammering his delighted surprise, Drinkwater shook hands with Calvert and was pulled ashore with the Elder Brother. Having seen Calvert off in the post chaise, Drinkwater turned his steps to the vicarage.

Autumn was in the air but he strode along without a care in the world, his heart thumping at the prospect of seeing Elizabeth again.

He swung back the gate. At the door he hesitated, his hand actually in the act of drawing back the knocker. Changing his mind he moved to a side window. It was the parson's study. Peering in, he saw the bald dome of the old man's head, the white locks from the sides and nape of his head falling sideways in the relaxation of sleep.

Drinkwater crept round to the rear of the house. He found Elizabeth in the garden. She was unaware of his presence and for a moment he stood watching her.

She was picking fruit from a tree whose gnarled boughs were bent under a load of russet apples. As she stretched out to pluck the fruit her face was in profile. The lower lip was caught in her teeth in an expression he recognized as one of concentration. There was something sweetly pastoral in the scene to one whose eyes had become accustomed to the monotony of the sea.

He coughed and she started, losing hold of her apron. A cascade of apples ran out on to the grass. "Oh! . . . Nathaniel . . . !"

He laughed, running over to help pick them up. "I'm sorry to have startled you."

She smiled at him. Kneeling, their faces were very close. He felt her breath on his cheek and was about to throw caution to the winds when she stood, brushing a wisp of hair behind her neck.

"I am glad that you have come. How long can you stay?"

Drinkwater had not given the matter much thought. He shrugged.

"How long would you have me stay . . . ?" he smilingly asked.

It was her turn to shrug. She laughed, refusing to be drawn, but he could tell she was pleased.

"I ought to return to Plymouth tomorrow . . . well I *ought* to return today but . . ." he shrugged again, "well let us say I am recuperating . . ."

"The New York packet is due and there'll be a post leaving soon, stay till then?"

"Well, er, I, er . . ."

"Father will be delighted, please stay . . ."

She uttered the last words pleadingly, so that Nathaniel had little choice and less inclination to choose. He looked into her brown eyes. They waited for his reply anxiously . . .

"Would you wish it that I stayed?"

She smiled. She had given away too much already. She gathered the last of the apples and moved towards the house.

"Do you like apple pie, Nathaniel?" she called over her shoulder.

The day passed delightfully. *Cyclops*, Morris, and the anxieties and fears of the past months might have been the experience of another person, a callow frightened youth compared to the vibrantly energetic young man.

As his daughter had said, the old parson was delighted to entertain the midshipman. He took great pride in showing Drinkwater his library and it was clear that the collection of books constituted practically the whole of Bower's possessions, since the artifacts of the house were the property of the absent clergyman. Closer acquaintance with Isaac Bower revealed him to be a man of considerable learning who had not only brought his daughter up but educated her himself. She was, he told Nathaniel with an air of confidentiality, the equal of most men and the superior of many in her knowledge of mathematics, astronomy, Greek and Latin, while her literary tastes encompassed those French authors who did not abjure the existence of God. Had there been any doubts about Elizabeth's talents in other directions these were swiftly dispelled at dinner when a roasted chicken was followed by an apple pie of generous proportions.

After dinner Drinkwater found himself alone in a darkening room with a bottle of port that Bower had unearthed in his host's cellar. He had drunk two glasses when the old man came into the room. He threw some logs onto the fire and poured himself a glass.

"I, er, had a little news the other day . . . after you had left. My Lord Bishop of Winchester had appointed me to a parish near Portsmouth. It is a poor parish, I believe, but . . ." the old man shrugged resignedly, ". . . that is of no matter. At least," he continued on a brighter note, ". . . it will bring us nearer you brave naval fellows and, I trust," he looked pointedly at Nathaniel, "I trust you will continue to visit us there."

Warmed by the wine, Nathaniel replied enthusiastically. "I shall be delighted, sir, absolutely delighted . . . After my last visit I found the prospect of reacquainting myself with you and Eliz . . . Miss Bower most comforting . . ."

Bower asked him something of his own circumstances and he told the parson of his widowed mother. Elizabeth joined them for a while before she announced she was retiring and the conversation was relaxed and informal. After she had left Nathaniel said, "I am, sir, very grateful for your kindness to me . . . it has meant a great deal to me . . ."

The two men drained the bottle. Nathaniel's remark unsprung the older man's greatest fear. "My boy, I do not expect to remain much longer in this world. I have no fortune to leave after me but my daughter and on her account I am oppressed in spirit . . ." he coughed a little self-consciously.

"I would have her left with one friend, for I fear she has had no opportunity to establish herself anywhere whilst following me upon my travels . . ." he paused diffidently, then, with a note of firmness in his voice he said. "D'ye take my meaning . . . ?"

"I am sure, sir," said Nathaniel, "that I shall do all in my power to assist your daughter should she need my protection . . ."

The old man smiled into the darkness. He had known it the instant the boy told them his name . . . Nathaniel . . . in the Hebrew tongue it meant a gift from God. He sighed with contentment.

The unusual sound of birdsong woke Drinkwater next morning. Realization that he lay under the same roof as Elizabeth woke him to full consciousness. He was quite unable to sleep so rose and dressed.

Quitely descending the stairs, he moved through the kitchen and unlatched the door. The invigorating chill of early morning made him shiver as he strode out on the dew-wet grass.

Without thinking he began pacing up and down the lawn, head down, hands behind his back, plunged in thoughts of last night's conversation with the old parson.

He felt a surge of excitement and relief at Bower's approval and smiled inwardly with self-congratulation. He stopped midway between the apple trees and the house. "You're a lucky dog, Nathaniel," he muttered to himself.

The creak of an opening window and the ring of laughter brought him back to reality.

From the kitchen window Elizabeth, her hair about her shoulders, was smiling at him.

"Are you pacing your quarterdeck, sir," she mocked.

Nathaniel was suddenly struck by the ridiculousness of his actions. With the whole of Cornwall at his feet he had paced over an area roughly equal to a frigate's quarterdeck.

"Why . . ." he raised his hands in a shrug, ". . . I never gave it a thought." Elizabeth was laughing at him, the sound of her laughter coming out of the window borne on the scent of frying eggs.

The haunting paradoxes of *Cyclops* and the malice of Morris seemed no longer important. All that mattered now was the laughter and the smiling face . . . and the sizzling freshness of fried eggs.

"Y're a lucky dog, Nathaniel," he muttered again as he crossed the grass to the kitchen door.

The London mail left Falmouth later that day with Nathaniel perched on its exterior bound for Plymouth. By the time it reached Truro Nathaniel, riding on the crest of growing confidence, had ascertained he possessed sufficient funds for the fare to London and back.

The weather remained fair and the experience of hurtling through towns and villages so agreeable and in harmony with his spirits that he decided the Plymouth guardship could do without him for a further three or four days. The idea had come to him while pacing the lawn that morning. Discussion of his family had filled him with a longing to return home, no matter how briefly. There had been no news of *Cyclops* when he had left Plymouth in the Trinity Yacht and Poulter, he knew, would not put into Plymouth to inform the authorities that he had landed him at Falmouth. It was, therefore probable that a few days of additional absence would go unnoticed.

He came to an arrangement for a half-price fare riding on the "conveniency" and settled down to enjoy the unprecedented pleasure of a journey through the green of southern England on an uncommonly fine day.

It was late in the afternoon following when, stiff from

the long journey and tired from the trudge of the Great North Road, Drinkwater reached Barnet. He pressed on to Monken Hadley, reaching the small house at last.

His desire to see his mother and brother had increased with the growing love he felt for Elizabeth. The strong attraction of her home had reminded him of his own and Bower's infirmity had emphasised the effect of passing time upon his remaining parent. His stay in Falmouth was limited by propriety yet he did not wish to kick his heels aboard that festering guardship.

Nathaniel, despite his fatigue, was pleased with himself. The freedom and independence he had experienced on *Algonquin* and the Trinity Yacht had served to mature him, the responsibility of the prize had stamped its imprint upon his character. His growing relationship with Elizabeth, certain in at least its foundation, lent him both hope and stability, banishing many of the uncertainties of the past.

His altered outlook had found expression and practical reward. He had looted King's small hoard of gold from the *Algonquin* somewhat shamefacedly, aware that his morality was questionable despite the usages of war. When this had been supplemented by Calvert's respectably acquired guineas and, most important of all, his certificate of examination as master's mate, he had a degree of autonomy for the first time in his life. It lent a jauntiness to the final steps to his mother's front door.

He knocked and lifted the latch.

Afterwards, when there was time to think, he realized he was right to come. His mother's pleasure in his visit was only clouded by its brevity. To him, however, her failing health and increasingly obvious penury were distressing and oppressive. He had not stayed long. He had talked and read to his mother and, when she dozed, slipped out to ask the Rector to engage someone from Barnet to attend to some of her needs. Calvert's guineas had gone there, and from the Rector he had learned that Ned was rarely seen in Monken Hadley. Nathaniel's brother had found employment as a groom at West Lodge with his beloved horses, had taken a common-law wife from among the maids there and come near to breaking his poor mother's heart. The Rector had shaken his head and muttered, "Like father, like son . . .", but he promised to do what he could for Mrs. Drinkwater, closing his hand over the gold.

Nathaniel sat in the quiet of the room watching motes of dust in the oblique shaft of sunlight that streamed in through the little window. He would return to Plymouth on the morrow; he felt the inactivity, the strange silence, discomposing. His mother dozed and, recalling the reason for his visit, he quietly resumed his letter to Ned. It was badly phrased, awkward in admonition but it spoke with the new found authority of the young man.

"What are you doing?" the old lady's voice startled him.

"Oh! Mother! . . . You are awake . . . just a note to Ned, to tell him to take more care of you . . ."

He saw her smile.

"Dear Nathaniel," she said simply, "You cannot stay longer?"

"Mother, I must return to duty, already I . . ."

"Of course my dear . . . you are a King's officer now . . . I understand . . ."

She held out her hand and Nathaniel knelt by her chair. He felt her frail arthritic hand brush his hair. He could think of no words adequate to the moment and had lost the means to say them.

"Do not be too hard on Edward," she said quietly. "He has his own life to lead and is very like his father . . ."

Nathaniel rose and bent over his mother, kissing her forehead, turning away to hide the tears in his eyes.

When he left next morning it was still dark. He did not know it but his mother heard him leave. It was only then she wept.

Chapter Twelve November 1780–January 1781

A Change of Orders

Drinkwater joined *Cyclops* again on the last day of October 1780. She had been in Plymouth Sound some days recruiting her prize crews and taking in fresh water, and the tale of the retaking of *Algonquin* had preceeded him, borne on board by Hagan and the others. Drinkwater therefore found himself something of a hero to the lower deck with whom he was already popular after his beating of Morris.

The latter, however, had re-established something of his former ascendancy in the cockpit. Drinkwater's absence had helped, but a few new appointees to the frigate in the form of very young midshipmen had given Augustus Morris more victims. There was, though, one new member of the mess whom Drinkwater was quick to realize was a potential ally. Midshipman Cranston, a silent man of about thirty, had little liking for Morris's bombast or bullying. A former seaman, Cranston had fought his way up from the lower deck by sheer abiity. He was clever and tough, and utterly unscrupulous. Drinkwater liked him instantly. He also liked another, though much younger addition to the mess. Mr. White was a pale, diminutive boy of thirteen. White was the obvious choice for victimization by Morris.

In the course of the succeeding weeks, the now overpopulated cockpit, whose members varied in age and pursuits, was to become a bedlam of noise and quarrels.

Towards the end of November, Captain Hope expressed himself ready once more to cruise against the enemy and the frigate left Plymouth, beating west and south to resume her station. The weather was now uniformly foul. Depression succeeded depression and a cycle was established of misery below decks and unremitted labor above. The outbreaks of petty thieving, fighting, insubordination and drunkenness that were the natural consequences of the environment broke out again. When a man was flogged for petty theft Drinkwater wondered if it was the same man who had been instrumental in the retaking of the *Algonquin*. At all events he no longer balked at such a spectacle, inured now to it, though he knew other methods existed to keep men at unpleasant labor. But they had no part here, in the overcrowded decks of *Cyclops*, and he felt no anger with Captain Hope for maintaining discipline with the iron hand that enabled the Royal Navy to sustain its ceaseless vigilance.

To the ship's company of *Cyclops* it was the dull, monotonous routine of normality. A fight with the enemy would have come as a blessed relief to both officers and men.

Captain Hope appeared on deck as little as possible, nursing a grievance that he had not yet received his share of the prize money for the capture of the *Santa Teresa*. Lieutenant Devaux showed signs of strain from similar motives, his usual bantering tones giving way to an uncharacteristic harassment of his subordinate lieutenants, especially Mr. Skelton, a young and inexperienced substitute for the late Lieutenant Price.

Old Blackmore, the sailing master, observed all and said little. He found these peevish King's Officers, deprived of their two-pence prize money and behaving like old maids, distasteful shipmates. Bred in a hard school, he expected to be uncomfortable at sea and was rarely disappointed.

Mr. Surgeon Appleby, ever the philosopher, shook his head sadly over his blackstrap. He ruminated on the condition of the ship to anyone who cared to listen.

"You see, gentlemen, about you the natural fruits of man's own particular genius: Corruption." He enunciated the word with a professional relish as if sniffing an amputated stump, seeking gangrene. "Corruption is a process arrived at after a period of growing and maturation. Medically speaking it occurs after death, whether in the case of an apple which had fallen from the bough and no longer receives sustenance from the tree, or, in the case of the human body which corrupts irrevocably after the heart has ceased to function. In both cases the span of time may be seen as a complete cycle.

"But in the case of spiritual corruption, I assure you, the process is faster and independent of the heart. Observe our noble ship's company. A pride of lions in battle . . ." Appleby paused to fortify his monologue with blackstrap. ". . . They are corrupted by the fetid atmosphere of a frigate.

"Sit down, Mr. Drinkwater, sit down and remember this when you are an Admiral. As a consequence all manner of evils appear; drunkenness, quarreling, insubordination, sodomy, theft, and worst of all, for it is a crime against God and not merely man, discontent. And what nurtures that discontent?"

"Why prize money!"

"*What* damned prize money, Bones?" interrupted Lieutenant Keene.

"*Exactly* my friend. *What* prize money? *You* won it. *You* were awarded it, but *where* the deuce is it? Why, lining the pockets of Milor' Sandwich and his Tory toadies. *Someone* is growing fat on merely the interest. God's blood they too are as corrupted as this stinking ship. I tell you, gentlemen, this will rebound upon them one day. One day it will not only be the damned Yankees that defy their Lordships but Tom Bowline and Jack Rattlin . . ."

"Aye and Harry Appleby!" shouted a voice.

A bored laugh drifted round the gloom of the gunroom. *Cyclops* plunged into a sea and expletives exploded in short, exasperated grunts from several voices.

"Who'd be a god-damned sailor?"

* * *

To Drinkwater, these weeks were less painful than to most. It is true he dreamed of Elizabeth but his love did not oppress him. Rather it sustained him. Blackmore was delighted that he had acquired his certificate from Calvert and tutored him in some of the more abstruse mysteries of celestial navigation. He also struck up a firm friendship with Lieutenant Wheeler of the Marines. Whenever the weather moderated sufficiently to allow it Wheeler and Drinkwater engaged in fencing practice. The frequent sight of his "enemy" thus engaged was a painful reminder of his humiliation to Morris; and the longer Drinkwater seemed immune from Morris the more the latter wished to revenge himself upon the younger man. Morris began to form his earlier alliances with like-minded men amongst the least desirable elements of *Cyclops*'s company.

Only this time there was more purpose to the cabal. Morris was degenerating into a psychopathic creature to whom reality was blurred, and in whom hatred burned with a flame as potent as love.

Christmas and New Year came and went almost unnoticed as they can only at sea. It was a dull day in the middle of January before any event occurred to break the monotony of life aboard the frigate.

"Sail Ho!"

"Where away?"

"Lee beam, sir!"

Lieutenant Skelton sprung into the mizen rigging and levelled his glass. Jumping down he turned to Drinkwater. "Mr. Drinkwater!"

"M'compliments to the Captain and there's a sail to starboard, might be a frigate."

Drinkwater went below. Hope was asleep, dozing in his cot when the midshipman's knock woke him. He hurried on deck.

"Call all hands, Mr. Skelton, and bear away to investigate."

A topsail was clearly visible now, white as a gull's wing against a squall, for a grey overcast obscured what sun there was. Occasionally a fleeting glimpse of a pale lemon orb appeared which Morrison patienty strove to capture in the horizon glass of his quadrant. The two ships closed rapidly and after an hour came up with one another.

Recognition signals revealed the other to be friendly and she turned out to be *Galatea*. The newcomer hove to under *Cyclops's* lee and a string of bright bunting appeared at her foremasthead.

"Signal, sir," said Drinkwater, flicking the pages of the codebook, "Repair on board."

Hope bridled. "Who does Edgecumbe think he is, damn him!"

Deavaux supressed a smile as Wheeler muttered *sotto voce*: "A Tory Member of Parliament, perhaps . . ."

After a little delay, just long enough for it to be impertinent, Hope snapped, "Very well, acknowledge!"

"Your gig, sir?" asked the solicitous Devaux.

"Don't smirk, sir!" rasped Hope irritably.

"Beg pardon, sir," replied Devaux still smiling.

"Huh!" Hope turned away furious. Edgecumbe was a damned, worthless time-server half Hope's age. Hope had as much time as lieutenant to his credit as Edgecumbe had time at sea.

"Gig's ready, sir."

Drinkwater laid the gig alongside *Galatea*. He watched his captain's spindly legs disappear to a twittering of pipes. A face looked down at him.

"Moornin' lad." It was Lieutenant Collingwood.

"Morning sir."

"I see you have clean ducks on today," the officer smiled before bursting into a violent and debilitating fit of coughing. When he had caught his breath he held out a bundle wrapped in oiled paper.

"I have some mail for *Cyclops*," he called. "I believe there's an epistle from a Miss Bower . . ."

Elizabeth!

"Thank you, sir . . ." answered the delighted and surprised Drinkwater as the bundle was tossed into the boat. Collingwood began coughing again. It was the tuberculosis that a posting to the West Indies would shortly aggravate and which eventually killed Wilfred Collingwood. It was his brother Cuthbert who became Nelson's famous second-in-command.

Elizabeth!

Strange how the mention of her name out here on the heaving grey Atlantic had the power to cause his heart to thump in his breast. The man at stroke oar was grinning at him. He smiled back self-consciously. Then he realised the man was Threddle.

In *Galatea's* stern cabin Hope was sipping a glass of excellent claret. But he was not enjoying it.

Sir James Edgecumbe, his prematurely florid face and popeyes a contrast to Hope's thin, leathery countenance, was trying to be pleasantly superior and only succeeded in being offensive.

"I shall overlook the slackness in acknowledging my signal as due to the quality of your midshipmen, Captain. I had the experience of meeting one of 'em. A snotty boy with filthy garments. Clearly no gentleman, eh Captain?" He snorted a contemptuous laugh that was intended to imply that as captains they had problems only appreciated by other commanders. Hope bridled at the insult to *Cyclops*, wondering who the offending middy had been. He said nothing beyond a grunt, which Edgecumbe took for agreement.

"Yes, well, m'dear fella, the problem of rank, don't you know."

Hope said nothing. He was beginning to suspect Sir James of having an ulterior motive in summoning him.

"Well, as I say, Captain, problems of rank and exigencies of the Service. I'm not helped by m'Parliamentary duties either, B'God. Makes m'life in the public service a most arduous task I do assure ye."

"This leads me to a question, M'dear fella. How much food and water have ye?"

"About two months provisions I suppose, but if you're relieving me I don't see . . ."

Edgecumbe held up his hand.

"Ah, there's the rub, m'dear fella. I'm not you see . . ." Edgecumbe interrupted.

"More wine? At least," he said slowly in a harder voice, an edge of malice in it, ". . . at least I don't intend to." Hope swallowed.

"Are you trying to tell me something unpalatable, Sir James?"

Edgecumbe relaxed and smiled again. "Yes m'dear Captain. I would deem it a great favor if you would relieve me of a rather odious and fruitless task. In fact m'dear fella," he lowered his voice confidentially, "I have to be in Parliament shortly to support the Naval vote and one or two other measures. In these times every patriot should do his utmost. Don't you agree Captain. And I'm best serving my country, and you brave fellas, by strengthening the navy." He dropped the sham and the note of menace was again detectable. "It wouldn't do *either* of us any good if I missed it, now would it?" Hope did not like the inflections in Edgecumbe's speech.

He had the feeling he was being boxed into a corner.

"I trust Sir James that you will do your utmost to ensure that ships like *Foudroyant*, *Emerald* and *Royal George* are properly dry-docked . . ." Edgecumbe waved his hands inconsequentially.

"Those are mere details, Captain Hope, there are competent authorities in the dockyards to deal with such matters . . ."

Hope bit off an acidic reply as, from nowhere, the servant of Sir James appeared with a new bottle of claret. Edgecumbe avoided Hope's eyes and sorted through some papers. He looked up with a smile and held out a sealed envelope.

"Life's full of coincidences, eh Captain? This," he tapped the envelope, "is a draft, I believe, on Tavistock's Banking House. Had a bit of luck with prizes I hear, well, well, my wife's a daughter of old Tavistock. He's a mean old devil but I expect he'll honour an Admiralty draft for £4,000."

Hope swallowed the contents of his glass. He swore mentally. Righteous indignation was no weapon to use against this sort of thing. He wondered how many people had connived to get this little scene to run its prescribed course? So that he, Henry Hope, should do something unpleasant on behalf of Sir James in order that the latter should occupy his seat in Parliament. Or worse, perhaps Sir James had other reasons for not carrying out his orders. Hope felt sick and swallowed another glass of claret.

"I presume you have my change of orders in writing, Sir James," Hope asked suspiciously although he already knew he would be compelled to accept the inevitable.

"Of course! Did you suspect that I was acting unoffically, m'dear sir?" Edgecumbe's eyebrows were raised in outrage.

"Not at all, Sir James," replied Hope with perfect honesty, "Only there are occasions when one doubts the wisdom of their Lordships . . ."

Edgecumbe looked up sharply. Hope found the suspicion of treason vastly amusing. Edgecumbe held out another envelope.

"Your orders, Captain Hope," he said with asperity.

"And the odious and fruitless task, Sir James?"

"Ah!" breathed Edgecumbe, reaching for a strong box that had all the while been lurking by his chair.

In the cockpit the single lantern swayed with *Cyclop*'s violent motion. Its guttering flame cast fitful and fantastic shadows that made reading difficult. Drinkwater had waited until it was Morris's watch on deck. He had a vague feeling that if he attempted to read Elizabeth's letter in his presence it would somehow sully his image of her. For, although Morris had made no attempt to reassert himself as Drinkwater's superior, Nathaniel knew instinctively that Morris was playing a waiting game, covertly watching his fellow midshipman, probing for an opening that he could exploit. Reading Elizabeth's letter in his presence would almost certainly afford him some such opportunity.

Drinkwater opened the little package. Inside was a

second packet and a letter. The letter was dated a few days after his departure from Falmouth.

My Dear Nathaniel,

Lieutenant Collingwood had just come to say that he believes his frigate will be meeting Cyclops *early in the New Year. He came to settle the account for your (sic) funeral and when father said that it should be borne by your own ship he said he would reimburse himself when he met your Captain.*

Drinkwater bit his lip, annoyed that he had not thought of that himself. He read on,

All of which is a poor way of wishing you well. I hope you like the enclosure, father tells me you sea officers are inordinately vain of your first commands. It was done the morning after your first visit, but I did not think it good enough to give you before.

We have news that we shall move to Portsmouth in April and I pray that you will visit us there. Please God that you are unscathed by battle or disease, for I fear your Service uses men barbarously as poor Lieutenant Collingwood's cough testifies.

The weather had turned now and we expect a miserable winter. Father says prayers regularly now for the Navy. Now I must conclude in haste for L. Collingwood is just leaving.

God bless you,
Ever yours,
Elizabeth.

Drinkwater read the letter four times before opening the packet.

Inside, set in a small frame, was a tiny watercolor. It showed a sheet of water set round by green shores and the grey bastion of a castle. In the foreground was a ship, a little dark schooner with British over Yankee colours.

"*Algonquin*," he muttered aloud, holding the picture to the lantern. "*Algonquin* off St. Mawes . . ."

He tucked the picture safely in the bottom of his sea-chest, scrambled into his hammock and re-read Elizabeth's letter.

Elizabeth wished him safe and well. Perhaps Elizabeth loved him.

He lay basking in the inner warmth the news gave him. A kind of bursting laughter exploded somewhere inside his chest. A feeling of superhuman triumph and tenderness welled up within him, so that he chuckled softly to himself as *Cyclops* creaked to windward in the gale.

The month of January 1781 was one of almost continuous bad weather in the North Atlantic. The "families" of depressions that tracked obliquely across the great expanse of water dashed a French fleet to pieces on the rock-girt coasts of the Channel Islands. Two thousand French soldiers had embarked to capture the islands but hundreds perished as their troopships were smashed to bits. Eight hundred who got ashore at St. Helier almost succeeded in taking the town until twenty-six year old Major Pearson led a desperate bayonet charge in which the French were routed but the young man lost his life.

But it was not only the French fleet that had suffered. Earlier, in October of 1780, Rodney's West Indies Fleet had been virtually destroyed in a hurricane. Most of Hotham's squadron had been dismasted and six ships lost. Although Sir Samuel Hood was even then proceeding to Rodney's aid, things were going ill for British arms. The situation in North America, handled in a dilatory fashion by Lord North and Lord George Germaine, had become critical. None of the principals were to know it at the time but the combination of the Franco-American armies around an obscure peninsula on the James River in Virginia was to prove decisive. As Lord Cornwallis fought his way through the swamps and barrens of Carolina with a pathetically small army, Nathaniel Greene opposing him, "fought and ran, fought and ran again," slowly exhausting the British who staggered from one Phyrric victory after another in ever diminishing numbers.

In Gibraltar, Augustus Elliot and his little garrison

held out whilst *Cyclops* suffered the battering of the elements, herself like a half-tide rock.

Topgallant masts were struck and twice the frigate drove off before the wind, heading back towards the Europe that Hope strove to leave astern, bound as he was for the coast of Carolina.

Life between decks had resumed its dismal round, so familiar to the ship's company. Damp permeated every corner until fungi grew freely and men sickened with lassitude and discomfort. Once again the lash was employed with nauseating regularity. The men became surly and the atmosphere thick with discontent.

In this climate it was not only the spores of floral parasites that flourished. Such conditions seemed to release the latent energies of Midshipman Morris, perhaps because the ship was less efficiently policed, perhaps because in the prevailing environment men were less interested in reminding him of previous humiliation.

Morris's position as the senior midshipman was a puissant one, and young White was the chief recipient of Morris's unpleasantness. No sarcasm was too trifling but the opportunity must be taken to hurt the hapless child, for his voice had not yet broken and as yet no hair grew upon his upper lip. He was made to "fag" for Morris, although the latter was careful not to make this too obvious in either Drinkwater's or Cranston's presence. This treatment, served chiefly to terrorize the weak into a cringing obsequiousness that may possibly have served them well if they entered public life, but was no training for the officers of a man o' war.

One night, black and blue from a beating by Morris, the unfortunate White had lain unable to sleep. Tears had come to him and he lay quietly sobbing in the subterranean blackness of the cockpit.

On deck it had come on to rain. Drinkwater slipped below for his tarpaulin and found the boy weeping. For a moment he stood listening in the darkness, then, remembering Morris discovering him in identical circumstances, he went over to the boy.

"What's the matter, Chalky?" he inquired softly. "Are you sick?"

"N-no, sir."

"Don't 'sir' me, Chalky . . . it's me, Nat . . . what's the matter?"

"Nnn . . . nothing, Nnn . . . Nat . . . it's nothing."

It was not very difficult for Nathaniel to guess the person responsible for the boy's misery, but it was a measure of his worldliness that he assumed the crime fouler than mere bullying.

"Is it Morris, Chalky?"

The silence from the hammock had an eloquence of its own.

"It is, isn't it?"

A barely perceptible "Yes" came out of the gloom.

Drinkwater patted a thin and shaking shoulder. "Don't worry, Chalky, I'll fix him."

"Thanks . . . N . . . Nat," the boy choked and as Drinkwater crept away he heard a barely audible whisper: "Oh mmm . . . mother . . ."

Returning to duty Nathaniel Drinkwater received a rebuke from Lieutenant Skelton for leaving the deck.

The following day was Sunday and after divine service the watch below were piped to dinner. Drinkwater found himself at mess with Morris. Several other midshipmen were in the cockpit struggling with their salt pork. One of them was Cranston.

Drinkwater swallowed the remains of his blackstrap and then addressed Morris in tones of deliberate formality.

"Mr. Morris, as you are senior midshipman in this mess I have a request to make."

Morris looked up. A warning sounded in his brain as he recalled the last time Drinkwater had uttered such formal words to him. Although he had scarcely exchanged any word with his enemy beyond the minimum necessary to the conduct of the vessel he regarded Drinkwater with suspicion.

"Well, what is it?"

"Simply that you cease your abominable tyranny over young White."

Morris stared at Drinkwater. He flushed, then began casting angrily about.

"Why the damned little tell-tale, wait till I get hold of him . . ." he rose, but Drinkwater objected.

"He told me nothing Morris, but I'm warning you: leave him alone . . ."

"Ah, so you fancy him do you . . . like that fancy tart you've got at Falmouth . . ."

Drinkwater hadn't expected that. Then he remembered Threddle in the boat and the letter lying in his sea chest . . . for a second he was silent. It was too long. He had lost the initiative.

"And what will you do, Mister Bloody Drinkwater . . ." Morris was threatening him now . . .

"Thrash you as I did before . . ." maintained Drinkwater stoutly.

"Thrash me, be damned you had a cudgel . . ."

"We both had single st . . ." Drinkwater never finished the sentence. Morris's fist cracked into his jaw and he fell backwards. His head hit the deck. Morris leapt on him but he was already unconscious.

Morris stood up. Revenge was sweet indeed but he had not yet finished with Drinkwater. No, a more private and infinitely more malevolent fate would be visited on him, but for the present Morris was content . . . he had at least re-established his superiority over the bastard.

Morris dusted himself off and turned to the other midshipmen.

"Now you other, bastards. Remember ye'll get the same treatment if you cross me."

Cranston had not moved but remained seated, his grog in his hand. He brought the patient wisdom of the lower deck to confound Morris.

"Are you threatening me, Mr. Morris?" he asked in level tones. "Because if you are, I shall report you to the first lieutenant. Your attack on Mr. Drinkwater was unprovoked and constituted an offense for which you would flog a common seaman. I sincerely hope you have not fatally injured our young friend, for if you have I shall ensure you pay the utmost penalty the Articles of War permit."

Morris grew as pallid as *Cyclops*'s topsail. Such a long speech, from a normally silent man, delivered with such sonorous gravity gripped him with visceral fear. He looked anxiously at the prostrate Drinkwater.

Cranston turned to one of the other occupants of the mess. "Mr. Bennett, be so good as to cut along for the surgeon!"

"Yes, yes, of course . . ." The boy dashed out.

Morris stepped towards Drinkwater but Cranston forestalled him. "Get out!" he snapped with unfeigned anger.

Appleby entered the midshipmen's berth with a worried Bennett behind him. Cranston was already chafing the unconscious midshipman's wrists.

Appleby felt the pulse, "What occurred?" he enquired.

Cranston outlined the circumstances. Appleby lifted the eyelid.

"Mmmmmm . . . lend a hand . . ." Between them they got Drinkwater propped up and the latter held some smelling salts under the patient's nose.

Drinkwater groaned and Appleby felt around the base of the skull. "He'll have a headache but he'll mend." Another groan escaped Drinkwater's lips and his eyelids fluttered open, closed and opened again.

"Oh God, what the . . ."

"Easy, lad, easy. You've received a crack on the skull and another on the jaw but you'll live. You midshipmen get him into his hammock for a little while. You'll bear witness to this?" The last remark was addressed to Cranston.

"Aye if it's necessary," answered Cranston.

"I shall have to inform the First Lieutenant. It will remain to be seen whether the matter goes further." Appleby picked up his bag and left.

Devaux regarded the matter seriously. He was already

aware of some doubt as to the exact nature of Midshipman Morris's sexual proclivities and, though he was ignorant as to the extent Morris exerted an influence over certain elements of the ship's company, he realized the man was a danger. With the prevalent sullen atmosphere on board it only needed some stupid incident like this to provoke more trouble. With the rapidity of a bush fire one such outbreak led to another and it was impossible to hush such things up. The unpunished breach of discipline in the midshipman's mess might lead to God knew what horrors. He sought an interview with Captain Hope.

He found Hope more concerned with their landfall on the coast of the Carolinas than with the future of Mr. Midshipman Augustus Morris.

"Do you think fit, Mr. Devaux," he said without looking up from the chart, "now I pray your attention on this chart . . ."

For a few moments the two men studied the soundings and coastline.

"What exactly is our purpose in making a landfall here, sir?" asked Devaux at last.

Hope looked up at him. "I suppose you had better be aware of the details of this mission since any mishap to myself necessitates the duty devolving upon yourself . . . we are to make a landing here . . ." Hope pointed to the chart.

"We will rendezvous with a detachment of troops at Fort Frederic, probably the British Legion, a provincial corps under Colonel Tarleton. An accredited officer will accept the package in my strong box. In the package are several millions of Continental dollars . . ."

Devaux whistled.

"The Continental Congress," Hope continued, "has already debased the credit of its own currency to such a state that the flooding of the markets of rebel areas will ruin all credibility in its own ability to govern, and bring large numbers of the Yankees over to the Loyalist cause. I believe large raids are planned on the Virginny tobacco lands to further ruin the rebel economy."

"I see, sir," mused Devaux. The two men considered the matter, then the younger said, "It does seem a deucedly odd way of suppressing rebellion, sir."

"It does indeed, Mr. Devaux, decidedly odd. But my Lord George Germaine, His Majesty's Secretary for the Colonies, seems to be of the opinion that it is infallible."

"Ha, Germaine!" snorted the indignant Devaux. "Let's hope he exercises better judgment than at Minden."

Hope said nothing. At his age youthful contempt was an expenditure of energy that was entirely fruitless. He took refuge in silent cynicism. Germaine, North, Sandwich, Arbuthnot and Clinton, the naval and military commanders in North America, they were all God's appointed . . .

"Thank you Mr. Devaux."

"Thank you, sir," replied Devaux, picking up his hat and leaving the cabin.

Morris was below when the first lieutenant summoned him. Ironically it was White who brought the message. Sensing no threat from the boy Morris swaggered out.

"Sir?"

"Ah, Mr. Morris," began Devaux considerately, "I understand there has been some difference of opinion between you and your messmates, is this so, sir?"

"Well, er, yes as a matter of fact that is so, sir. But the matter is settled, sir."

"To your satisfaction I presume," asked the first lieutenant, scarcely able to disguise the sarcasm in his voice.

"Yes, sir."

"But not to mine," Devaux looked hard at Morris. "Did you strike first?"

"Well, sir, I, er . . ."

"Did you, sir, did you?"

"Yes, sir," whispered Morris, scarcely audible.

"Were you provoked?"

Morris sensed a trap. He could not claim to have been provoked since Cranston would testify against him and that would further militate in his disfavor.

He contented himself with a sullen shrug.

"Mr. Morris, you are a source of trouble on this ship and I ought to break you, never mind stretching your neck under the Twenty Ninth Article of War . . ." Morris's face paled and his breath drew in sharply. "But I shall arrange to transfer you to another ship when we rejoin the fleet. Do not attempt to obtain a berth aboard any ship of which I am first lieutenant or by God I'll have you thrown overboard. In the meantime you will exert no influence in the cockpit, d'ye understand?"

Morris nodded.

"Very well, and for now you will ascend the foretopgallant and remain there until I consider your presence on deck is again required."

Chapter Thirteen February 1781

The Action with La Creole

His Britannic Majesty's 36-gun frigate *Cyclops* was cleared for action, leaning to a stiff southwesterly breeze, close hauled on the port tack. To windward the chase was desperately trying to escape. As yet colors had broken out at her peak, but the opinion current aboard *Cyclops* was that she was American.

She had the appearance of an Indiaman but cynics reminded their fellows that Captain Pearson had been compelled to surrender to Paul Jones in the *Bonhomme Richard*. She had been an Indiaman.

On his quarterdeck Hope silently prayed she would be a merchant ship. If so she would prove an easy prey. If she operated under letters of marque she might prove a tougher nut to crack. What was more important was that Hope wished his arrival on the coast to be secret. Whatever the chase turned out to be Hope wanted to secure her.

Devaux urged him to hoist French colors but Hope demurred. He had little liking for such deceptions and ordered British colors hoisted. After a while the chase brailed up his courses and broke out the American flag.

"Ah there! He's going to accept battle. To your posts, gentlemen, this will be warm work. Do you likewise with the courses, Mr. Blackmore, and take the topgallants off her . . ."

Shortened down for the ponderous maneuvers of formal battle, *Cyclops* closed with her enemy. In the foretop Drinkwater peered under the leech of the fore-topsail.

There was something odd about the ship they were approaching.

"Tregembo . . . clap your eyes on yon ship . . . do you notice anything peculiar . . . ?"

The Cornishman left his swivel and peered to where the enemy vessel lay to, seemingly awaiting the British frigate.

"No zur . . . but wait, there's siller at her rail. No . . . it's gone now . . ." He straightened up, scratching his head.

"Did you see flashes of silver?"

"Aye, zur, leastways I thought I did . . ."

Drinkwater looked aft. Cranston in the main-top waved at him and he waved back, suddenly making his mind up. He swung himself over into the futtock shrouds.

On the quarterdeck he bumped into Morris who was now signal midshipman.

"What the hell are you doing aft?" hissed Morris, "Get forward to your station, pig!" Drinkwater dodged round him and hovered at Hope's coat tails.

"Sir! Sir!"

"What the devil?" Hope and Devaux turned at the intrusion of their vigilant watch on the closing American.

"Sir, I believe I saw the sun on bayonets from the foretop . . ."

"Bayonets, by God . . ." Wheeler too whirled at the military word. Then he turned again and clapped his glass to his eye. Briefly visible the sun caught the flash of steel again.

"Aye bayonets by God, sir! He's a company or two there sir, damned if he hasn't . . ." exclaimed the marine officer.

"You'll be damned if he has, sir," retorted Hope, "so he wants to grapple and board with infantry . . . Mr. Devaux, lay her off a little and aim for his top hamper."

"Aye, aye, sir." Devaux went off roaring orders.

"Thank you, Mr. Drinkwater, you may return to your station."

"Aye, aye, sir . . ."

"Lickspittle!" hissed Morris as he passed.

Hope's assessment had been correct. The enemy ship had indeed been a French Indiaman but was then operating under a commission signed by George Washington himself. Despite her American authority she was commanded by a Frenchman of great daring who had been cruising under the rebel flag since the Americans first appealed for help from the adventurous youth of Europe.

This officer had on board a part battalion of American Militia who, though recently driven out of Georgia by their Loyalist countrymen, had recovered their bravado after receiving a stirring harangue from their ally and were now eager to fire their muskets again.

Although Hope had correctly assessed his opponent's tactics he was too late to avoid them. As the two vessels opened fire on one another the enemy freed off a little and bore down towards the British ship. As they closed her name was visible across her transom: *La Creole*.

La Creole's main yard fouled *Cyclops*'s cro'jack yard and the two vessels came together with a jarring crash. The pounding match already started continued unabated, despite the fact that the gun muzzles almost touched. Already the adjacent bulwarks of the two ships were reduced to a shambles and the deadly splinters were lancing through the smoke laden air. *Cyclops*'s shot had destroyed the enemy's two boats on the gratings and the stray balls and resultant splinters were unnerving the militia. The French commander, knowing delay was fatal, leapt on to the rail and waved the Americans on. His own polyglot crew followed him.

The tide of boarders swirled downwards over the upper deck gunners and Wheeler brought his after guard of marines forward in a line.

"Forward! Present! Fire!" They let off a volley and reloaded with the ease of practice, spitting the balls into their muzzles and banging the musket stocks on the deck to avoid the time consuming ritual of the ramrod.

Back in the foretop, Drinkwater discharged the swivel into the throng as it poured aboard. He reloaded then turned to find Tregembo wrestling with a sallow desperado who had appeared from nowhere. Looking up, Drinkwater saw more men running like monkeys along the enemy's yards and into *Cyclops*'s rigging. In the main top Cranston was coolly picking off any who attempted to lash the yards of the two ships, but men were coming aboard via the topsail yards and sliding down the forestays in a kind of hellish circus act.

On the maindeck the gun crews continued to serve their pieces. Occasionally the rammer working at the exposed muzzle would receive a jab from an enemy boarding pike until Devaux ordered the ports closed when reloading. It slowed the rate of fire but made the men attentive and reduced the risk of premature explosions through skimpy sponging. Small arms fire crackled above their heads and a small face appeared at Lieutenant Keene's elbow. It was little White.

"Sir! Sir! Please allow the starboard gun crews on deck, sir, we are hard pressed . . ."

Keene turned. "Starbowlines!" he roared, "Boarding pikes and cutlasses!" The order was picked up by the bosun's mates and the men, assisting their mates at the larboard guns, ran for the small arms recks around the masts.

"Skelton, do you take command here!"

Keene adjusted the martingale of his hanger on his wrist. Turning to White he managed a lopsided smile, "Come on young shaver . . ."

White pulled out his toy dirk.

"Starbowlines! Forrard Companionway! Follow me!"

A ragged cheer broke out, barely audible amid the thunder of the adjacent guns. But it broke into a furious yell as the men emerged onto the sunlit deck where the mêlée was now desperate. Although the attempts of the rebels to enter *Cyclops* through the main deck ports had been repulsed, on the upper deck it was a different story.

The initial shock of the boarding party had carried them well on to the British frigate's quarterdeck. At the extreme after end Wheeler and his marines were drawn into a line loading and firing behind a precise hedge of bayonets. After a few sallies the boarders drew back and turned their attention to the forward end where the resistance, led by Lieutenant Devaux, was fierce but piecemeal, the seamen and officers defending themselves as best they might.

Although the American militia were unsteady troops they fought well enough against the seamen and gradually began to overwhelm the defenders. Once the Americans reached the waist in force they could drop down into the gundeck and their possession of the British frigate was only a matter of time. The fighting was fierce, a confusion of musketry, pistol flashes and slashing blades. Men screamed with rage or pain, officers shouted orders, their voices hoarse with exhaustion or shrill with fear and all the while the two ships discharged their main batteries at each other at point blank range in a continuous cacophony of rumbling concussions, the smoke of which rolled over the frightful business above.

Poor Bennett, forced over a gun, died of a bayonet wound. Stewart, the master's mate, weakened by the consequences of his amorous adventure at Falmouth, parried the French commander's sword but failed to riposte. The Frenchman was quicker and Stewart fell in his own gore on the bloody deck.

From the foretop Drinkwater was uncertain of the progress of the fight below since it was obscured by powder smoke. Between the fore and main tops the treat of aerial invasion via the rigging seemed to have been stemmed when Drinkwater heard the yells of Keene's counter attack. He was on the American where more men were assembling to attack. They sent a case of langridge into the Rebel waist: men fell, dispersed and reassembled. Drinkwater's gun fired again.

"Two rounds left, zur!" Tregembo shouted in his ear.

"Blast it!" he shouted back. "What the hell do we do then . . . ?"

"Dunno zur." The man looked below. "Join in down there, zur?" Drinkwater looked down. The gunfire seemed to have eased and the wind cleared some of the smoke. He saw White, his dirk flashing, shoved aside by an American who lunged at a British warrant officer. The master's mate took the thrust on the thigh and the American grimaced as the spurned White stabbed him in the side. Devaux, with his hanger whirling in one hand and a clubbed pistol in the other, was laying about himself like a maniac urging on Keene's men and the remnants of the upper deck guncrews.

Aft of him Drinkwater saw Cranston out on the main yard arm cutting away any gear that bound the two ships together.

Of course, they must pry *Cyclops* away from the rebel ship.

"We must separate the two ships, Tregembo!"

"Aye, zur, but she'm to wind'ard."

It was true. The wind's pressure was holding *La Creole*'s hull alongside *Cyclops* as efficiently as if they were lashed together. Drinkwater looked below again and his eyes rested on the anchors. Earlier in the day Devaux had had the hands bending a cable to the sheet anchor as they closed the American coast. All they had to do was to let it go.

"The sheet anchor, Tregembo!" he shouted excitedly, pointing downwards.

Tregembo instantly grasped the idea. They both leapt for the forestay. The anchor was secured to the starboard fore channels by chain. The chains terminated in pear links through which many turns of hemp lashing were passed, securing the anchor to the ship.

Snatching out his knife Tregembo attacked the stock lashing whilst Drinkwater went for that at the crown.

The shouting, screaming mass of struggling men were only feet away from them yet, because *La Creole* had come aboard on *Cyclops*'s port quarter, the fo'c's'le was a comparative haven. Then someone in the privateer's tops opened fire with a musket. The ball struck the anchor fluke and whined away in ricochet. Sweat rolled off the two men and Drinkwater began to curse his fine idea, thinking the seizing would never part. His head throbbed with the din of battle and the bruise that Morris had given him. Another ball smacked into the deck between his feet. His back felt immensely huge, a target the marksman could not fail to hit at the next shot.

Tregembo grunted, his seizing parted and the sudden jerk snapped the remaining strands of Drinkwater's. The anchor dropped with a splash.

"I hope to God the cable runs . . ."

It did, enough at least to permit the anchor to reach the bottom where it bit, broke loose and bit again, snubbing the two ships round head to the current that runs inexorably north east up the coast of Florida and Carolina. The current pulled each hull, but *Cyclops* held, her anchor bringing her up against the force of it. Drinkwater moved aft. He was the first to detect a grinding between the ships that told where *La Creole* slowly disengaged herself from her foe.

"She's off lads, we've got 'em!" One head turned, then another, then all at once the British rallied, seeing over their heads the movement in the enemy's ship.

They took up the cry and with renewed vigor carried on the work of stabbing and cutting their adversaries. Looking over their shoulders the Franco-Americans began to realise what was going on. The militia were the first to break, running and scrambling over friend and foe alike.

La Creole scraped slowly aft, catching frequently and only tearing herself finally clear of *Cyclops* after a minute or two. Sufficient time elapsed for most of her men to return to her, for the exhausted British let them go. The final scenes of the action would have been comic if they had not occurred in such grim circumstances with the dead and dying of three nations scattered about the bloody deck.

Several men leapt overboard and swam to where their comrades were lowering ropes over the side. One of these was the French commander who gesticulated fiercely from the dramatic eminence of the frigate's rail before plunging overboard and swimming strongly for his own ship.

On *Cyclops's* gangway a negro was on his knees, rolling his eyes, his hands clasped in an unmistakable gesture of submission. Seeing Drinkwater almost alone in the forepart of the ship, the negro flung himself down at his feet. Behind him Devaux seemed bent on running him through, a Devaux with blood lust in his eyes . . .

"No, no massa, Ah *do* surrenda sah! Jus' like that Gen'ral Burgoyne, sah, Ah do surrenda!" It was Wheeler who eventually overcame the first lieutenant and brought him to his senses by telling him the captain wanted him aft. The negro, thankfully ignored, attached himself to Drinkwater.

The two ships were now two cables apart. Neither of them was in a fit condition to re-engage immediately.

"That," said Captain Hope to Mr. Blackmore as they emerged from the defensive hedge made for them by Wheeler and his marines, "that was a damned close thing!"

The sailing master nodded with unspoken relief. Hope barked a short, nervous laugh.

"The devil'll have to wait a little longer for us, eh Blackmore?"

La Creole drifted astern.

"Cut that cable, mister," ordered Hope when Devaux eventually reached him, "and find out who let the anchor go."

"Might I suggest we weight it, sir . . ."

"Cut it, dammit, I want to re-engage before he spreads the news of our arrival on the coast . . ."

Devaux shrugged and turned forward.

Hope turned to the sailing master. "We're in soundings then."

"Aye, sir," said the old man, recollecting himself.

"Make sail, we'll finish that rebel first."

But *La Creole* was already shaking out her canvas. She was to leeward and soon under way. Fifteen minutes later *Cyclops* was before the wind, two and three quarter miles astern of the privateer.

That was still the position when darkness set in.

Below, in the cockpit, Drinkwater sat having his shoes polished by the negro. He was unable to rid himself of the encumbrance and in the aftermath of action no one seemed to bother about the addition to *Cyclops*'s complement.

"What's your name?" he asked, fascinated by the ebony features of the man.

"Mah name, sah, is Ach'lles and Ah am your serbant . . ."

"My servant?" said Drinkwater, astonished.

"Yes sah! You sabe ma life. Ach'lles your best fre'nd."

Chapter Fourteen March 1781

The Best Laid Plans of Mice and Men . . .

Daylight revealed *Cyclops* alone within the circle of her visible horizon. *La Creole* had given her the slip and Captain Hope was furious that her arrival on the coast would now be broadcast. He now had no alternative but to execute his orders as speedily as possible.

He waited impatiently for noon and Blackmore's meridian altitude. When the master had made his calculations he brought the answer to Hope: "Our latitude is thirty four degrees twelve minutes north, sir. That is," he glanced at his slate, "that is forty three miles to the north of our landfall although we shall have to weather Frying Pan shoals."

Hope nodded. "Very well, make the necessary arrangements and be kind enough to attend me with the first lieutenant . . . and, er, Mr. Blackmore, have young Drinkwater bring your charts down here . . ."

When the master reappeared with Devaux, Hope cordially invited them to sit. Drinkwater spread the charts out on the table between them.

"Ah, hhmmm, Mr. Drinkwater," began Hope. "The first lieutenant has informed me that it was you that let go the sheet anchor during the late action with *La Creole*?"

"Er, yes, sir. I was assisted by Tregembo, fore-topman, but I take full responsibility for the loss of the anchor . . ."

"Quite so, quite so . . ."

"If you'll permit me to observe, sir," broke in Devaux, "it may well have saved the ship."

Hope looked up sharply. There was the smallest hint of reproach in Devaux's voice. But Hope had not the energy for anger, his glance caught Blackmore's. Barely perceptibly the old master shrugged his shoulders. Hope smiled to himself. Old men saw things differently . . .

"Quite so, Mr. Devaux. Mr. Drinkwater, I wish to congratulate you on your initiative. It is a quality which you appear to possess in abundance. I shall do what I can for you and if I fail I am sure Mr. Devaux will prompt me . . . in the meantime I would be delighted if you and Mr. Cranston together with Lieutenant Wheeler, Mr. Devaux and yourself, Master, would join me at dinner. Who will have the watch, Mr. Devaux?"

"Lieutenant Skelton, sir."

"Very well, we had better have Keene and of course no dinner aboard *Cyclops* would be complete without an after-dinner speaker in the shape of the surgeon. Please see to it . . . Now Mr. Drinkwater, the charts . . ."

The men bent over the table, their bodies moving automatically to the motion of the frigate.

"Our destination," began the captain, "is the mouth of the Galuda River here, in Long Bay. As you observe there is a bar but within the river mouth there is a small fort: Fort Frederic. Our task is to enter the river, pass to the garrison such stores and munitions as they require and to hand a certain package to some sort of agent. The details of this are known to Mr. Devaux and need not concern us here . . ." Hope paused and wiped his forehead. He resumed. "When we close the coast we will send boats in ahead to sound the channel into the anchorage."

Devaux and Blackmore nodded.

"To be on the safe side we will clear for action as we enter the river, and put a spring on the cable when we anchor. I do not intend being here a moment longer than is absolutely necessary, for I fear our late adversary will come looking for us with reinforcements." Hope tapped the chart with the dividers.

"Any questions, gentlemen?"

Devaux cleared his throat. "If I am not mistaken, sir, you are as apprehensive of this operation as I am . . . ?" Hope said nothing, merely stared at the lieutenant.

"I mislike the whole thing, sir. It had a smell about it, I . . ."

"Mr. Devaux," bristled Hope, "it is not part of your duties to question orders, I imagine their Lordships know their business." Hope spoke with a conviction he was far from feeling, his own misgivings lending his voice an asperity that was over-severe.

But Devaux knew nothing of the circumstances of Hope's reception of his orders. To him Hope was no longer the man who had towed the *Santa Teresa* off the San Lucar shoal. The tedious weeks of patrol had wearied him, the worry over prize-money had worn him and he had learned from Wheeler how Hope and Blackmore had taken an abject refuge behind a steel hedge of bayonets in the recent fight. Devaux's reaction was jaundiced for he, too, had been subject to the same strains for similar reasons. But he saw Hope now as a timid old man, blindly obeying the orders dished up by a hated Tory cabal . . . he mastered his impatience with difficulty; events had conspired against him . . .

"With respect, sir, why send us to this remote spot to cripple the rebel economy with counterfeit bills?" Blackmore looked up with sudden interest and Drinkwater had the sense to remain absolutely motionless. Hope opened his mouth to protest but Devaux ploughed on. "Why not get them through New York where Clinton's agents must have a clearing house? Or Virginny where the rebel wealth really comes from? Even New England is better than the Carolinas . . ."

"Mr. Devaux! I must remind you that what I told you was in confidence . . . but since you lack the self-control I had thought to be an attribute of your class I will explain, as much for your benefit as for these other gentlemen here . . . And I must ask you to treat the matter with confidence . . . The Carolinas are in Lord Cornwallis's hands, Mr. Devaux. I assume the notes are for him. He is, I believe, extending operations under Major Ferguson into the back country where, I presume, the money is required. That is all, gentlemen . . ."

Drinkwater left the captain with a profound sense of disquiet. He knew his presence had been an embarrassment to Captain Hope, who might have dealt more sharply with the first lieutenant had the midshipman not been there. But there was more than the rift between captain and first lieutenant to set his mind working. The negro Achilles had been telling odd stories in the cockpit. Stories that did not tally with Hope's pat summary of the military situation in the Carolinas.

After some thought Drinkwater sought out Wheeler and consulted him. It was a breach of the captain's confidence in him but, under the circumstances that appeared to prevail ashore, he felt confident in so doing.

"Well, young shaver, we'd better go and have a word with your friend . . . what d'ye say he is . . . your servant?"

"He claims the right. Says I saved his life . . ."

"Get him to come up to the gunroom . . ."

They found Achilles to be an intelligent man who had been a plantation slave. When the British Military authorities offered freedom to any negroes who took up arms against the rebels, Achilles had forthwith escaped and promptly obtained his release from bondage. Soon obtaining a post as officer's servant to a lieutenant in the 23rd Foot, he had been separated from his master at the battle of Camden and, by an evil fate, captured by the son of his former owner who was then a captain in the militia battalion that later embarked in *La Creole*.

His unique position, ready wit and intelligent powers of observation had made him a favorite with officers of the 23rd and made him privy to many of their conversations. This had given him a reasonably accurate idea of the real military state of South Carolina. Wheeler set about extracting as much information as possible. He had little trouble since Achilles had a great love of the splendid scarlet soldiers and enjoyed their attention and amusement, contrasting their indolent disinterest with his former owner's ferocity.

"Yes, sah, dis war is no good, sah. Dere is not enuff ob de reg'lar sojers in de Carolinas, sah. Dat Major Ferguson, he dam' fine sojer, sah, but dey Tory milisha all dam' trash an' no more join afta Maj' Ferguson get kill up on dat ole King's Mount'n."

Wheeler whistled. So the brilliant Patrick Ferguson was dead. The best shot in the British Army, who had invented a breech loading rifle, who fenced with his left hand when he lost the use of his right at the Brandywine, had been killed. The negro rolled his eyes dolorously.

"What about Lord Cornwallis then, Achilles?"

"He dam' fine sojer too, sah! He lick dat Yankee rebel Gates and whip him proper at Camden. Gates he ride sixty mile after de battle, yesss sah! But poor Ach'lles, sah, Ah get the wrong side o' sum trees an' ah run smack inta mah old boss's son who is mighty mad, cos he'm runnin from dey redcoats . . ."

"Yes, yes, Achilles, you've told us all that but what about his Lordship . . . ?"

"He keep marchin'," replied the negro sitting bolt upright and making little swinging gestures with his arms, "an' he keep fi'tin' but he nebber stop, so de officers ob the Twenty Third, they say he nebber win nuffin'."

"What do you mean?"

"Well, sah. Afta Gen'ral Gates gone back to dam' Congress wiv his lil' ole tail hangin' 'tween his legs they send Gen'ral Greene down an' Gen'ral Greene he wun dam' fine sojer too, eben s'posin' he a rebel 'cos all de officers of de Twenty Third say so, sah!" Achilles was defensive, as if in admiring Greene he be thought to sympathize with the rebels. Then a puzzled look came over his face.

"Ah don' rightly unnerstand but dat Genr'l Greene he jus' don' know when he' beat. He fight, then he run, then he fight an' run agen . . . but he jus' don' get beat . . ." Achilles shook his head in incomprehension, his eyes rolling expressively.

"Ma Lord Cornwallis he send dat Lord Rawdon here an' dere, an' he send dat Co'nel Tarleton here and dere and dem two fine sojers dey charge up an' down the swamp lands tryin' for to catch de Swamp Fox an' de Gamecock . . ."

"The *what*?" queried Wheeler, grinning in spite of himself.

"Dey de names of de rebel raiders, sah. Dam' clebber men. Dey say dey look jus' like trees all de time. Dey nearly get caught by Tarleton one, two time but always de 'scape. Maybe dey nobody," Achilles hinted darkly, ". . . Maybe de voodoo . . ." Again Achilles shook his head and rolled his eyes.

"De war no good for us Loy'lists, sah. De reg'lar loy'lists fight like wild cats, sah. De reg'lar redcoat sojers dey fight better'n any dam' Yankees but dere jus' ain't enuff, sah. Dat's all, sah. Ach'lles tell you truth, sah. Ebbery word. I hear all de officers say dis, plenty times, sah, and de Twenty Third one dam' fine corp' of fine fuzileer, sah."

Despite the seriousness of his news Wheeler could not stifle his laughter at the negro. At the end of his monologue Achilles had risen to his feet and come stiffly to attention to give due importance to the mention of His Majesty's Royal Welch Fusileers. Regrettably his zealous action had ended in sharp contact with the overhead deckbeams which were too low to accomodate the negro at full height. His swift reduction to a crouching position caused Wheeler and Drinkwater to burst out laughing.

"Very well, Achilles. And what about you . . . you may volunteer for service in the navy . . ."

"Don' know nuffin' 'bout no navy, sah," said Achilles with feeling rubbing his bruised head . . . "Achilles dam' fine servant, sah . . ."

"Well in that case I think you had better attend to me . . ."

"Ac'lles dis gennelman's servant, sah." He indicated Drinkwater loyally.

Wheeler looked at Drinkwater. "I don't know what the Hon. John will say to that, cully . . . I should get him appointed to messman . . ."

Wheeler took the news to Devaux who snorted with exasperation when he heard it.

"Young Nat was pretty perceptive to realize the significance of the nigger's intelligence."

"Not really," said the first lieutenant, still angry with Hope. He tossed off a tankard of flip and wiped the back of his hand across his mouth. "He was in the cabin when the Old Man re . . . oh, dammit, when *I* blew up and revealed all . . . still perhaps it's an ill wind. At least my suspicions are confirmed . . ."

"What'll we do?" Devaux thought for a bit, then poured another tankard of flip.

"Listen, Wheeler, I'll raise it conversationally at dinner tonight. Do you back me up . . ."

It was inconceivable that the mission should not come up during the meal as the prime subject of conversation. The poor quality of the food served to remind them all that they had been pitched across the North Atlantic with insufficient provisions for a prolonged stay on the coast. Indeed it was Hope who broached the subject in general terms, explaining their presence off the Carolinas.

"I still don't see why they had to send a frigate to this desolate destination of ours. It doesn't make military, naval or any other kind of sense to me," opined Devaux cautiously, seeking to channel the drift of talk. But Appleby, sensing an opening for more expansive dialogue, beat Hope to the breach. Drinkwater sat open-mouthed at the pedagogic delivery of the surgeon.

"If you will permit me, gentlemen, to offer an opinion on your preoccupation . . ." Devaux sighed resignedly and Hope could scarcely suppress a smile. "Your naivety does you great credit, Mr. Devaux . . ." Devaux protested. "Nay, hear me out, I beg. It seems to me, and with all due respect to Captain Hope, that this operation of ours is a political expedient not a military or naval exercise and therefore, if I may say so, not so readily comprehensible to you gallant gentlemen of the sword."

Well, well, thought Hope. Either Appleby was psychic or omniscient.

"Imagine, messieurs, it was obviously conceived by a politician, who else has been passing Coercive Acts and playing at warfare with Parliamentary statutes? Why politicians! Milords North and Germaine hatched this one up! Germaine probably told North this was the very thing to do. Wouldn't cost much. Print a few million notes, ruin the rebel economy, bring Congress to its knees. No need for more troops, no credit to general officers or admirals but . . . and here's the beauty of it . . . brilliant stroke by Milordships!"

There was a rumble of appreciation from the officers assembled round the table and lounging back in their chairs.

"You perceive the outline, gentlemen. The idea hatched by a man cashiered for cowardice after Minden but with a skin as thick as hide . . . and a changed name to hide under."

"Sackville by God!" exclaimed Wheeler, ignoring Appleby's pun. "I had clean forgot. Didn't the king himself strike Sackville off the Army list with an injunction that he was never to serve again in a military capacity?"

"Exactly so, my dear sir, the late king certainly did. And what is this creature now? Why, none other than the virtual director of military operations in the Americas, a continent of which he knows nothing. Baré does, but the Government ignores the good colonel. Burke and Fox and Chatham realized, but nobody took any heed of them. So here *we* are!" Appleby expelled his breath contentedly looking round as if expecting applause.

"You are not quite right about Germaine, Mr. Appleby." Appleby frowned and looked round to see who dared to contradict him. It was Cranston.

"I *beg* your pardon?" he said archly.

"Lord George Germaine might well be exactly what

you say but he has as his Secretary an American Loyalist who is reckoned to be an expert in several fields. His name is Benjamin Thompson."

"Pah!" retorted Appleby. "Thompson is his catamite!" Drinkwater had not the slightest notion what a catamite was except that it was clearly something suspect, for sniggers and grins appeared on several faces.

"I think Mr. Appleby, that Cranston has a point," Hope spoke with quiet authority but Appleby was not to be gainsaid.

"I disagree sir."

"So do I sir. The facts alone speak for themselves. Surely Thompson, if he is the genius he claims to be, knows far more damage can be done the rebels by us arriving off Charleston or New York?" Devaux tried again to manipulate the conversation's direction.

"Ah! There's the rub don't you see," plunged in Appleby once again. "Germaine turns to Thompson. 'Damme Benjamin,'" he mimicked Germaine's reputedly haughty tones, "'I don't like Clinton, irresolute little fella and that damned traitor Arnold's in his suite, probably playing a double game. Best not send the cash there.' Germaine turns to map: 'Where shall we send it then Benjamin? To Cornwallis, damme never liked his wall-eyes, or his second, young Rawdon, or that dammed know-all Ferguson . . .'"

"Ferguson's dead," Wheeler intoned flatly.

Appleby raised his eyebrows imploringly heavenward at the interruption.

"'. . . no, no that won't do at all. Benjamin. Bring that map nearer; now which bit is Carolina? Ah yes, well how about there!'" Eyes closed Appleby stabbed the damask tablecloth with his finger, then opened them and looked down at the imaginary map. "'That will do fine, Benjamin, see to it for it is now five of the clock and I must to the tables for an hour or two's relaxation . . .' Picks up hat, exeunt." Appleby sat back at last, smirked and folded his hands across his stomach.

Several officers clapped languidly. They all smiled smugly with the generous contempt sailors reserve for politicians . . . after all, the smiles seemed to say, what does one expect . . .

Hope clearly had to dispel such thoughts from the minds of his men. It was an attitude that begot carelessness.

"I find your assessment amusing, Mr. Appleby, but inaccurate. That *Cyclops* has been ordered to carry out a part which to us seems incomprehensible is scarcely a new situation in naval war. The whole essence of the naval service is an adherence to orders without which nothing can be achieved . . ."

"Sir," said Devaux slowly and deliberately, "Lieutenant Wheeler has interrogated the negro who surrendered from *La Creole*. The blackamoor informs us that the Carolinas are in a state of utter confusion with no man knowing who has the upper hand. Lord Cornwallis has insufficient troops to do more than hold a few posts and chase the rebels."

It was enough for hope. "Mr. Devaux,." he almost shouted, "What do you expect a damn nigger to say—he's a rebel. D'ye think he's going to tell us we're winning . . . ?"

But Devaux was equally flushed. "For God's sake hear me out, sir," he altercated, "in the first place he's Loyalist with papers to prove it, and that's no mean achievement considering he's been with the rebels, in the second he's a slave freed by ourselves so hardly likely to sympathize with the rebels and voluntarily submit to slavery, and in the third he's been batman to a lieutenant in the 23rd Foot."

"And I suppose," replied Hope sarcastically, "that you consider all that cast iron proof that every word is true . . . ?" He was really, deeply angry now. Angry with Devaux and Appleby for voicing the doubts in his own heart, angry with himself for submitting so tamely to the blandishments of Edgecumbe and the £4,000 prize money which was not one whit the more use to him on this side of the ocean, and angry with the whole system that had created this ridiculous situation.

"Time will tell, sir, which of us is right . . ."

"That's as may be, mister, but it will not stop us all doing our duty," the captain looked meaningfully round the assembled officers. Their averted gazes and embarrassed complexions further angered him.

He rose and the officers scrambled to their feet. "You, Mr. Devaux, may take such measures as you see fit in the way of precaution. Good night, gentlemen!"

A screech of chairs and buzz of retreat accompanied the departure of the officers. Devaux's words rang in his ears:

"Time will tell, sir, which of us is right . . ."

The trouble was Hope already knew . . .

Drinkwater left the dinner with the uncomfortable feeling that he had witnessed something he should not have done. He had hitherto considered Hope's position as unassailable and was shocked by Devaux's outspoken attack. In addition he was surprised at the giggling of some of the dinner guests, particularly Devaux and Wheeler, who seemed in some curious way pleased with what they had achieved. But perhaps it was the face of Blackmore that he remembered most. The old man's white hair was drawn severely back and his face passed the midshipman like a kind of fixed figurehead. The expression it bore as it passed Wheeler and Devaux was one of utter contempt.

Drinkwater followed Cranston below. In the shadows of the orlop an arm reached out and grabbed his elbow. His exclamation was silenced by a face with a commanding finger held to its barely visible lips. It was Sharples.

"What do you want?" whispered Drinkwater, unable to shake off the foreboding engendered by the recent conversation. Somehow the appearance of Sharples, whom he had ignored for months now, came as no surprise.

"Beg pardon, sir. You ought to know I believe Threddle and Mr. Morris are hatching something up, sir. Thought you ought to know, sir . . ." Drinkwater felt his arm released and Sharples melted away in the shadows . . .

Drinkwater entered the cockpit.

"So you are back from your dinner at the captain's table, eh?"

Morris's voice was loaded with venom. At first Drinkwater did not reply. Then, aware that Cranston was still in the mess he decided to bait his enemy.

"Tell me Morris, why do you hate me?"

"Because, lickspittle, you are less than a dog's turd, yet you have been a source of trouble for me ever since you came aboard this ship. You are an insufferable little bastard . . ."

Drinkwater's fists clenched and he shot a look at Cranston. The older man was disinterestedly climbing into his hammock. "I'll call on you for satisfaction when we get to New York for that remark . . ."

"Ah! But now now, eh? Not so bloody bold without a cudgel are you? Bit more careful of our pretty face since we got that little whore in Falmouth aren't we, or is it because you're keeping company with the officers now, Wheeler's quite a dandy-boy now isn't he . . ." Drinkwater paled at the allusion to Elizabeth but he held his rage. He saw Cranston, sitting up in his hammock, making negative motions with his hands. Morris was working himself up into a violent rage, a torrent of invective streaming from him in which he worked through every obscenity known to his fertile and warped imagination. Drinkwater grabbed his boat cloak and went on deck . . .

"Why don't you shut your filthy mouth, Morris?" asked Cranston from the shadows.

But Morris did not hear Cranston. Hatred, blind and unreasoning hatred, burned in his heart with the intensity of fever. There could be no justification for such bitter emotion any more than there was explanation for love. Morris only knew that from thwarted purpose Drinkwater had come to represent all that had dogged Morris's career: ability, charm, affability and a way of inspiring loyalty in others, qualities in which he was lacking.

Morris was a victim of himself: of his own jealousy, of his sexuality and its concomitants. Perhaps it was the onset of disease that upset his mental balance or perhaps the bitter fruits of a warped and twisted passion; a frustrated love that suffered already the convolutions of self-torture by its very perversity.

Chapter Fifteen March–April 1781

. . . Oft Times go Astray . . .

If the ship's company of *HMS Cyclops* expected a dramatic coastline for their landfall they were disappointed. The Carolinian shore was low and wooded. Blackmore, the navigator, had the greatest difficulty in locating the least conspicuous feature with any confidence. In the end the estuary of the Galuda River was found by the long-boat scouting inshore.

It was afternoon before the onshore breeze enabled Hope to take the frigate into the shoaling waters with confidence.

Leadsmen hove their lines from the forechains on either bow and the long-boat, a loaded four-pounder in her bow, proceeded ahead under Lieutenant Skelton, sounding the channel. Behind her under topsails, spanker and staysails the frigate stood cautiously inshore.

The Galuda River ran into the Atlantic between two small headlands which terminated in sandspits. These twin extensions of the land swung north at their extremity where the river flow was diverted north by the Gulf Stream. Here a bar existed over which the frigate had to be carefully worked.

Once into the estuary the river banks were densely wooded, seamed by creeks and swamps as the Galuda wound inland. Just within the river mouth itself the land was a little higher, reaching an elevation some thirty feet above high water. Here the trees had been removed and Fort Frederic erected.

It was towards the fort that attention aboard *Cyclops* was directed once the dangers of the bar had been negotiated. The serrated stockade rampart was just visible over the surrounding trees. No Union Flag was visible from its conspicuously naked flagpole.

"Shall I fire a gun, sir?" enquired Devaux.

"No," replied Hope. The tension in the situation blotted out the memory of their former disagreement. *Cyclops* crept slowly onwards, the leadsmen's chants droning on. The frigate was abeam of the headlands into the main river; slowly the fort drew abeam. There was not a soul in sight and the very air was pregnant with the desolation of withdrawal.

"Abandoned, by God!"

"We will bring the ship to her bower, Mr. Devaux," said the Captain, ignoring Devaux's outburst, "kindly see to it."

The longboat was brought alongside and a party of seamen and marines detailed into it. Drinkwater watched the boat pull away from the ship.

A small wooden jetty, obviously for use by the garrison, facilitated disembarkation. His hanger drawn, Wheeler advanced his men in open order. Drinkwater watched as they ran forward in a crouching lope. The seamen followed in a ragged phalanx. At the boat the four-pounder covered the assault.

The occupation of Fort Frederic was carried out without a shot. The fort was empty of men, ammunition or provisions of any kind. There was not the slightest clue as to where or when the garrison had gone. But it had a weird, sinister atmosphere about it as some deserted places do. It made the stoutest hearts shiver.

Devaux, who had commanded the landing party turned to Wheeler. "If he's going to stop here we'd better occupy the place," Wheeler agreed. "We can put swivels here and . . . er, over there. My marines can manage. Will you row a guard boat all the time?" Devaux smiled at the scarlet-coated figure, gorget glinting in the sunshine. Wheeler was nervous. Devaux looked around him. "This *is* a bloody business, Wheeler and I like none of it, I'll report to Hope. Yes, of course we'll row a guard. I wouldn't leave a dog in a place like this . . ." Wheeler shivered despite the sun's heat. He was not given to premonitions but he was put in mind of another American river. Wheeler had lost his father on the Monongahela . . .

He shook off the oppressive feeling. He began shouting orders to Hagan and the seamen to put Fort Frederic into a state of defense . . .

Cyclops was a ferment of activity. As "a precautionary measure" Devaux had her topgallant masts struck down so that they might not appear above the surrounding trees. Three boat guns and few swivel guns were mounted in Fort Frederic of which Wheeler, losing his earlier misgivings, was appointed commandant. He embraced the post with enthusiasm and it was not long before properly-appointed sentinels were mounted and patrols were sent out into the surrounding woods. Wheeler's only regret was that Hope forbade him to hoist British colors over the fort.

"It is conceivable that we may have to abandon the post in haste, I have no wish to appear to surrender a British fort," Hope explained, and with that Wheeler had to be content.

As a precaution against attack from seaward the longboat was sent to cruise on the bar commanded by a midshipman or a master's mate. The other boats were variously employed ferrying men and stores ashore.

After twenty-four hours no contact had been made with friend or foe and Hope decided to despatch an expedition inland to reconnoiter. A spring had been secured to the frigate's cable so that her broadsides might bear on either bank, up, or down stream. But it was from seawards that the captain expected trouble and a lookout was kept at the main-topmast cap. From here the longboat was assiduously watched.

That second evening *Cyclops* had been placed in a defensive position and the final preparations were made by rigging boarding nettings. These extended from the ship's rails to lines set up between the lower yardarms. As the sun set and the red ensign fluttered down from *Cyclops*'s stern the sick, brought on deck for some air, were taken below as the bites of the mosquitoes rendered their position on deck untenable. But the insects that infested the forested banks of the Galuda River boarded unperturbed. The restless moans of the sick and hale as they endured the torment of the biting parasites floated away from the frigate over the twilit water, punctuating the sinister stillness of the surrounding foliage.

Thus did *Cyclops* pass two nights waiting for some news of British or Loyalist forces.

The following morning Wheeler was relieved of his command to take over the entire marine detachment in support of Lieutenant Devaux and a party of seamen who were to undertake a probe inland. It was a desperate attempt by Hope to fulfill his orders; if the prophet would not go to the mountain then some attempt must be made to bring the mountain to Mahomet . . .

Thus reasoned the captain as he wiped his perspiring forehead. He poured himself a glass of rum grog and walked aft. The slick waters of the Galuda bubbled under *Cyclops*'s stern, chuckling round the rudder which moved slightly with a faint creak and soft grind of tiller chains.

In the corner of his vision he could just see the landing party forming up after disembarking. He saw Wheeler throw out an advanced picket under Hagan and lead off with the rest of the marines. In a less precise column he saw Midshipman Morris follow with a squad of seamen. Midshipman Drinkwater brought up the rear followed by a file of marines under their corporal. The head of the column had already disappeared in the trees when he saw Devaux, after addressing a few final words to Keene left as fort-commander, look back at the ship then take to his heels in chase of his independent command . . .

Hope tossed off the rum and looked seawards. The longboat was down there under Cranston. Skelton was the only other commissioned officer left on board. With a surprising pang of affection he thought anxiously of Devaux and the gaudy but competent Wheeler . . . he thought idly of young Drinkwater . . . so very like himself all those years ago . . . he sighed again and watched the Galuda run seawards . . . out to the open sea . . . "From whence cometh our help," he muttered in silent cynicism to himself . . .

Drinkwater had little taste for the inland expedition. Once they had lost sight of the frigate it seemed to him that the whole party was instantly endangered. The sea was their element and, as if to confirm his worries, seamen ahead of him, men as nimble as monkeys in the rigging, were tripping and stumbling over tree-roots and cursing at the squelching morasses that they began immediately to encounter. He was also overshadowed by the earnest entreaties of Achilles who had refused to come with Drinkwater but who impressed upon the midshipman the folly of going inland. Drinkwater therefore plunged into the forest with his nerves already highly strung, with every fiber of his being suspicious of the least faltering of the head of the column, of the least exclamation no matter how innocent the cause . . .

Despite the nature of the terrain the landing party made good progress along the track that led inland from Fort Frederic. About five miles from the fort they came across a cleared area with a saw pit and indications of some sort of logging post. There was also evidence that its occupants had made a hurried departure. A few miles further on they came across a small plantation with a clapboard house and outbuildings. The house had been partially burned and the outbuildings were a mass of flies. Carrion eaters were feeding on the decomposing corpses of cattle.

The stink of that burnt out farm seemed to linger with the little column as it made its way through the oppressively empty pine barrens. They crossed a creek that drained north into the Galuda and set up a bivouac for the night. The men were now grumbling in a murmur that soon became an uproar as the mosquitoes began biting. Devaux had no zeal for this kind of service but Wheeler, able to assume the unofficial leadership through his military training, was revelling in his own element. Watches were posted and the party settled down to eat what they had brought with them.

About sunset, having ascertained his watch duties for the night, Drinkwater went off into the surrounding forest to answer a call of nature. After the sweaty progress of the day, the incessant grumbling of the men and the struggle to keep them going towards the end, he was feeling very tired. Squatting over a tree root he became light-headed, convinced that this was not really him, Nathaniel Drinkwater, who squatted thus, emptying his bowels God knows how many thousand miles from home. He looked down. Was this soggy, mossy undergrowth really the fabulous Americas? It seemed so illogical as to be impossible. As so often happened at such private moments he found his thoughts drifting to Elizabeth. Somehow the image of her was more real than this ludicrous actuality . . .

So strongly was he able to fantasise that he seemed to see himself telling Elizabeth of how, once, many years ago, he had sat across the roots of a pine tree in somewhat indelicate circumstances in far away Carolina thinking of her. So disembodied were his instincts that he failed to hear the crack of a dead branch behind him.

Even when Morris pitched him forward on his face he did not react immediately. Only when it dawned on him that he had his face pressed in a mossy hummock and his naked backside revealed to the world did he come to.

"Well, well, what a pretty sight . . . and how very appropriate, eh, Threddle?"

At the sound of that voice and the mention of the name he tried to turn, putting an arm out to push himself up. But he was too late. Even as he took his weight a foot came down on his elbow and his arm collapsed. Almost instinctively he drew his knees up, twisting his head round.

Threddle stood on his arm, a cutlass in his hand.

There was a cruel glitter in his eyes and the corners of his mouth smirked.

"What *shall* we do with him, eh, Threddle?" Morris remained behind him, out of sight but Drinkwater felt horribly exposed, like a mare being steadied for the stallion. As if reading his own fear Morris kicked him. The wave of nausea that spread upwards from his genitals was overwhelming, he fought for breath as the vomit emptied from him. Suddenly he felt Threddle's hand in his hair, twisting his face round so that he faced his own excrement . . .

"What a very good idea, Threddle . . . and then we will bugger him, eh? That'll cut him down to his proper size . . ." Drinkwater had no power to resist, all he could do was clamp his mouth and eyes shut. But even as the smell of his own ordure grew stronger in his nostrils the pressure of Threddle's hand ceased and pulled sideways. The big man fell with a squelchy thud.

"What the . . . ?" Morris half turned to see in the gathering twilight the figure of a man holding a boarding pike. Its end gleamed wetly as it was pointed at Morris.

"Sharples!"

Sharples said nothing to Morris. "Are you all right Mr. Drinkwater?" The midshipman rose unsteadily to his feet. He leaned against the tree and, with trembling fingers, buttoned his ducks. Still not trusting his voice he nodded dumbly.

Morris made a move but ceased as Sharples jabbed the point at his chest.

"Now, *Mister* Morris, take the pistol out of your belt and no tricks . . ." Drinkwater lifted his head to watch. It was getting quite dark but there was still light enough to see the furious gleam in Sharple's eyes.

"No tricks now, *Mister* Morris I want you to place that pistol at Threddle's head and blow his brains out . . ." the voice was vehemently insistent. Drinkwater looked down at Threddle. The pike had pierced his abdomen, entering below the rib cage and ripping through the digestive organs. He was not dead but lay with blood flowing across his belly and gobbets of gore trickling from his mouth. Occasionally his legs twitched weakly and the only thing about him that seemed not to be already half dead were the eyes that screamed a silent protest and cry for mercy . . .

"Cock it!" ordered Sharples, "Cock it!" He jabbed the pike into Morris's buttocks, forcing the midshipman round to face Threddle. The click of the hammer coming back sounded in Drinkwater's ears. He roused himself. "No," he whispered, "for God's sake Sharples, no!" His voice gathered strength but before he could say more Sharples shouted "Fire!"

For perhaps a split second Morris hesitated, then the boarding pike made his muscles involuntarily contract. The pistol cracked and Threddle's face disintegrated.

No one moved for perhaps thirty seconds.

"Oh, my God!" managed Drinkwater at last. "What the hell have you done, Sharples?"

The man turned. A soft, childish smile played around his mouth. His eyes were deep pools in the near-night, pools of tears. His voice when it came caught on breathless sobs.

"It came in the mail, Mr. Drinkwater, the mail we got from *Gal'tea* . . . the letter that tol' me my Kate was dead . . . they *said* she died in chil'birth but I know better'n that, sir . . . I know better'n that . . ."

Drinkwater mastered himself at last. "I'm sorry, Sharples, really sorry . . . and thank you for your help . . . But why did you kill Threddle?"

"Because he's shit, sir," he said simply.

Morris looked up. His face was deathly white. He began to walk unsteadily back towards the encampment. With a final look at Threddle Sharples followed, then, sensing Drinkwater lagged behind, he turned back.

"It ain't no good crying over spilt milk, Mr. Drinkwater . . ."

"Shouldn't we bury him?"

Sharples snorted contemptuously. "No."

"But what am I to tell the first lieutenant . . . ?" Sharples was already tugging him away from the darkening clearing. There was the sound of branches breaking underfoot. Ahead of them they saw Wheeler and two marines, their white cross-belts glowing in the gathering night, close round Morris.

Sharples let go of the boarding pike.

They came up with the others. "What's going on?" demanded Wheeler looking pointedly at Morris's hand which still held the pistol. Morris's face remained an impassive mask, he looked through, rather than at, Wheeler.

Drinkwater came up. "Just a stupid mistake, Mr. Wheeler. I was emptying my bladder when Morris thought I was a rebel . . . Sharples was doing the same thing about ten yards away . . ." he managed a smile. "That's right isn't it Morris?"

Morris looked up and Drinkwater felt ice-cold fingers of apprehension round his heart. For Morris smiled. A ghastly, complicit smile . . .

"If you say so, Drinkwater . . ."

And it was only then that Drinkwater realized that by explaining their actions with lies he had become a party to the crime . . .

At dawn the next morning, the camp was astir with discontent. Unable to comprehend the seemingly pointless purpose of the march, employed outside their own environment and stung into a half-crazy state, the men were now openly mutinous. Devaux did his best to placate them but lacked conviction for he shared their belief, with more justification, that their mission was an ill-conceived waste of time.

"Well, Wheeler," he said, "we may be marching along a fine "military road" but I see few of the fine military upon it, barring your goodself, of course. For my money we may as well retrace our steps before being utterly consumed by these damned bugs." Here he slapped his face, missing the offending insect and presenting a ludicrous spectacle to those near him.

Wheeler considered the matter and a compromise was reached. They would march until noon then, if they still found nothing, they would turn back.

An hour later they set off . . .

* * *

Out on the bar of the Galuda River Midshipman Cranston served biscuit and water to the long boat's crew. Despite their cramped and aching bodies after a night in the boat, the seamen were cheerful. Cruising offshore there was either a land or sea breeze and the insect life was negligible. They looked forward to a pleasant day, a yachting excursion comparable with that enjoyed by the wealthy members of the Duke of Cumberland's fleet. It all seemed to have little to do with the rigorous duties of a man o' war. Fitted with a lugsail the longboat cruised with little exertion necessary from her crew. Lulled into such complaisance it was a rude shock to discern the topgallants of a large vessel offshore.

Cranston put the long boat off before the wind and headed for the Galuda estuary. He was certain the stranger was *La Creole* . . .

The sun had almost reached its zenith when they came upon the mill. It was another weatherboard edifice and indicated the presence of human habitation since the farther trail was better cleared and recently trod. Nevertheless it was deserted despite a partially-filled sack of flour and a dumped cartload of indian corn.

"That's been left in a deuced hurry," said Wheeler pointing to the pile.

"Very perceptive," said Devaux, annoyed that, just as it seemed he would have his way and return they were going to find people.

"D'ye think they fled at our approach?"

"I don't know . . ." said Devaux flatly.

"Shall we feed the men before proceeding further, for I don't like this." Wheeler's confidence was shaken for the first time. Devaux noted this and pulled hismelf together. He was in command of the party. First they'd eat and then decide what was to be done.

"D'ye attend to it, Wheeler, and a couple of men at the top of the mill will set our minds at ease, eh?"

"Aye, aye," answered the marine officer, biting his lip

with chagrin that he had overlooked such a very elementary precaution.

The men settled to another meal of dried biscuit and water. They lay in languid poses scratching themselves and grumbling irritably. Having posted his sentinels Wheeler flung himself down in the shade.

All morning Drinkwater had toiled in the heat, trying desperately to forget the events of the night before. But his testicles ached and from time to time the gorge rose in his throat. He choked it manfully down and avoided all contact with Morris. Sharples swung along with the seamen, a benign smile on his face. Drinkwater was filled with the overwhelming sense of relief when they lay down in the shade of the mill. He closed his eyes and drifted into semi-consciousness.

Then the rebel horse were on them.

The raiders swept into the clearing in a sudden thunder of hooves and dust and the sparkle of sabres. Most of the British were caught lying prone. Surprised in the open, the seamen were terrified at the appearance of horses. The flying hooves and flaring nostrils were unfamiliar and horrifying to these men who gave their lives without protest in the claustrophobic darkness of a gundeck. They defended themselves as best they might, stark terror adding to their confusion.

Wheeler and Devaux came to their feet blaspheming.

"To me, sergeant! Oh, Christ Jesus! To *me* sergeant, damn you!" The marines began to fight their way through to the base of the mill, coalescing in little groups to commence a methodical discharge of musketry.

The general mêlée lasted ten long minutes in which a third of the seamen had been cut down and there was a scarce a man in the entire force who had not received a cut or graze.

Drinkwater leaped up with the rest. He had brought a cutlass with him and lugged it out, its clumsy unbalanced blade awkward to his hand. A man on a bay plunged towards him. Drinkwater parried the blow but the impetus of the horse threw him over and he rolled to one side to avoid the hooves. A pistol ball raised dust by his head as he struggled to his feet again. Weakness overcame him as he was filled with the overwhelming desire simply to lie down. He rolled on to his back, half submitting to the impulse. A man ran past him with a musket. He dropped to one knee and fired at the horseman, now turning to make another pass. It was Sharples. He discharged the musket and half dragged Drinkwater closer to the mill. The horseman swerved and rode off to attack four seamen fighting back to back and already going down before the slashing sabres.

Drinkwater got to his feet. He saw Devaux and Wheeler with a group of men forming a defensive group. He pointed and Sharples nodded. Suddenly another man had joined them. It was Morris. He pushed Drinkwater, who staggered back against the mill. Sharples turned and thrust the barrel of his musket between them. Morris fired his pistol and Sharples doubled over, a great hole in his chest. Drinkwater was dazed, his vision blurred. He comprehended nothing.

Another horseman rode up and slashed at them. Morris turned away, running round the corner of the mill. The horseman followed. Drinkwater took one brief look at Sharples. He was dead.

He looked up again, the little group round the two lieutenants had grown. In a blind panic he put down his head and ran, dodging among the whirling sabres and stamping horses' legs with animal instinct.

The rebel cavalry had played out their advantage of surprise. Used as they were to attacking lonely farms or ambushing parties of raw Tory militia, the horsemen were used to speedy and uncontested victory. Having fought the intruders for some minutes the surviving seamen steadied. Devaux was among them, his teeth bared in a snarl of rage. They began to rally, their cutlasses slashing back at the horses or the riders' thighs, concentrating on the bright red spot which, through the swirling dust, marked where the marines were forming a disciplined center of resistance.

The American officer felt his squadron's will to fight was on the ebb. Seeking to rally his force he yelled out:

"Tarleton's quarter, my lads! Give the bastards Tarleton's quarter!" This reference to the leader of the British Legion, a force of Loyalist Americans under British officers, who let not a rebel escape them if they could help it, had its effect and they renewed their attack. But the resistance of the British was now established and the Americans gradually drew off, reining in their steaming horses just out of short musket range.

Slowly the dust subsided and the two contending parties glared at each other across a no-man's-land of broken bodies and hamstrung horses. Then the enemy wheeled their mounts and vanished into the trees as swiftly and silently as they had come.

The news of the arrival of *La Creole* off the Galuda came as no surprise to Hope. On receiving Cranston's intelligence the captain ordered Skelton to the mainmast cap to watch the enemy privateer. It was with some relief that the lieutenant reported that *La Creole* had stood offshore towards the late afternoon, thus buying valuable time for the British. Why she had done so Hope could only guess, possibly the enemy commander wanted time to make preparations, perhaps he did not think he had been observed and wished to make his attack the following day. Perhaps, and Hope hardly dared believe this, perhaps *Cyclops* had not been spotted and *La Creole* was working her patient way southward still searching. At all events the captain was too old a campaigner to worry when fate had dealt him a card he did not expect.

The appearance of *La Creole* enabled him to make up his mind in one direction. He would recall Devaux and the landing party immediately. The indecision that had manifested itself earlier and annoyed Devaux was gone now, for it had been caused, not by senility, but lack of faith in his orders. Hope ordered the garrison of Fort Frederic to be withdrawn and the frigate's defenses strengthened against a night boat attack.

At a conference of officers he called for a volunteer to take the message of recall to Devaux. The pitifully small group of officers regarded the silent forest visible through the stern windows with misgiving.

"I'll go," said Cranston at last.

"Well done, Mr. Cranston. I shall endeavor to do everything possible for you for such a service. Will no-one else support Mr. Cranston . . . ?"

"There's no need, sir. I'll take the blackamoor."

"Very well, you may draw what you require from the purser and small arms from Lieutenant Keene. Good luck to you."

The officers shuffled with relief at Cranston filling such a dangerous office. When they had gone Hope poured himself a glass of rum and wiped his forehead for the thousandth time that day.

"I'll be bloody glad when Devaux and Wheeler get back . . . I pray heaven they're all right . . ." he muttered to himself . . .

The landing party reached their bivouac of the previous night dragging with them the remnants of their expedition. The men collapsed on the banks of the creek to bathe their wounds or drink the bloody water. The badly injured groaned horribly as the mosquitoes renewed their assaults and several became delirious during the night.

Drinkwater slept badly. Although unwounded beyond a bruised shoulder from the flat of a sabre and the endemic scratches collected on the way, the heat, fatigue and events of the preceding hours had taken their toll. He had marched from the mill in a daze, his mind constantly fastening unbidden on images of Threddle lying dead in the gloaming and Sharples stiff with blackened blood in the heat of noon. Between these two corpses floated Morris, Morris with a pistol still smoking in his hand, Morris with the smile of triumph on his face and, worst of all, the superimposition of Morris over his image of Elizabeth.

He fought hard to retain her face in his mind's eye but it faded, faded beyond recall so that he thought he might go mad in this forested nightmare through which they trudged.

And when night came there was no rest, for the mosquitoes reactivated the exhausted nervous system, constantly recalling to wakefulness the mind and body that only wished to sleep. Death, thought Nathaniel at that midnight moment, would be a blessed relief.

Wheeler, too, slept little. He constantly patrolled his outposts, apprehensive lest the enemy renew their attack on the sleeping men. He shook his head sadly as a grey dawn revealed the encampment. The men were tattered, their limbs scarred and gashed by briars and branches, dried blood blackening improvised bandages and flies settling on open wounds.

Several of the wounded were delirious and Devaux ordered litters improvised and an hour after dawn the party moved off, resuming its painful march.

At mid-morning they found Cranston and Achilles.

The negro had been tied to a tree and flayed alive. His back was a mass of flies. Hagan, himself badly wounded limped forward and cut the body down. Achilles was still alive, his breath coming in shallow gasps.

Cranston had evidently put up a fight. He had been hanged from a tree but it was obvious he had been dead before the rebels strung him up. Or at least Devaux hoped so. Scarce a man there refrained from vomiting at the sight of the mutilation inflicted on Cranston's body. Devaux found himself wondering if the man had a wife or a mistress . . . and then he turned away.

Wheeler and Hagan laid the negro gently on the ground, brushing the flies from his face. Devaux stood beside him and touched his shoulder. Wheeler stood up, "Bastards," he choked.

Achilles opened his eyes. Above him he saw the scarlet coat and gold gorget. His hand moved slightly in salutation before dropping back to death.

The two officers had the midshipman cut down and crudely buried with the negro, then the column pressed on.

In the evening they emerged from the forest and staggered down to the landing jetty. Wheeler could raise no protest when he saw no men in the little fort and

Devaux felt relief flood through him. Relief from the tension of independent command, and relief that very soon he would see the comfortable old face of Henry Hope.

All Nathaniel Drinkwater saw was the frigate, dark and strangely welcoming in the twilight and he waited impatiently for the boat to ferry him off.

"Are you all right, Nat?"

It was little White, sunburned and bright from new responsibility.

Drinkwater looked at him. It did not seem possible that they belonged to the same generation.

"Where's Cranston?" asked White.

Drinkwater raised a tired arm and pointed at the surrounding forest. "Dead in the defense of His Majesty's dominions," he said, aware that cynicism was a great relief, "with his bollocks in his mouth . . ."

Somehow he found White's shocked look amusing . . .

Chapter Sixteen April 1781

The Cutting Out

If the remnants of the landing party expected rest after their labors they were to be disappointed. After a bare three hours exhausted sleep, several found themselves rowing a guard-boat cautiously downstream to prevent a surprise attack by *La Creole* or her boats. Hope was especially concerned since he had seen the enemy stand southwards.

Although he did not know it *La Creole* had missed *Cyclops* in her search, but the last of the onshore breeze the next afternoon brought her back. An hour before sunset she had anchored on the bar. There was no longer any doubt that she had found her quarry.

The twenty four hours that had elapsed since the return of the landing party had proved tiring and trying for all. Without exception the members of the expedition had about them the smell of defeat and their low morale affected the remaining men. The immediate failure of the mission was forgotten in the urgent necessity of alleviating the sufferings of the wounded and preparing the frigate for sea. The topgallant masts were re-hoisted and the upper yards crossed. It may well have been this that discovered her to *La Creole* but no one now cared. Action was infinitely preferable to lying supinely in the stinking jungle-surrounded Galuda a moment more than was necessary. Appleby and his mates worked harder than anyone else, patching up the walking wounded so that they might man their guns again, or easing the sufferings of the badly wounded with laudanum.

The time passed for Drinkwater in a daze. Outwardly he carried out his duties with his customary efficiency. When the roll was called he answered for Sharples having been killed at the mill.

When Threddle's name was called his mouth clamped shut. His eyes swivelled to Morris. The enigmatic smile still played around the mouth of his adversary but Morris said nothing.

Strain and fatigue continued to play havoc with Drinkwater's nerves as the day wore on until, when the news of the arrival of *La Creole* on the bar spread rapidly through the ship, he seemed to emerge from a tunnel. He had found his second wind. Morris was just Morris, an evil to be endured; Achilles had been a brief and colourful intrusion into his life and was so no more; Cranston was dead, just that, dead; and Threddle . . . Threddle was discharged dead too, killed in action at the mill . . . or so the ship's books said . . .

It was only when he received the summons to attend the Captain, however, that his mind received the final jerk that returned him to sanity. As he entered the cabin in company with all the other officers, he found himself standing next to Morris. It came to him then, the awful truth, the fact that his numbed mind had automatically excluded in its pain . . .

Sharples had not died in action. Sharples had been shot down in cold blood under the cover of action. And the man next to him had done it . . .

"Well, gentlemen . . ." Hope looked round the ring of tired yet expectant faces. They were all here. The welcome features of Devaux and Wheeler, the careworn, lined face of old Blackmore, the younger Keene and youthful Skelton. Behind the commissioned officers the mature warrant officers; the gunner, the bosun and the carpenter, and the eager yet apprehensive faces of his midshipmen and master's mates.

"Well gentlemen, it seems our friend has returned, I suspect with reinforcements. I imagine he will attempt a cutting out so I am not intending to warp the ship round. If we see *La Creole* approaching then we shall have to do so and for that eventuality the spring is already rigged, but I do not foresee this. The wind during the night will be offshore and therefore favor an attack by boats. I have a mind to bait a trap and for that purpose have summoned you all here . . . Moonset is about two o'clock. We may, therefore, expect his boats soon after in order that, having taken us," here Hope looked round and swept what he believed to be a sardonically inspiring grin around the company, ". . . he may carry the *terral* to sea . . ."

A little shuffle among the officers indicated a stirring of interest. Hope breathed a silent sigh of relief. "Now, gentlemen, this is what I intend that we should do . . ."

Cyclops settled down to await the expected attack. The hands had been fed and the galley fire extinguished. The men had been sent to their stations and the most elaborate dispositions made. Apart from a watch the hands were, for the time being, ordered to rest on their arms.

Anxious to stimulate the morale of his crew, Hope had accepted several suggestions for improvisation in the frigate's defense. Of these the best had been suggested by Wheeler. *Cyclops*'s two largest boats were hoisted by the yardarm tackles fitted to the extremities of the fore and main yards. By this means the boats were slung outboard of, and higher than, the frigate's sides. In each boat a party of the ship's best marksmen lay hidden, awaiting the order to open fire upon the anticipated boarders as they scrambled up *Cyclops*'s sides.

The lower deck gunports were all secured and the hands issued with small arms.

An hour after moonset the faint chuckle of water under a boat's bow was heard from downstream. Peering intently from the stern cabin windows Devaux touched Hope's arm.

"Here they come, sir," he whispered. He turned to

pass word forward but Hope held him back. "Good luck Mr. Devaux . . ." Hope's voice cracked with age and emotion. Devaux smiled in the darkness. "Good luck to you, sir," he replied warmly.

The first lieutenant slipped through into the gundeck, passing a whispered warning to the men stationed there. Emerging onto the upper deck, he ordered the men to lie down. In a crouching position he moved up one side and down the other. At each post he found the men waiting eagerly.

Drinkwater was one of the party waiting in the forward gundeck. Commanded by Lieutenant Skelton, their task was to counterattack once the enemy had boarded in the manner that had been so successfully used in the previous action. Up on the fo'c's'le O'Malley, the Irish cook, scraped a melancholy air on his fiddle and several men sang quietly or chatted in low voices as might be expected from a casually maintained anchor watch . . .

The boats came alongside at several points. Faint grunts and bumps told where they secured. Devaux waited. A hand reached over the rail and grasped the hammock netting, another followed. One groped upwards and a moment later a knife was sawing through the boarding netting, another followed. Another hand came over the opposite rail. It was followed by a head.

"Now!" bellowed Devaux, expelling his pent-up breath in one mighty roar that was taken up by the waiting seamen. The tension burst from them in smoke, flame and destruction. Fifty or sixty twelve pound cannon balls were dropped overside to plummet down through the bottoms of *La Creole*'s boats. From her own boats, suspended high above, *Cyclops*'s marksmen opened a lethal fire on the invaders. This desperate refinement quickly cleared the frigate's sides.

From the deck too a withering fire was poured down at the hapless privateersmen now struggling in the river . . .

Aft the attacks had been driven off with similar success. Hope looked round. He was suddenly aware that his ship was swinging, her head falling off from pointing up river. Someone forward had cut *Cyclops*'s cable and instinct prompted Hope to stare over the stern, searching in the darkness for the spring. Shouting anxiously for Blackmore to get sail on the ship, he sprung himself for the wheel in case the spring parted and the ship was in danger of going aground.

Forward the rebels had had more success than the mere severing of the frigate's cable. Having driven a boat in under *Cyclops*'s figurehead where access was comparatively easy via the bowsprit rigging and the foretack bumpkins, twenty or thirty men had gained access to the deck under an enterprising officer, and a fierce hand to hand engagement now took place. Several of the privateersmen were engaged in turning one of the bow chasers inboard along the length of *Cyclops*.

The situation became critical and Devaux shouted for Skelton's reserve.

Hearing the shouts and screams from above, Lieutenant Skelton was already on his way, leading the counter attackers out of the stygian gloom of the gundeck. Behind him Drinkwater drew his dirk and followed.

On the fo'c's'le the French privateer officer was achieving a measure of success. His men had swung the starboard bow chaser round and were preparing to fire it. He was determined to destroy the British frigate if he could not take her. If he could force her aground and fire her . . . already she was head downstream . . . it occurred to him that she should be broadside on . . .

He turned to shout orders to two men remaining in the boat to bring combustibles on board, then he swung round to rally his men for a final attempt to secure the upper deck in the wake of the bow chaser's discharge.

A British lieutenant appeared in front of him, leading a fresh body of men that had appeared from nowhere. The lieutenant slashed at the Frenchman but before Skelton's blade even started its downward path the latter executed a swift and fatal lunge.

"*Hela*!" he shouted. Skelton reeled backwards carrying with him two seamen coming up behind. The French officer's eyes gleamed in triumph and he turned to order his men to discharge the cannon.

"*Tirez*!" A thin youth confronted him. The Frenchman grinned maliciously at the dirk his opponent held. He extended his sword arm. Drinkwater waited for the lunge but the other recovered and the two stood for a second eyeing each other. The Frenchman's experience weighed the midshipman . . . he lunged.

Skelton's blood flowed freely across the deck. The French officer slipped as Drinkwater half turned to avoid the blade. The sword point, raised involuntarily by his opponent's loss of balance, caught his cheek and ripped upwards, deflected out of the flesh by the cheekbone. Drinkwater had gone icy cold in that heart-beat of suspension, he already knew he had his man as his fencer's instinct told him the other was losing his balance. Now the sting of the wound unleashed a sudden fury in him. He stabbed blindly and savagely, giving the thrust impetus by the full weight of his body. The dirk passed under the man's bicep and buried itself in his shoulder, piercing the right lung. The Frenchman staggered back, recovering his balance too late, dropping his sword, blood pouring from his wound.

Drinkwater flung away the dirk and grabbed the fallen sword. It leapt in his hand, balanced exquisitely on the lower phalange of his forefinger. He threw himself into the fight, screaming encouragement to the seamen struggling for possession of the deck.

In twenty minutes it was over. By then *Cyclops* had brought up to her spring and Drinkwater, the only officer left standing forward, was joined by Devaux and they began securing the prisoners . . .

Instead of travelling slowly downstream beam on, the frigate's spring had the effect of re-anchoring her by the stern since it was led out of an after gun port and secured to the anchor cable below the cut. This fortuitous circumstance permitted Hope to set the topsails so that the vessel strained at her anchor as the sails bellied out to the *terral*.

Drinkwater hurried aft, touching his forehead.

"All the boarders secured, sir, what orders?"

Hope looked astern. He could make out the splashes of men struggling in the water and the taut spring rising, dripping with water from the tension on it.

Devaux hurried up. "Get those boats cut down and you, Drinkwater, get the spring cut . . ."

The two ran off, "Mr. Blackmore!"

"Sir?"

"Take the conn, have a man in the chains and a quarter master back at the wheel. Pass word to the leadsman that I want the soundings *quietly*." Hope emphasised the last word as Keene came up. "Work round the deck, Mr. Keene, not a word from anyone . . . anyone do you understand?"

"Aye, aye, sir."

Drinkwater ran up again. "Spring cut, sir." He reported.

"Well done, Mister." Hope rubbed his hands gleefully, like a schoolboy contemplating a prank. "I'm going out after that fella, Mister Drinkwater," he confided, pointing ahead to somewhere in the darkness where *La Creole* awaited them. "She'll be expecting us under her cutting out party—we'll give 'em a surprise, eh cully?" Hope grinned.

"Aye, aye, sir!"

"Now run off and find Devaux and tell him to man the starboard battery and have topmen aloft . . . oh, and men at the braces . . ." Drinkwater ran off with his message.

Blackmore was letting the wind and current take the frigate downstream, trusting that the run of the water would serve her best. As the ship cleared the wooded headlands he adjusted the course and trimmed the yards. Drinkwater was ordered forward to keep a lookout for *La Creole*.

He strained his eyes into the night. Small circles danced in his vision. He elevated his glance a little from the horizon and immediately, on the periphery of his retina a darker spot appeared to starboard. He clapped the battered glass to his eye.

It was *La Creole* and at anchor too!

He raced aft: "She's two points to starboard, sir, and at anchor!"

"Very well, Mr. Drinkwater." Then to Blackmore, "starboard a point."

Blackmore's voice answered, "Starboard a point, sir. By my reckoning you are just clear of the bar . . ."

"Very well. Mr. Drinkwater, get a cable on the second bower!"

Cyclops slipped seawards. *La Creole* was just visible against the false dawn. Hope intended to cross *La Creole*'s stern, rake her and put his helm down. As he turned to starboard and ran alonside the enemy ship he would anchor. It was his last anchor, except for the light kedge and it was a gamble. He explained to his principal officers what he intended . . .

Drinkwater found two bosun's mates and a party of tired seamen hauling an eight-inch rope up to the ring on the second bower. The two ships were closing fast.

"Hurry it up there," he hissed between clenched teeth. The men looked up at him sullenly. After what seemed an interminable delay, the cable was secured.

Returning to report the anchor ready, Drinkwater passed the prisoners. In the haste they had been trussed up to the foremast bitts and a sudden thought occurred to him. If these men shouted a warning, *Cyclops*'s advantage would be lost. Then another idea came to him.

He ordered the marine sentries to herd them below, all of them except the French officer who lay groaning on the deck. Drinkwater still had the man's sword in his hand. He cut the rope securing the man to the bitts.

"Up mister!" he ordered.

"*Merde*," growled the man.

Drinkwater pointed the sword at his throat: "Up!"

The man rose reluctantly to his feet, swaying with dizziness. The midshipmen prodded him aft, he ordered the last marine to go below to slit the throat of the first man that so much as squealed. Afterwards his own ruthless barbarity surprised him, but at the time it seemed the only logical thing to do under the uncompromising prompting of a desire to survive.

He arrived on the quarterdeck. "What the devil?" queried a startled Hope, to be reassured by a sight of his own midshipman, a drawn sword in his hand, behind the Frenchman.

"Anchor's ready, sir. I thought this fella would help allay any suspicions, sir. Shout to the enemy, sir, tell 'em the ship's his . . ."

"An excellent idea, Drinkwater. Speaks English, eh? Must do with that polygot rebel crew. Probably uses French with his commander. Prick him a little, sir," said the captain.

The man jerked. Hope addressed him in English, his voice uncharacteristically sinister and brutal:

"Now you dog. I have an old score to settle with your race. My brother and my sister's husband died in Canada and I've an unchristian hankering for revenge. You tell your commander that this ship is yours and you'll anchor under his lee. No tricks now, I've the best surgeon in the fleet and he'll see to you, you've my word on that but," here Hope looked significantly at Drinkwater and paused, "but one false word and it's your last. D'ye understand, *canaille*?"

The man winced again. "*Oui*," he nodded, breathing through clenched teeth. Drinkwater shoved him to the main chains. Hope turned away.

"Pass the word to Mr. Devaux to have the gun crews stand by. On the command I want the ports opened and the guns run straight out and fired."

"Aye, aye, sir," a messenger ran off.

Cyclops was less than one hundred yards of *La Creole* now, crossing her stern from starboard to larboard. A hail came from the big privateer.

"Very well, Mr. Drinkwater, prompt our friend."

The Frenchman drew a breath.

"*Ca va bien! Je suis blessé, mais la frégate est prise!*"

A voice replied across the diminishing gap between the two ships. "*Bravo mon ami! Mais votre blessure?*"

The French officer shot a glance at Drinkwater and took a deep breath.

"*Affreuse! À la gorge!*" There was a moment's silence then a puzzled voice:

"*La gorge? . . . Mon Dieu!*" A shout of realization came from *La Creole*.

Hope swore and the Frenchman, his left hand to his chest where his punctured lung gave him great pain, turned triumphantly to Drinkwater. But the midshipman could not kill him in cold blood, indeed he only half comprehended what had transpired . . .

But events now moved in rapid succession so that Drinkwater's dilemma was short lived. The French officer slumped to the deck in a faint as *La Creole*'s people ran to their guns. A gust of wind filled *Cyclops*'s topsails so that she accelerated a little and suddenly the privateer's stern was drawing abeam.

"Now Devaux! Now by God!"

The ports opened, there was a terrible squealing rumble as the starboard battery of twelve-pounders were run out. Then the concussion of the broadside overwhelmed them all, rocking the frigate. In the darkness of the gundeck Keene and Devaux were leaping up and down with excitement and a fighting madness. They had double shotted the guns and topped off the charges with canister. The devastation thus inflicted upon *La Creole* almost destroyed her resistance at a blow. As the guns recoiled inboard, *Cyclops* swung to starboard. Her impetus carried her alongside *La Creole* and a further broadside smashed into the ex-Indiaman's hull. A few bold souls aboard the American fired back and the engagement became general, though all the advantage lay with the British.

Drawing a little ahead, *Cyclops* lost way. Her anchor was let go and her sails clewed up. Veering the cable *Cyclops* settled back and brought up on *La Creole*'s larboard quarter.

For twenty dreadful minutes the British poured shot after shot into her. Aboard the American ship men died bravely. They got eight guns into action and inflicted some damage on their opponent but in the end, lying in his own gore, his ship and crew a shambles around him, the French commander ordered his ensign struck and an American officer complied.

The pale light of dawn revealed to Hope the limp bunting lying across the jagged remnants of what had once been a handsome carved taffrail and he ordered his cannon to cease fire . . .

Later in the morning Drinkwater accompanied his commander aboard the enemy ship. Captain Hope did not consider her worth taking as a prize. His depleted crew were barely enough to guard the prisoners and work *Cyclops*. The rebel ship had been old when the Americans commissioned her and the damage that she suffered at the hands of *Cyclop's* gun crews had been frightful.

Drinkwater gaped at the desolation caused by the frigate's broadsides. The planking of her decks was ripped up, furrowed by ball and canister into jagged lines of splinters reminiscent of a field of petrified grass. Several beams sagged down into the spaces below and cannon were knocked clean off their carriages. Trunnions had been sheered and three had had their cascabels cut off as if with a knife. Scattered about all this destruction were petty items of personal gear. A man's stocking hat, a shoe, a crucifix and rosary beads, a clasp knife and a beautifully painted chest split to fragments . . .

Grimmer remains of what had once been men lay in unseemingly attitudes and splashes of vivid color. Dried blood was dark beside the ochreous pools of vomit, the stark white of exposed bone, the blue of bled flesh and the greens and browns of intestines. It was a vile sight and the hollow eyes of the surviving members of the crew regarded the British captain with a dull hatred as the author of their fate. But Hope, with the simple faith of the dedicated warrior, returned their gaze with scorn. For these men were nothing but legalized pirates, plundering for profit, destroying merchant ships for gain, and visiting upon innocent seamen a callous indifference to their fates.

The captain ordered out of her such stores as might serve the frigate, and had combustibles prepared to fire her. Lieutenant Keene boarded *La Creole* at sunset to ignite her. As the offshore *terral* began to blow seawards, *Cyclops* weighed her anchor. *La Creole* burned furiously, a black pall rolling seawards away from the coast of that benighted land.

Cyclops was standing well offshore when *La Creole's* magazine exploded. An hour later she altered course for Cape Hatteras and New York.

Chapter Seventeen April–October 1781

Decision at the Virginia Capes

The weather was once more against them. Off the dreaded Cape they met a gale of unbelievable ferocity which tried the gear severely. The main topgallant mast went by the board and took with it the fore and mizen topgallants. During this blow the wounded were, of course, confined below. The cockpit was a scene of utter degradation. The filth in the bilge was augmented by the water made by the straining frigate as she labored in the seaway and the whole slopped about the bottom of the ship, driving the rodent population higher. The rats ran almost unchecked over the bodies of the dying, who retched and urinated without relief. For die they did. Scarce a man who received anything more trivial than a scratch escaped gangrene or blood poisoning of one kind of another.

Drinkwater was one of the fortunate few. His cut, a superficial one, was disfiguring rather than dangerous. Appleby sutured it for him. An Appleby who had lost much rotundity and whose pitifully few medicines were exhausted as he fought disease and sepsis with his own diminishing energies. At last, utterly worn with fatigue and exasperation, he wept angry and frustrated tears in the darkness of his hellish kingdom.

Hope buried the bundles in their hammocks. Six one day, nine another as the wind howled, the frigate bucked and the spray drove inboard in hissing sheets. The burial service became curtailed into the briefest formality.

Although the weather was poor, it allowed *Cyclops* to limp north undetected. For she was in no condition to fight. In addition to the heavy losses incurred at the Galuda River, the ship's company now had to subsist on rotten stores. Opening the last casks of salt provisions Copping, the purser, had discovered the usually tainted pork was uneatably putrid and the misery of *Cyclops*'s company immeasurably increased.

At last she made her number to the guardship at Sandy Hook and, in company with the members of the North American Squadron, let go her anchor in the Hudson River.

For the last months of effective British rule in any part of her thirteen colonies, His Britannic Majesty's frigate *Cyclops* lay passive. Arriving at New York on the last day of April 1781 she lay in the mouth of the Hudson without positive orders beyond the general directive of effect repairs to her fabric.

Admiral Arbuthnot did not appear to take a great interest in her arrival as she was not on the establishment of the North American Station. Indeed he seemed rather offended that she should make her appearance anywhere in his command without his receiving prior notice, and visited his displeasure on Captain Hope whom he greeted with icy politeness.

Secretly angry that he had ended up between two stools, Hope claimed his mission had been confidential but, when challenged as to its success, was compelled to report failure. His explanation was received with disbelief, the admiral firmly maintaining the Carolinas were in British hands. Hope also wished to rid himself of the Continental currency, but this was too much for Admiral Arbuthnot, who studied the captain through rheumy eyes.

"You arrive on my station sir, occupy a British post without authority, fail in a mission you claim is secret yet was given you by the captain of a frigate and now you wish *me* to rid *you* of an embarrassing sum of rebel currency." The admiral rose. "You may retain the stuff until you report to y're own flag officer, Admiral . . . Admiral . . .

"Kempenfelt, sir."

"Exactly." Arbuthnot appeared to consider the matter closed.

"But sir, I have to refit my to'gallants . . ."

"Your topgallants, sir, are your topgallants and not mine . . . I suggest you contact Admiral Kempenfelt on the matter. Good day, sir."

Hope left.

Eventually Arbuthnot's secretary received instructions from London to render such assistance as might be necessary to the frigate *Galatea.* A note was appended to the effect that due to political circumstances of the greatest importance, *Galatea* had been retained in home waters and her mission undertaken by *Cyclops*, Captain Henry Hope, R.N.

The secretary therefore prepared an order for her to come in and draw such stores as she required and refit her gear. Arbuthnot signed the order without comment since he was at that time prone to sign almost anything, being nearly blind.

On receipt of these orders *Cyclops* moved to a berth at the Manhattan Dockyard to commence her repairs. On that evening Hope and Devaux dined together. Over their port, several cases of which had been removed from *La Creole*, hope drew Devaux's attention to a decision that the weather and the frigate's cranky tophamper had deferred.

"Assuming that we eventually receive definite orders, Devaux, we have to consider the matter of a replacement for Skelton. Cranston was a loss to us and the Service as a whole . . ."

"Yes," agreed Devaux, nodding. His mind slid back to the dense forest and the sight of Cranston's mutilated body . . . He tore his mind away from the grisly memory.

"D'ye have any opinions?" asked the Captain.

The first lieutenant recollected himself. "Well sir, the next senior is Morris. His journals are poorly kept, though he's served the six years . . . I consider him quite unsuitable and I would appreciate his removal from the ship . . . indeed I threatened him with it I seem to remember . . . I am of the opinion that young Drinkwater is a likely candidate for an acting lieutenancy." He paused. "But surely, sir, there's a junior in the fleet hereabouts . . ." Devaux indicated the riding lights of several warships visible through the stern windows.

"An Admiral's favorite d'ye mean, Mr. Devaux?" asked Hope archly.

"Just so, sir."

"But Admiral Arbuthnot informed me that the ship is under Kempenfelt's flag. Who am I to question his decision," he inquired with mock humility, and then in a harder tone, "besides I am not disposed to question him on the matter of my midshipmen." He sipped his port. "Furthermore I submitted a list of casualties that clearly indicated the state of our complement of officers. If he does not see fit to appoint someone he can go to the devil." He paused. "Besides I rather suspect Kempenfelt would approve our choice . . ." Hope smiled benignly and tossed off the glass.

Devaux raised an eyebrow. "Old Blackmore will be pleased, he's had Drinkwater under his wing since we left Sheerness." The two officers refilled their glasses.

"Which," said Devaux choosing his moment, "brings me to the matter of Morris, sir. I'd be obliged if a transfer could be arranged . . ."

"That is a little drastic, is it not, Mr. Devaux. What's behind this request?"

Devaux outlined the problem and added the remark that in any case Morris would resent serving under Drinkwater. Hope snorted.

"Resent! Why I've resented serving under half the officers I've submitted to. But Morris is fortunate, Mr. Devaux. Had I known earlier I'd have broken him. Another time I'll trouble you to tell me as soon as you have any inkling of this kind of thing . . . it's the bane of the service and produces officers like that loathsome Edgecumbe . . ." Hope added expansively.

"Yes, sir," Devaux changed the subject hastily. "What are the Admiral's intentions, sir?"

Again Hope snorted. "Intentions! I wish he had some. Why, he and General Clinton sit here in New York waving the Union Flag with enough soldiers to wipe Washington off the face of the earth. Clinton shits himself with indecision at the prospect of losing New York and saves face by sending General Philips into Virginny."

"However I hear that Arbuthnot's to be relieved . . ."

"Who by, sir?"

"Graves . . ."

"Good God, not Graves . . ."

"He's a pleasant enough man, which is more than I found Arbuthnot."

"He's an amiable incompetent, sir. Wasn't he court-martialled for refusing battle with an Indiaman?"

"Yes, back in 'fifty seven . . . no 'fifty six. He was acquitted of cowardice but publically reprimanded for an error of judgement under the 36th Article of War . . . you must admit *some* Indiamen pack a punch . . ." Both officers smiled ruefully at memories of *La Creole*.

"D'ye know, John, it's one of the great ironies that on the very day the court at Plymouth sentenced Tommy Graves, a court at Portsmouth got John Byng for a similar offense which was far more strategically justifiable. You know what happened to Byng. They sentenced him under the 12th Article . . . he was shot on his own quarterdeck . . ." Hope's voice trailed off.

"*Pour encourager les autres* . . . ," muttered Devaux. "Voltaire, sir," he said in explanation as Hope looked up.

"Ah, that Godless French bastard . . ."

"Does anyone know what's happened to Cornwallis, sir?"

Hope stirred. "No! I don't believe any of 'em know

anything, John. Now what about my main to'gallant . . . ?"

The next morning Devaux sent for Drinkwater. The lieutenant was staring north up the Hudson River to where the New Jersey Palisades could be seen, catching the early sunlight.

"Sir?"

Devaux turned and regarded the young man. The face had matured now. The ragged line of the wound, rapidly scarring, would hardly alter the flesh over the cheekbones, though it might contrast the weathered tan. The figure beneath the worn and patched uniform was spare but fit. Devaux snapped his glass shut.

"That hanger you had off *La Creole's* lieutenant . . . D'ye still have it?"

Drinkwater colored. At the end of the action he had found himself still clasping the small sword. It was a fine weapon and its owner had not survived long after the capture of his ship. Drinkwater had regarded the thing as his own part of the spoil. After all the gunroom officers wallowed in the captured wine for weeks afterwards and he felt the weight of a dirk too useless for real fighting. The sword had found its way to the bottom of his sea chest, where it lay wrapped in bunting. He did not know how Devaux knew this but assumed that omniscience was a natural attribute of first lieutenants.

"Well, sir?" queried Devaux, a note of asperity in his voice.

"Er, yes, sir . . . I, er, do have it . . ."

"Then ye'd better clap it on y're larboard hip!"

"Beg pardon, sir?" The young man frowned uncomprehendingly.

Devaux laughed at Drinkwater's puzzled expression. "The captain is promoting you acting third lieutenant as of now. You may move your chest and effects up on to the gundeck . . ." He watched the effect of the news on Drinkwater's face. The lad's mouth dropped open, then closed. He blinked, then smiled back. At last he stammered his thanks.

* * *

Cyclops lay at her anchor with Arbuthnot's squadron through May and June. During this time Drinkwater's prime task was to get a new broadcloth coat from a New York tailor. The ship had recruited its complement from the guardships, but there was little for the men to do. Then, on July 12th, things began to happen. Admiral Graves arrived, a kind, generous but simple incompetent who was to be instrumental in losing the war. Then Rodney's tender *Swallow* arrived with the intelligence that Admiral De Grasse had left the West Indies with a French fleet bound for the Chesapeake. Graves chose to ignore the warning despite its significance. Since May, Lord Cornwallis had abandoned the Carolinas and was combining his force with General Philips's in Virginia. If Cornwallis had De Grasse sitting on his communications with New York, he would be cut off. Captains and officers had themselves rowed about the fleet while they grumbled about their admiral's failure to grasp the simplest strategic facts. Cornwallis was retreating to the sea for the navy to support him . . . but the navy was in New York . . .

Once again the opinion was expressed that in executing Byng their Lordships had taken more leave of their senses than was usual; they had shot the wrong man.

Another message arrived via *Pegasus* that urged Graves to sail south and join Sir Samuel Hood, to whom Rodney had relinquished command through ill health. But the fleet remained supinely at anchor.

At the beginning of August Clinton decided to act, not against Virginia, but against Rhode Island where French troops and men o' war were based. Admiral Graves ordered a number of ships down to Sandy Hook in preparation. One of these was *Cyclops*.

It was at this time that Midshipman Morris left the frigate.

When *Cyclops* left the Galuda, her ship's company were hard put to fight the elements, guard their prisoners and simply survive. The remaining lieutenants were on watch and watch, with the mates and midshipmen equally hard pressed. Drinkwater and Morris were in opposite watches and the preoccupations of working and sleeping allowed no one the luxury of contemplating the events of past weeks objectively. It would not be true, however, to say that the events and circumstances that had occured were forgotten. Rather they lay at a level just above the subconscious, so that they influenced conduct but did not dominate it. Drinkwater was particularly affected. The horrors he had seen and the guilt he felt over his involvement in the death of Threddle impinged on his self-esteem. And his knowledge of the manner of Sharples's death lay like a weight upon his soul.

Although Sharples had been the true murderer of Threddle, Drinkwater knew that he had been driven to it. Morris's cold-blooded execution of the seaman at the mill, however, was another matter.

To Drinkwater's mind it was a matter for the law or, and he shuddered at the thought, a matter for vengeance.

When *Cyclops* arrived at New York there was time, too much time, for the mind to wander over possible causes and effects and the consequences of action.

In the midshipmen's mess some contact with Morris was unavoidable and there had been potentially disruptive scenes. Drinkwater had always avoided them by walking out, but this action had given Morris the impression of an ascendancy over Nathaniel.

Morris had entered the mess some time after, but on the day that Drinkwater had been told of his promotion.

"And what's our brave Nathaniel up to now?" There was silence. Then White came in. "I've taken your boat-cloak and tarpaulin to your cabin, Nat . . . er, sir . . ."

Nathaniel smiled at his friend. "Thanks, Chalky . . ."

"Cabin? Sir? What bloody tomfoolery is this . . . ?" Morris was coloring with comprehension. Nathaniel said nothing but continued to pack things in his chest. White could not resist the chance of aggravating the bully at whose hands he had suffered, particularly when he had a powerful ally in the person of the acting third lieutenant.

"Mr. Drinkwater," he said with gravity, "is promoted to acting third lieutenant."

Morris glared as he assimilated the news. He turned to Nathaniel in a fury.

"The devil you are. Why you jumped-up little bastard, you don't have time in for lieutenant . . . I suppose you've been arselicking the first lieutenant again . . . I'll see about this . . ." He ran on for some minutes in similar vein.

Drinkwater felt himself seized again by the cold rage that had made him so brutal with the wounded French lieutenant of *La Creole*. It was a permanent legacy of that horrendous march inland and was to stamp his conduct in moments of physical confrontation. As the influence of his widowed mother had made him soft clay for Morris's viciousness, the events of the Galuda had tempered the latent iron in his soul.

"Have a care, sir," he said, his voice low and menacing, "have a care in what you say . . . you forget I have passed for master's mate which is more than you have ever managed . . . you also forget I have evidence to have you hanged under two Articles of War . . ."

Morris paled and Drinkwater thought for a moment he was going to faint. At last he spoke.

"And what if I tell of your conduct over Threddle?"

Drinkwater felt his own heart thump with recollection but he retained his head. He turned to little White, who was staring wide-eyed between one and the other of the older midshipmen.

"Chalky, if you had to choose between evidence I gave and evidence Morris gave whose would you favor?"

The boy smiled, pleased at the dividend his revenge was receiving, "Yours, Nat, of course . . ."

"Thank you. Now perhaps you and Morris would be kind enough to carry my chest to my cabin."

Drinkwater luxuriated in the privacy of his little cabin. Situated between two twelve-pounders on the gundeck it dismantled when the frigate cleared for action. He no longer had to endure the constant comings and goings of the cockpit and was able to read in privacy and quiet. Perhaps the greatest benefit his acting rank conferred upon him was the right to mess in the gunroom and enjoy the society of Wheeler and Devaux. Appleby, though not at that time technically a member of the commissioned officers' mess, was a frequent, indeed a usual, visitor. In New York Drinkwater obtained new clothes and cocked hat without braid so that his appearance befitted his new dignity without ostentation, though he was rarely on deck without his captured sword swinging, as Devaux put it, "upon his larboard hip".

His acquaintance with the multifarious duties of a naval officer increased daily as there was a constant stream of boats between the ships and town of New York, but his social life was limited to an occasional dinner in the gunroom of another vessel. Unlike Wheeler or Devaux he eschewed the delights of the frequent entertainments given by New York society for the garrison and naval officers. This was partly out of shyness, partly out of the deference to Elizabeth, but mostly due to the fact that the other occupants of the gunroom now had a junior in their midst sufficiently subordinate not to protest at their abuses of rank.

Drinkwater's chief delight at this time was reading. In the bookshops of New York and from the surgeon's small travelling library he had discovered Smollett and made the consequential acquaintance of Humphry Clinker, Commodore Trunnion and Roderick Random.

It was the latter that led his thoughts so often to Elizabeth. The romantic concept of the waiting woman obsessed him so that the uncertainty of Elizabeth's exact whereabouts worried him. That he loved her was now beyond a doubt. Her image had sustained him in the dreary swamps of Carolina and he had come to think of her as a talisman against all evil, mostly that of Morris.

There was more to his enmity with Morris than a poisonous dislike. He was convinced that the man was an evil influence over his life. Buried deep in the natural fear of the green young midshipman of two years earlier, this idea had grown as successive events had seemed to establish a pattern in his imagination. That they had served to strengthen him and his resolution seemed inconsequential. Had he not been made aware of Morris's depravity and the fate of Sharples? Could not someone else have come in from the yardarm that night the topman had begged for help? Could not another midshipman have been sent forward to ask Kate Sharples to leave the deck that day in Spithead?

But now there was a more vivid reason for attributing something supernatural to Morris's malevolence. For Drinkwater was subject to a recurring dream, a nightmare that had its origins in the swamps of Carolina and haunted him with an occasional but persistent terror.

It had come first to him in the exhausted sleep after the taking of *La Creole* and occurred again in the gales off Cape Hatteras. Twice while *Cyclops* lay in New York he had suffered from it.

There was always a white lady who seemed to rear over him, pale as death and inexorable in her advance as she came ever nearer, yet never passed over him entirely. Sometimes she bore the face of Cranston, sometimes of Morris but, most horribly of Elizabeth, but an Elizabeth of Medusa-like visage before which he quailed, drowning in a vast noise like the clanking of chains, rythmically jerking . . . or of *Cyclops*'s pumps . . .

It was therefore with relief that Drinkwater learned of Morris's transfer. Since his promotion, he had not sought to impose his new found authority upon Morris and simply heard that he was joining a ship in Rear Admiral Drake's division with an inner and secret lightening of the heart.

Perhaps, after all, his fears were the groundless suppositions of an overtaxed nervous system . . .

But on the morning of Morris's departure, Drinkwater was again in doubt.

He was reading in the confined privacy of his tiny cabin when the door was flung unceremoniously open.

Morris stood on the threshold. He was drunk and held in his hand a piece of crumpled paper.

"I've come to shay good-by, Mishter Fucking Drinkwater . . ." he slurred, his hooded lids half closed, ". . . I want to tell you that you and I have unfinished businesh to attend to . . ." he managed a mirthless chuckle, spittle bubbling round his mouth.

"Ish funny really . . . you and I could've become friends . . ." Tears were visible in the corners of his eyes and Drinkwater slowly realised the awful, odious implication in the man's words. Morris sniffed, drawing his cuff across his nose. Then he began chuckling again.

"I've a letter from my shishter here . . . she knows a man or two at the Admiralty. She promishes me to use her four-poshter to make me a posht Captain . . . now don't you think thatsh bloody funny Mishter Drinkwater? Don't you think thatsh about the funniesht thing you've ever heard . . . ?" he paused to chuckle at the ribald pun, then his smile vanished and with it his drunken laxity. The threat he had come to utter reinforced by rum was from his heart:

"And if as a consequence I can ever destroy you or your Miss Bower I will . . . by God I will . . ."

At the mention of Elizabeth's name, Nathaniel felt the terrible icy rage that had despatched the French privateer officer flood his veins. Morris fell back abruptly and stumbling, sprawled on the deck. Drinkwater had the captured sword half out of its scabbard when the abject spectacle of his adversary quailing before him brought him to his senses. He slammed the fragile door to his cabin and snapped the sword down in its sheath. Outside he heard Morris's feet scrape on the deck as he staggered upright.

Drinkwater stood stock still in the center of the room, his breathing slowly returning to normal. He began shaking like an aspen leaf in a breeze and found himself looking at the little picture of the *Algonquim* that Elizabeth had given him and that his new-found privacy had allowed him to hang.

He reached out a shaking hand to reassure himself of its reality . . .

On August 16th, 1781, the ships at Sandy Hook sighted sails to the southward. Sir Samuel Hood arrived in a lather, furious to find Admiral Graves still in New York. The Rear Admiral had himself rowed up the harbor to harangue Graves when he found the latter ashore in his comfortable house. Though junior to Graves, Hood impressed his superior of the size of the French fleet in North American waters. In view of Grave's apparent pusillanimity he suppressed details of the unseaworthiness of his own squadron, one ship of which was actually in a sinking condition.

Graves was suddenly infected with the panic of rapid action and ordered his fleet to sea.

But it was still the end of the month before the twenty-one line of battleships were proceeding south. De Barras at Rhode Island, with eight of the line, had already sailed and the previous day Admiral De Grasse had anchored his own twenty eight of the line, numerous frigates and transports in the Chesapeake. He had also landed 3,000 troops to surround an obscure peninsula called Yorktown.

Lord Cornwallis was cut off, for Washington and Rochambeau were marching south from the Hudson Highlands, across New Jersey, their flank exposed to the inactive Clinton at New York, to join up with LaFayette and close the iron ring round the hapless Earl.

What happened to Cornwallis is history. The British fleets sailed south too late. Graves flung out his frigates and *Cyclops* stood to the eastward, thus taking no part in the forthcoming battle.

The fleet fought an action with De Grasse which was indecisive in itself. But it was enough for Graves. De Grasse retained possession of the Bay of the Chesapeake. At the time De Barras had not arrived but when Graves, realizing the enormity of his blunder, tried a second time to draw out De Grasse, the British Admiral found De Barras had reinforced the Comte and drew off.

Cornwallis was abandoned.

A gallant effort was made to cross the James River under cover of darkness to where Tarleton held a bridgehead at Gloucester, but, after the first boats had got over, a violent storm rose and the breakout to New York was abandoned. A few weeks later Lord Cornwallis surrendered and the war with America was effectively, if not officially, over.

Cyclops, scouting eastward, missed both the action off the Virginia Capes and a sight of De Barras's squadron. She eventually returned to New York to receive belated recognition from the new Commander in Chief that she belonged to the Channel Fleet. After despatching the fast tender *Rattlesnake* with the news of the loss of Cornwallis's Army at the end of October, Admiral Graves recollected that although fast she was lightly armed and a vulnerable prey to a French cruiser or a marauding Yankee privateer. In typical fashion he vacillated, fretting about the fate of *Rattlesnake*, worrying that his report might fall into enemy hands. Eventually he decided to send a frigate with a duplicate set of dispatches.

It seemed a good idea, his secretary advised, to take the opportunity of sending *Cyclops* back to Kempenfelt.

Acting Lieutenant Nathaniel Drinkwater stopped pacing to stare up at the main topgallant. His body balanced effortlessly as the ship moved beneath him, a near southwesterly gale thrumming in the rigging and sending a patter of spray over the starboard quarter rail.

He studied the sail for a moment. There was no mistaking the strain on the weather sheet or the vibration transmitted to the yard below. It was time to shorten sail.

"Mr. White!" The boy was immediately attentive: "My compliments to the captain and the wind's freshening. With his approval I intend furling the t'gallants."

"Aye, aye, sir."

Drinkwater stared into the binnacle. The two helmsmen grunted and sweated as they fought to hold *Cyclops* on course. He watched the gently oscillating compass card. Advancing daylight already rendered the oil lamp superfluous. The heaving grey Atlantic lifted the frigate's quarter, sent her scudding forward until it passed under her and she dragged into the trough, stabbing her bowsprit at the sky. Then her stern lifted again and the cycle repeated itself, over and over, all the three thousand miles from New York to the chops of the Channel . . .

Drinkwater felt none of the shame being experienced by Captain Hope shaving in the cabin below. For Hope already knew the heady wine of victory, having fought through the glorious period of the Seven Years War. To end his career in defeat was a bitter blow, a condemnation of the years of labor and a justification of his cynicism that was only alleviated by the draft on Tavistock's for four thousand sterling.

To Drinkwater, the events of the last few weeks had been a culmination. In their fruitless search for De Barras they had boxed the compass off Long Island and the New England coast. To Nathaniel, free of the oppressive presence of Morris, it had been a glorious time, a fruitful splendid time in which, cautiously at first, but with growing confidence, he had handled the ship.

He looked up at the now furled topgallants. His judgement was vindicated for *Cyclops* had not slackened her pace.

He saw Captain Hope ascend the companionway. He vacated the windward side, touching his hat as the captain passed.

" 'Morning, sir."

"G'morning, Mr. Drinkwater." Hope glanced aloft. "Anything in sight?"

"Nothing reported, sir."

"Very well." Hope looked at the log slate.

"Should raise the Lizard before dark, sir, by my reckoning," volunteered Drinkwater. Hope grunted and began pacing the weather quarterdeck. Drinkwater moved over to the lee side where young Chalky White was shivering in the down-draught of the main topsail.

"Mr. Drinkwater!" The captain called sharply.

"Sir?" Drinkwater hurried over to where the captain was regarding him with a frown. His heart sank.

"Sir?" he repeated.

"You are not wearing your sword!"

"Sir?" repeated Drinkwater yet again, his forehead wrinkling in a frown.

"It is the first morning you have had your present appointment that you have not worn it."

"Is it, sir?" Drinkwater blushed. Behind him, White giggled.

"You must be paying the correct attention to your duties and less to your personal appearance. I am pleased to see it."

Drinkwater swallowed.

"Y-yes, sir. Thank you, sir."

Hope resumed his pacing. White was in stitches, the subject of Mr. Drinkwater's sword having caused much amusement between decks. Drinkwater turned on him.

"Mr. White! Take a glass to the foremasthead and look for England!"

"England, Nat . . . Mr. Drinkwater, sir?"

"Yes, Mr. White! England!"

England, he thought, England and Elizabeth . . .